A DANCE OF HEARTS

"I believe this is my dance, Miss Whitney," Standford said, bowing.

"So it is," she replied, a gentle smile curving her lips.

Leading her out onto the dance floor of the Blarewoods' large ballroom, Standford paused to study her while they waited for the music to begin. "I am delighted to have this opportunity to speak with you privately."

Glancing around at the other dancers, Lydia smiled. "Somehow, my lord, I never think of 'being private' in the middle of a crowded room."

"Ah, Miss Whitney, when *you* are in a room, one has eyes for no other."

Lydia's eyes widened at the flattery. "I think Her Grace has greatly underestimated your gift for flirting, my lord."

"Flirting?" The earl was startled. Was that what he was doing? Somehow he simply felt at ease with this beautiful lady.

As the strains of the waltz began, Standford took Lydia in his arms. The sweet intoxicating scent of flowers wafted up from her as he drew her close. They twirled around the dance floor in perfect unison. A surge of warmth rushed through him when he gazed down at her sweet face. Why did this young woman attract him as no lady of the *ton* ever had?

WATCH FOR THESE ZEBRA REGENCIES

LADY STEPHANIE   (0-8217-5341-X, $4.50)
by Jeanne Savery
Lady Stephanie Morris has only one true love: the family estate she has managed ever since her mother died. But then Lord Anthony Rider arrives on her estate, claiming he has plans for both the land and the woman. Stephanie soon realizes she's fallen in love with a man whose sensual caresses will plunge her into a world of peril and intrigue . . . a man as dangerous as he is irresistible.

BRIGHTON BEAUTY   (0-8217-5340-1, $4.50)
by Marilyn Clay
Chelsea Grant, pretty and poor, naively takes school friend Alayna Marchmont's place and spends a month in the country. The devastating man had sailed from Honduras to claim his promised bride, Miss Marchmont. An affair of the heart may lead to disaster . . . unless a resourceful Brighton beauty finds a way to stop a masquerade and keep a lord's love.

LORD DIABLO'S DEMISE   (0-8217-5338-X, $4.50)
by Meg-Lynn Roberts
The sinfully handsome Lord Harry Glendower was a gambler and the black sheep of his family. About to be forced into a marriage of convenience, the devilish fellow engineered his own demise, never having dreamed that faking his death would lead him to the heavenly refuge of spirited heiress Gwyn Morgan, the daughter of a physician.

A PERILOUS ATTRACTION   (0-8217-5339-8, $4.50)
by Dawn Aldridge Poore
Alissa Morgan is stunned when a frantic passenger thrusts her baby into Alissa's arms and flees, having heard rumors that a notorious highwayman posed a threat to their coach. Handsome stranger Hugh Sebastian secretly possesses the treasured necklace the highwayman seeks and volunteers to pose as Alissa's husband to save her reputation. With a lost baby and missing necklace in their care, the couple embarks on a journey into peril—and passion.

Available wherever paperbacks are sold, or order direct from the Publisher. Send cover price plus 50¢ per copy for mailing and handling to Penguin USA, P.O. Box 999, c/o Dept. 17109, Bergenfield, NJ 07621. Residents of New York and Tennessee must include sales tax. DO NOT SEND CASH.

A Game of Chance

Lynn Collum

ZEBRA BOOKS
KENSINGTON PUBLISHING CORP.

ZEBRA BOOKS are published by

Kensington Publishing Corp.
850 Third Avenue
New York, NY 10022

Zebra and the Z logo Reg. U.S. Pat. & TM Off.

First Printing: August, 1996
10 9 8 7 6 5 4 3 2 1

Printed in the United States of America

For my father,
James Alford Lee Collum

One

"Come down from that tree at once, Lady Sophia," Miss Lydia Whitney called sternly to her young charge. Circling under the girl, the governess eyed the tree with trepidation at the thought of going up after the mischievous child. Lydia knew she could ill afford to lose another post, but three weeks with the devil-child on the limb made her doubt her ability to survive to the end of the present week.

"I won't," Lady Sophia stated rudely. "I can see all over the grounds from here, and I want to look at the pretty dresses." The dark-eyed minx settled upon a sturdy limb to study the garden party in progress at Pemberton Hall.

"Then I shall come up after you," Lydia threatened. "You know your mother is most insistent you be in bed by eight of the clock and you have not even dined yet." She hoped to avoid calling a footman to fetch the child, for the servants reported all of her failures to Lady Pemberton.

When her charge remained stubbornly perched on the limb, Lydia gave a resigned sigh, then slowly climbed the tree. Reaching the branch where Sophia was seated, she concentrated on her footing. She turned and settled on the solid bough to catch her breath.

"Well done, Miss Whitney. You are the first governess ever brave enough to come up after me." The ten-year-old eyed her pursuer with grudging approval.

"I am not surprised to find you played this trick upon your former governesses." Lydia gazed out through the leaves at the colorfully clad people who moved about near the Hall in the fading evening light. Hoping to impress upon Sophia that she could not be bested, the young woman added, "You should know that I climbed trees as a young girl, also. However, I gave up such hoydenish pranks by the time I reached your advanced age."

With a toss of her dark curls, Sophia responded, "*I* am Dashing Jack's daughter and am therefore expected to be more adventurous than most young ladies."

That, thought Lydia, is the problem. Everyone filled the child's head with ridiculous stories about Lord Pemberton which only encouraged her high-spirited pranks. Like father, like daughter the servants said. Lydia knew from personal experience how children could idolize a ne'er-do-well father.

"Lady Sophia, you must remember that what is acceptable behavior in a gentleman is not correct behavior for a Lady of Quality. I would—"

Before Lydia could finish her reprimand, the child scrambled to her feet. Exhibiting the skill of a monkey, the girl swung from a small limb to one lower in the tree. Using this heartstopping method, she was soon on the ground. With a delighted giggle and a flash of petticoats, she disappeared toward the Hall.

Releasing her breath, Lydia felt only relief. At least the child was safe. She knew Sophia would soon tire of trying to evade her governess and would, no doubt, be found quietly eating when Lydia returned to the schoolroom.

Allowing herself a few moments of peace, she enjoyed the sounds of the music wafting through the trees from the party and gazed enviously at the elegant ladies moving about the lawn. *She* might be among the guests if only her grandfather had acknowledged the existence of his younger son's child. But it was useless to wish for a miracle. Years ago the Duke of Graymoor had completely cut off her father when he returned from Scotland with a wife not of the aristocracy. The duke had never relented, not even after her widowed father died last year. If not for dear Bertie, she would have been destitute.

Her old governess had found Lydia her first job with Mrs. Brisby. Little did Bertie know of the woman's lecherous husband. Lydia lasted a scant two months before being falsely branded a hussy and tossed out into the world.

As the sound of tinkling laughter drifted to her from the party, Lydia gave herself a shake. She'd been fortunate to secure her present position, mostly by the kind intervention of Mrs. Brisby's vicar, and she could not chance losing it now.

Watching the sun sink behind the Hall, she knew it was time to return to Sophia. Edging back along the limb toward the main trunk, she searched for a foothold. Then she noticed a bright pink hat with a large feather bobbing up and down as someone approached beneath her. Fearful of being caught in such an impossible position, Lydia shrank close to the tree.

A feminine voice floated upward. "My dear Standford, we are now alone. What is so important that it could not wait until later?" Lydia recognized the familiar tones of Mrs. Howell, a frequent guest at Pemberton. The lady sounded amused, but impatient.

Curious, Lydia peeked through the leaves. She could now see the elegant widow, clad in a revealing pink muslin gown with matching parasol. The woman was breathtakingly beautiful with auburn curls and green eyes.

"Mrs. Howell . . . Eugenie, I only came to this rather dreadful house party in hope of an opportunity to speak with you." The speaker was a tall gentleman in a dark blue coat and grey pantaloons. He must have just arrived at Pemberton, Lydia thought, or she would have met him last evening with the other guests. She prayed he would not look up, but she needn't worry. He was too intent on pleading his case with Mrs. Howell, though he went about it in a rather strange way.

His voice, utterly devoid of emotion, continued. "Despite

the obvious disadvantage of your widowhood, I think you would make an excellent countess. I, therefore, hope you will do me the honor of becoming my wife."

A bitter laugh escaped Eugenie Howell. "Standford, you obviously came by your nickname, Stiff-neck, honestly. 'Tis a pity. However, I spent two years of my life with a pompous curmudgeon, and henceforth, I intend to have laughter and gaiety around me. I know your consequence is so great you cannot fathom that a woman could resist an offer by a Marsh, but you may believe I would prefer to remain a widow all my days than to marry another stuffy bore, lord or no."

Lydia watched the gentleman's face become a haughty mask even while the lady addressed him. She felt a wave of pity for the unknown suitor. No man should be rejected in this cruel manner, no matter how proudly and coldly he behaved.

He took it well, bowing slightly. "Then I shall say no more, madam. I apologize for having mistaken your polite conversation for something of a more tender nature." His voice sounded angry, and Lydia could see the knuckles whiten on his clenched hands.

"Tender nature?" the lady snapped. "Do not speak to me of such, sir. I doubt you would recognize a genuine emotion if it ran over you like a runaway carriage. Do you think your excessively proud manner and staid demeanor are such to engage a lady's affections? You offer no gentle words or pretty compliments, but treat this proposal like one more task to be gotten through, my lord."

"I beg your pardon. I had not thought you to be of such a romantic nature, Mrs. Howell. Perhaps I should have paid more attention to my friend's hint that you are no better than you should be."

Lydia nearly fell backwards in shock when the lady's hand flashed against the gentleman's jaw. Mrs. Howell's fury was palpable and she hissed angrily, "You shall pay for that ill-judged remark, my lord. I need only drop a word to a few of my friends, and news of your absurd proposal will be all over Town. Stiff-necked Standford will be the laughing stock of the *ton*."

Mrs. Howell turned and disappeared from Lydia's view, leaving the gentleman standing rigidly, watching her retreating form. He stood motionless for so long, one would have thought him turned to stone.

Lydia's arms ached from clinging to the tree so long. She very much hoped Lord Standford would nurse his wounded pride back at the Hall. Shifting to a more comfortable position, she felt her sleeve snag on a small limb. Having only three gowns which befit her role as governess, she knew she must save the dress from serious damage. Focusing on her own problem, she forgot about the rejected suitor below.

A twig-like branch was entwined in the simple lace ruffle at the top of the green sleeve. In an effort to reach the entangled material, Lydia hooked her booted foot under a small branch so she might lean away from the tree. When she tilted backwards a loud crack could be heard as the wood gave way. Flailing desperately for a hold, she was left with her face pressed against the trunk.

A cracking limb startled Standford from his bitter musings. He turned his head sharply and spied a young woman in danger of falling from a bough where she was precariously perched. Instinctively, he moved closer to the tree while she teetered, but halted when he realized the woman had steadied herself by grasping the trunk.

Suddenly, the earl realized the unknown female must have witnessed his humiliating encounter with Mrs. Howell. A muscle twitched in his jaw as he ground his teeth in anger. "Well, madam, did you enjoy eavesdropping on a very private conversation?"

He angrily scrutinized her. She was dressed plainly in a drab green gown. Her ankles were indecorously exposed as they dangled beneath her. Silver-blonde hair, parted in the middle, was pulled into a tight knot at the back of her head.

There was nothing of the fashionable young lady about her. He suspected she was some upper servant, which made the pity in her eyes all the more enraging.

Pushing upright from the tree, the young woman tried to recover her dignity as she straightened her back and smoothed the loose silver tendrils with shaking hands. "I beg pardon, my lord. 'Twas an unfortunate accident that I overheard your . . . conversation."

"What the devil are you doing up there?" he demanded, unpacified.

"I was stranded here after I climbed up to get my charge."

Standford's gaze briefly scanned the tree. Scornfully, he said, "I see only you. Do you expect me to believe you are in charge of Pemberton's red squirrels? I half suspect you contrived this tale as an excuse to spy on your betters."

She flushed with anger and glared down at him. "Do not be absurd, my lord. I am Lady Sophia's governess. I could hardly know that you would choose this corner of the estate to offer for Mrs. Howell."

She spoke the truth, of course. Impossible to believe otherwise. He would not have accused her so rashly had he not been humiliated by the cutting refusal of his proposal. Eugenie's words burned in his mind and he sighed. "It would seem all of Society finds me absurd."

"We all have our absurdities, my lord. I find it such to be sitting in this tree."

He caught the amusement in her voice, and for a moment wondered if she were daring to make fun of him. Then he realized she was laughing at herself. Some of his anger evaporated. It was not this woman's fault that she'd witnessed his ignoble rejection. He wanted only to get away now, but he could not, in good conscience, leave her stranded. Reluctantly, he offered, "Is there anything I can do to assist you?"

"Thank you, my lord. 'Tis most kind of you. I really must hurry to find Lady Sophia before she gets into more mischief."

With a resigned sigh, he asked, "Do you wish me to come up and get you, Miss . . . ?"

"Whitney, sir. No, if you will but wait there I shall climb lower. I just wish someone to steady me while I descend." The young woman frowned as she searched for footholds.

The earl stepped beneath her. "Whenever you are ready, miss. I shall try to catch you if you should fall."

His words seemed prophetic. Her boot slipped from the branch, causing her to tumble straight down.

A small scream escaped her lips. The surrounding branches battered her. Tiny limbs clawed at her dress and hair like a frightened cat before she landed in the earl's out-stretched arms.

The suddenness of her descent caused Standford to stagger backwards. Trying to maintain his balance and hold her securely proved more than he could manage. The pair landed with a thud, sprawling in the leafy dirt beneath the tree.

Dazed, but in one piece, Lydia sat up. She looked at the gentleman beside her. Wavy chestnut hair, cut shorter than was fashionable, glinted brightly against the dark green of the leaves. A pair of azure-blue eyes surveyed her from a bemused face. She suspected he might be called handsome, were he to allow the sculpted planes of his face to relax into a smile.

"Sir, are you hurt?"

Rolling onto his elbow, Lord Standford stiffly responded, "I am fine, Miss Whitney. You should save your worries for your own . . . condition."

Lydia was suddenly aware of pale blond curls hanging about her face and shoulders. Indeed, she could feel the tresses brushing her bare skin. Looking down, she saw the white flesh of her exposed left shoulder.

Her cheeks burning with embarrassment, she glanced up to see the stranger's gaze shift to the bare expanse. Hurriedly she gathered the remnants of the tattered green sleeve to preserve her modesty.

"Fear not, Miss Whitney. I assure you I have no designs upon your person." His voice sounded husky despite his assertion.

"I did not think—"

"Miss Whitney! Lord Standford! What is the meaning of this unseemly display?" Lady Pemberton, a small woman with dark curls, stood in uncompromising disapproval as she surveyed the pair before her. The fringe of her Norwich shawl trembled, so great was her indignation.

"Not what you suppose," Standford responded grimly as he rose. He brushed remnants of leaves from his coat and pantaloons, then turned to assist Miss Whitney to her feet before facing his outraged hostess.

"I demand an explanation," Lady Pemberton fumed. It was unfortunate that she had caught her husband in many similar situations, and already had formed a very clear notion of what was going forward.

Annoyed, Standford snapped, "Do not allow your imagination to run away with you, madam. Your governess was stranded in this tree and I merely tried to assist her. Regrettably, we both took a tumble."

"Of all the ridiculous Banbury tales—do you take me for a green girl? I am not so gullible, Lord Standford, and it is plain to me you have fooled the entire *ton* with your stiff manners and airs. I will not have a guest forcing his attentions upon my staff. Your actions are contemptible, and I take leave to tell you that you are no longer welcome at Pemberton Hall."

The earl's blue eyes glinted with outrage as he stared down his nose at his petite hostess. "Madam, you are as big a fool as Jack. A Standford does not dally with servants. I shall gladly leave."

Stooping to pick up his hat, Lord Standford bowed rigidly to the ladies. With a final glance at Miss Whitney, which held a hint of an apology, he turned and walked briskly up the path toward the Hall.

Lady Pemberton settled her incensed stare on Lydia. "You, Miss Whitney, will pack your bags and be out of my home before night falls. Rogers will give you coach fare back to Town and money for a room at the inn. I do not wish to see you again.".

Lydia trembled beneath her employer's gaze, and attempted to explain. "But Lady Pemberton, I only—"

"That is enough, Miss Whitney. I have heard sufficiently of trees and such. I should have listened when Mrs. Brisby warned me of your nature, and had not the vicar interfered on your behalf, I would never have employed you. You may have pulled the wool over his eyes, but I will not be so easily gulled. You will leave at once." Satisfied she'd made her intentions plain, Lady Pemberton lifted her skirts and brushed by her former governess.

Lydia's shoulders slumped dejectedly. She knew it was useless to protest further. If Lady Pemberton would not believe Lord Standford, it was most unlikely she would ever listen to a mere servant.

Overwhelmed with defeat, Lydia wondered where she would go. Of course Bertie would take her in, for the dear soul had stood behind her in bad times before, but it went against Lydia's nature to impose on her former governess again. Feeling miserable, Lydia stole quietly up the path to the Hall to change and pack her meager belongings.

In the cramped bedchamber at the Brown Bull, Hadley busily brushed his lordship's coat, emitting periodic sighs of disappointment. The earl recognized the valet's act as one of wounded feelings. The old man was bursting with curiosity about the sudden removal from Pemberton Hall.

"Enough of these missish airs, Hadley. If you must know, Mrs. Howell refused me," the earl stated bitterly. Watching his aged valet, Standford regretted the necessity of confiding his plans to the old man. It made his rejection all the more humiliating. Then he remembered that Eugenie had promised to make certain the entire *ton* knew of his embarrassment. At least Hadley was sympathetic.

With a nod of his grey head, the valet inquisitively asked, "What's your plan for your aunt now that you aren't to marry, my lord?"

Andrew Marsh, sixth Earl of Standford, would not allow such an impertinent question from many people, but Hadley had practically raised him from a callow youth to a grown man. The earl thought Hadley still treated him like that young boy.

"I wouldn't wait too long to be thinkin' on it or the lady'll be done up afore you know it." The old man removed an imagined speck of lint from the coat he had just helped the earl don.

"Thank you, Hadley. I am aware I must do something, for Aunt Carolyn seems determined to ruin herself before the Season ends. I had no idea she was such a trial to Uncle Sydney."

Chuckling, the old retainer stepped back to survey his master in a black superfine coat with pale ivory pantaloons. Somehow the severe color fit the earl's somber mood. "That she was, my lord. 'Tis no wonder your uncle cocked up his toes at the earliest possible moment. I expect that's why he kept her quiet-like in the country. Have you thought of sendin' her back to Leeds?"

"Believe me, Hadley, if it were within my power to make her go, I would drive her the entire way myself. Unfortunately, I am only responsible for keeping her above the hatches. 'Twas all I could manage to get her to stay in Cavendish Square with me." The earl walked across the spacious room to the cheval mirror beside the door to inspect his cravat.

"Well, if you'll pardon my sayin' so, I thought it a daft idea to marry for the sake of finding someone who could bear-lead the lady."

"I think you forget yourself, Hadley," Standford said haughtily. He walked over and opened the chamber door.

"At my age I forget a great many things," the valet replied unconcerned, as he picked up the discarded clothes.

Standford frowned as he left the room. He knew he should think about replacing the old man, but Hadley seemed to belong with him, almost more like family than a mere servant, and he had not quite the heart to pension him off.

Shaking his head, he walked down the hall toward the stairs. He'd learned a great deal from his mistakes this dreadful day. For starters, he would never again confide in Hadley about his intentions to make an offer to a lady. Secondly, he would not allow his judgment to be swayed by a beautiful face. What he required was a nice girl of good breeding and a respectable portion. In the future, he would confine his search for a wife to the upper reaches of the *ton*. Surely, it should not be difficult to find a young lady who met his standards.

His aunt's escapades had precipitated his need to wed. He truly sought to provide her with a suitable companion. But beyond that, Standford was well aware of his obligation to produce an heir. His austere father had made it clear that a Marsh placed duty and honor above all else. At thirty he knew he must marry to ensure the continuity of the line. The beautiful Eugenie had suited his thoughts about what his future countess should look like—beautiful, witty, and socially at ease.

His lips thinned as he remembered Eugenie's anger. She'd reproached him for treating an offer as though it were some task to be performed, but that was exactly how he viewed it. He had an obligation to the family to wed, else he would not undertake a venture certain to disrupt the comfort of his home. His wife would be a countess. She would have both rank and wealth. Was that not sufficient to entice a lady? Eugenie had spoken of gentle words and pretty compliments. Was that what ladies desired? He had no idea. He'd been raised in a house devoid of females, except for serving maids. The creatures remained an enigma to him.

Walking down the stairs, the earl allowed his mind to drift to the final scene under the trees at Pemberton. He idly wondered about the young governess and hoped she'd persuaded Lady Pemberton to believe her tale.

A small twinge of guilt nudged his conscience for leaving the girl to fend for herself. He knew himself to be, in part, responsible for her predicament. Then he reminded himself that had Miss Whitney not climbed a tree like some hoyden, the incident need never have occurred. But his conscience was only partially mollified, and the image of the hapless governess lingered in his mind.

Pausing at the foot of the stairs, Standford surveyed the small crowd in the taproom. The group of rough-hewn men looked like a collection of locals who'd escaped from their homes to share a tankard of the Bull's excellent ale. The room reminded him much of the inn near his home of Crosswell. He longed to go back to his estate instead of returning to London. First, he had to deal with the problem of finding a wife and resolving the situation with Aunt Carolyn.

Turning to enter the private parlor Hadley bespoke on their arrival, the earl halted abruptly. The inn door had opened to reveal Miss Whitney. Standford scanned the girl's pale face beneath a drab brown bonnet. Despite her plain costume, she was surprisingly pretty for a governess. He'd forgotten how truly fine her tawny gold eyes were.

Pushing the thought from his mind, he advanced toward her. "Miss Whitney, it would appear my worst fears for your situation have been realized. I take it Lady Pemberton dismissed you without listening to the truth?"

"Yes, my lord. She has arranged for my transportation to Town on the morning stage." A deep blush flamed on the governess's cheeks, but her voice remained steady.

"Mayhap you would care to join me in a private parlor away from the prying eyes of the locals. I should like to discuss this matter further, and may I suggest a glass of sherry after your long walk from the Hall?" Standford opened the door to the room and stepped aside.

Miss Whitney glanced at the people in the public room, then tilted up her chin. "Thank you, my lord."

She walked with the bearing of a duchess into the low-ceilinged room. Entering behind her, he left the door correctly open. He watched her set a worn portmanteau near the fireplace. Her regal manner disappeared as she nervously clasped her hands before her and her slender shoulders sagged as though they bore the weight of the world.

"Please allow me to formally introduce myself. I am Andrew Marsh, the Earl of Standford." He bowed before walking to a table set with a decanter and glasses. "Shall it be this indifferent claret, a light sherry, or would you perhaps prefer tea?"

"In truth, sir, I would welcome a cup of tea." The hint of a smile played about her mouth as she stared back at Standford.

After the order was given to a freckled-faced maid, the earl suggested they be seated. Miss Whitney removed the unfashionable bonnet to display shining blonde hair, this time tightly wrapped in a neat chignon at the back of her neck.

"What are your plans for the future?" he asked.

Tensely clutching the bonnet in her lap, she looked up at him. "I fear I am forced to return to my old governess. She helped me after my parents died. I know it will be difficult, if not impossible, to find another post with no references."

All conversation ceased when the maid returned with the tray. After setting it on the table, she left the silent pair. The earl gestured for Miss Whitney to serve herself.

Standford watched her slender white hands while she poured out the tea. He was suddenly reminded of his troublesome aunt, Carolyn Trevor, currently acting as his hostess in Town. Looking back to Miss Whitney's face, Standford realized the truth of her words: Few ladies would want a governess so young and comely. She might be unable to obtain another post even if she had the proper references.

An idea, born partially of guilt and partially from the desire to help, struck him. He suggested tentatively, "I have need of a companion, Miss Whitney. Would you consider such a post?"

The cup rattled in the saucer when Miss Whitney placed it on the table. Wary shadows filled the golden eyes which stared back at him. Leaning back from the table, her dainty hands clutched the wooden arms of the straight-backed chair. She quietly asked, "What kind of companion, sir?"

Sensing her unease, the earl rose and walked to the window. "As you must have guessed, I had hoped to be married soon. A wife would have provided my aunt with the companionship she needs. Since that . . . event will not take place, I shall need to engage someone to fill the post."

Miss Whitney slowly released her grasp and placed her hands politely back in her lap. Smiling, she said, "I have no experience in being a companion, my lord, but I should very much like to try. I believe it could not possibly be as difficult a position as governess."

Her smile was of such radiance, it almost took his breath away. Dropping his gaze to the glass of claret which sat untouched on the table, he suddenly realized how improper it was to be alone with this gently bred young woman. It behooved him to bring the interview to an end. "The position is yours, Miss Whitney. I suggest you retire to a chamber, for we shall make an early start in the morning."

"Thank you, Lord Standford. I shall be ready. Good night, my lord." The tense look was gone from the young woman's face. Rising, she curtsied, then turned and left him.

He stood by the table wondering if he should warn her of the difficult task before her. No, he thought, he did not want to slander his aunt to Miss Whitney. She would learn soon enough.

Striding after the lady, the earl shouted for the landlord.

After arranging for a private chamber and a light meal to be served in her room, he returned to the parlor and the bland repast which the Brown Bull provided.

While the fire burned low in the hearth, Standford found himself thinking of the girl above stairs. His aunt would most certainly resist the idea of being saddled with a companion, but he was determined to make her accept Miss Whitney. He wondered idly about the lovely woman's first name. He would have to inquire in the morning, he thought, when the vision of golden eyes flashed through his mind.

An hour later, when he entered his chamber, Standford was surprised to find Hadley waiting.

"I understand from one of the maids that our party's been increased by one, sir," the valet remarked, staring at the earl curiously.

"I fear I was inadvertently responsible for Miss Whitney losing her post at Pemberton, and it occurred to me that she might make a suitable companion. Hopefully, she will be able to protect my aunt from her own folly."

"And did you explain to the young lady just what that would involve?" the valet asked as he rose to remove the earl's jacket.

"There is time enough to speak of my aunt's propensity for excessive gaming after Miss Whitney comes to know her. I did not want to frighten the girl off even before we returned to Town."

"Of course, sir. I just hope the young woman is up to the task."

As the delicate face of Miss Whitney came to mind, the earl said, "So do I, Hadley. So do I."

The cold night air smelled of smoke and the stables, Lydia thought, as she stood at the open window of the small room the earl had secured for her. Her spirits were enlivened since her conversation with Lord Standford. She would not have to impose on Bertie after all, thank goodness, for she could ill afford another charge. Lydia decided to write Bertie and inform her of the provident change of employers.

Thinking of the earl, Lydia's mind lingered on the way Standford had looked as she'd entered the inn. A strange fluttering occurred in her heart. He'd appeared very different from the way he'd looked at her at Pemberton. There he had been all frigid dignity.

She reminded herself that the handsome man was now her employer, and this was no time for silly schoolgirl fantasies about him. Still, his kindness overwhelmed her. The notion that perhaps he'd remained at the inn just to discover her fate, flashed through her mind. The idea warmed her even as she realized it was unbelievably foolish.

A knock startled her. Closing the window, she went to open the door. She smiled at the plump chambermaid who stood holding a covered tray.

"I brung you a tray what 'is lordship done ordered. Meg's me name, if you be needin' somethin' else, miss." The maid eyed Lydia closely. "Why, you be the new governess for Lady Sophy. I saw you in the family pew on Sunday."

The heat of a blush warmed Lydia's cheeks. "You did, indeed, but I am no longer employed there, Meg."

"Well, you been turned off quicker than most, but if it's any comfort, you ain't the first nor likely the last. There's been six or seven at the Hall just this year. Lady Sophy runs 'em ragged, but her mama won't hear a word against her." The maid set the tray down on the room's sole table. "I best warn you, Lady Pemberton's been known to tell tales 'bout them other governesses round the neighborhood. Wouldn't surprise me to find she'd 'ave a word with your new mistress if you remain 'ereabouts."

"Thankfully, I have a new position elsewhere," Lydia murmured, then frowned as she realized she didn't know exactly where.

"With the earl?" Meg asked, giving Lydia a doubtful look.

"I have been engaged as companion to his aunt," Lydia replied. "Is there something I should know about Lord Standford, Meg?"

"I don't know 'is lordship myself, but I just know 'is kind. Be careful, miss. Mighty 'igh in the instep that one is, and the same sort got me turned off from my last position. My advice is the less 'e knows 'bout you and yours, the better."

Lydia was surprised to find she acutely disliked hearing anyone disparage Lord Standford. But she knew Meg meant well and thanked her gently before closing the door.

After the maid left, Lydia lifted the cloth to reveal a bowl of soup and thick slices of bread with butter, but her appetite had fled. Although she had lightly dismissed the maid's words, doubts lingered. Lord Standford had not enquired about her past, but she knew with a certainty that he would be shocked. A man about Town like the earl would surely have faced her father over the green baize at some point during his notorious career. Fear knotted inside her at the thought. Had she gained a new position only to lose it because of her past?

Until Meg had spoken, Lydia had not given it a thought. But, in her heart, she knew Lord Standford would be appalled. He would be shocked to learn that until she was ten, she'd often accompanied her father to the less reputable gaming houses, sitting quietly in the corner until he was satisfied with the night's play. Only the arrival of Bertie in their household had finally put an end to such unseemly jaunts.

Lydia desperately needed this position. Envisioning a quiet life in retirement with an aged lady, she thought there was little chance of her meeting anyone who knew her from those gaming hells. And if she did not mention the matter, surely no one would connect her with her infamous father, Lord Frederick Whitney—the gentleman known to his intimates as Faro Freddie."

Two

Lydia gazed wide-eyed at the opulent surroundings while a footman took her pelisse. Somehow she'd gained the obviously mistaken impression that Mrs. Trevor resided at the earl's country estate. He'd given her little information during their interview and reverted to the cold, stern man of the house party by the time she had come down for breakfast that morning. Now she found herself standing by his side in this elegant London house.

"Chandler, where is my aunt?" Standford demanded, taking his York tan gloves off. He slapped them across one hand while he waited impatiently for an answer.

The austere old butler avoided looking at his master while he brushed road dust from the earl's greatcoat. "I believe Mrs. Trevor to be in the Rose Drawing Room, my lord."

Standford frowned at the butler's evasive manner. "Is she alone? I need to speak with her."

Clearly, the old man was determined to look anywhere but at his master. Lydia suspected something was amiss in the earl's household.

"My lord . . . um . . . I believe she is entertaining a guest."

Standford's mouth tightened as he glanced up the stairs. "Come along, Miss Whitney. I shall introduce you to my aunt."

Lydia followed the earl up the curved stairway, barely keeping up with his rapid stride. At the landing, he entered a set of double doors without knocking. She trailed along behind. The earl stopped so abruptly inside the room, she practically bumped into him.

She was so taken with the lavishly decorated apartment, she did not at first notice the pair who sat in the window seat across the chamber. A girlish giggle drew her attention. Lydia gasped as she noted the beauty of the youthful woman. Surely this wasn't the lady to whom she was to be a companion?

Glancing back to the earl, Lydia discovered his chin raised in haughty indignation. The maid at the Brown Bull had been correct. No one could appear more high in the instep than Lord Standford.

She followed his gaze to the lady across the room, observing that Mrs. Carolyn Trevor looked to be a widow of barely forty years. Honey-blonde hair, fashionably short, formed a delightful cap of curls through which a blue ribbon was threaded. The burnished locks framed a delicate porcelain face, with rosebud lips and sparkling blue eyes. Dressed in a daringly cut blue muslin gown, her new mistress possessed a decidedly girlish figure for one of her years.

A foppish gentleman of indeterminate age rose when he noticed them. His collar points were so high he had to turn his entire body to face the earl. "Standford . . . thought you were at Pemberton's house party."

"Oh, Andrew," Mrs. Trevor said, as wide eyes stared unhappily at the earl. A tinge of pink added color to her pale cheeks, and nervous fingers clutched a white lace fan.

"I am sure you can find your way out, Masten." Standford moved to the center of the room, coldly staring at the unwelcome guest. His back ramrod straight and his face a frosty mask, the earl left no one in doubt of his disapproval.

"Yes, must not overstay, though I hope to have the pleasure of seeing you soon, my dear," the man suavely addressed Mrs. Trevor. Raising her hand, he brushed a kiss across it.

He strolled across the room, briefly eyeing Lydia, before nodding to the earl. "Your servant, Standford."

Mrs. Trevor rose with a questioning look on her face as she approached her nephew. Having regained her composure, her cheeks were once again fashionably pale. "I must assume that your suit did not prosper, Andrew, or you would not have returned so soon."

"How the devil did you know about my . . . Hadley," the earl said with exasperation. "Never mind my personal affairs. Pray explain what you mean by entertaining Masten. The fellow is a loose screw and well you know it, Aunt Carolyn. I believe I made it clear I do not wish the family name linked to such a rogue."

"Heavens, Standford, must you go on so about my flirts? Is it so wrong of me to wish a little pleasure now that I have emerged from mourning? As for Sir Jasper, he is a delightful companion and received everywhere. You hold yourself too high." The widow turned from her nephew and took a seat on a rose satin sofa. "I might add I consider it rather rude of you to rake me down in front of a stranger. Who is this pretty child?"

Lydia blushed warmly while the lady's gaze moved up and down her rumpled traveling dress. Lord Standford stared at his aunt, frustration on his handsome face. With a noticeable sigh, he came and took Lydia's elbow, leading her to stand before his relative.

"Aunt Carolyn, this is Miss Lydia Whitney. I engaged her to be your companion."

"Companion!" Carolyn shrieked. She jumped to her feet, a flush of anger staining her cheeks as she confronted the earl. "Have you taken leave of your senses, Standford? I am not some doddering old matron who needs a girl to read and fetch for me."

"Calm down, madam. You mistake the situation," the earl said sharply, putting his hand on her arm. "I have matters to attend to at my estate and can ill afford to stay in Town every night. I thought you might get lonely and would enjoy having someone to accompany you to your routs and balls and such."

Pulling away from the earl, Carolyn turned and stalked toward the window. "Do you take me for a fool? I know what you want. You want to foist upon me some milk-and-water miss who will tell you my every move." Carolyn turned back and raked Lydia with an unfriendly gaze before stonily eyeing the earl. "Well, I tell you, I won't have it. I will not be spied on, Standford."

"You are being ridiculous, Aunt Carolyn. I am not your keeper."

"No? Yet you forced me to live in this house under your thumb," the lady countered.

"For reasons of economy. I *am* responsible for managing your income." The earl drew his arms behind him and clasped his hands together as if he were dealing with an errant child.

"And I agreed with the plan for that reason. But I tell you I refuse to allow you to turn me into some aged widow for all the *ton* to laugh at." Carolyn stamped her foot.

"If you choose to make a cake of yourself, there is little I can do or say. But, I can and will stop your funds if you behave in a manner which I feel brings disgrace on the family name. I hope you will remember that," Standford coldly stated.

"So you are my keeper after all." Carolyn turned her back on the earl, her blonde curls shaking with indignation.

"Madam," he angrily addressed her back. "You may call me anything you like, but you will treat Miss Whitney kindly for she is here to help you."

"So, I might call you anything I like. Well, Lord Nip Cheese, I take leave to tell you that my dear sister, your late mother, would be greatly disappointed in you."

Lydia, watching the scene with a mixture of horror and fascination, could tell by the clenched muscles in the earl's jaw that he was making a supreme effort not to return a stinging retort.

After a moment, Lord Standford took a breath, then quietly said, "Madam, I am going out. Since you agreed to act as my hostess, I suggest you compose yourself and arrange for a room for your new companion. Before I go, I would have your promise to treat Miss Whitney with kindness."

"As if I would do otherwise. Miss . . . Whitney is hardly to blame in this matter."

"Very well then, I shall bid you good day, ladies."

Standford marched stiffly from the room, leaving Lydia with the noticeably hostile Mrs. Trevor. Lydia nervously shifted from one foot to the other while she awaited her new mistress's attention.

When the silence lengthened, Lydia decided to try and soothe the lady's feelings. Clearing her throat, she said, "Mrs. Trevor, forgive me if I am out of line, but I must tell you that Lord Standford never suggested that I spy upon you."

"Of course not. He would never be so obvious, my dear child. An innocent like you would not realize that his polite questions about our evening would actually be an inquiry into where I went, what I did, and with whom I did it," Carolyn said as she turned to look appraisingly at Lydia.

Uncomfortable under Mrs. Trevor's suspicious gaze, Lydia knew her hair style was prim, her gown drab and unfashionable, but she still had her dignity and lifted her chin. "I assure you I would not allow myself to be used in such a manner, madam."

With a husky laugh, Carolyn said, "My dear, a straight-laced, country-bred miss like yourself would be no match for Standford."

The lady seemed convinced her companion was some stuffy paragon come to spoil her Season. Should Carolyn Trevor succeed in convincing the earl she did not need a companion, Lydia knew she would be without a post once again. She must persuade the lady she was no green girl.

Lydia came to a quick decision and confessed, "I feel I must be honest with you, Mrs. Trevor. You keep referring to me as straight-laced and country-bred, but I fear I am neither. I grew up right here in the heart of London. My father was . . . Lord Frederick Whitney."

Carolyn raised her gently arched brows, "Lord Frederick Whitney? Should that name mean something, my dear?"

With a sigh, Lydia answered, "Faro Freddie."

When Mrs. Trevor brought her hands up to cover her mouth, Lydia's heart sank. She had chanced that the information would soften the lady's attitude, but the look of astonishment in her eyes convinced Lydia she would be back at Bertie's by nightfall.

To Lydia's surprise, when Mrs. Trevor dropped her hands, she revealed a broad smile. "Why, Miss Whitney . . . Lydia, I met your father once. Such a delightful man."

"Yes, so everyone said."

Carolyn Trevor came toward her companion with arms extended in a welcoming gesture. Taking Lydia's hands, she said, "I apologize for my behavior, but Standford can be so . . . cork-brained about ladies. If he'd only told me—but never mind. Let me order some tea. We shall get to know each other better."

"Please allow me to order tea for you," Lydia said with a genuine smile. A wave of relief rushing through her, she walked over to pull the cord, then joined her employer on the sofa.

A warm look in her eye, Mrs. Trevor said, "I hope you will call me Carolyn, for I am sure that we shall be great friends."

The May wind, with its hint of late spring and the scent of flowers from the large stone pots beside the doorway, swirled around Standford. He stood on the steps outside the Duke of Atherton's town house awaiting admittance to his godfather's home. The walk from Cavendish Square to Oxford Street had cooled his anger sufficiently to realize he wanted to speak with his old friend. That wise fellow might have some useful advice.

Whaley admitted him and kept him waiting in the hall only for a brief moment or two, before escorting Standford to the library. His Grace was seated in a comfortably padded chair drawn sufficiently close to feel the warmth of the cheerful fire burning in the grate.

"Andrew, my boy, 'tis good to see you."

The duke rose and came forward to grasp Standford's hand. His grip was surprisingly strong for a gentleman nearing his sixtieth year. Observing him, Andrew thought the duke looked well. The snow-white hair was fashionably cropped and arranged, contrasting sharply with his tanned, hawk-like face. Today, he wore a stylish light blue coat and pale grey pantaloons—both of superior cut.

Andrew took the chair his godfather indicated, stretching out his long legs. "I am surprised and thankful to find you home on such a pleasant day."

"Normally I would be at my club by now, but my nephew's staying with me. Just arrived from the Indies and had some business to transact. I expect him back momentarily. Plan to put his name up for Brooks today. Now, what brings you by, my boy?"

"Well, sir, to be blunt I have made rather a mull of my personal affairs. I need some advice."

The duke raised a bushy white eyebrow. "Ah, of which widow do we speak?"

"I fear both, sir."

"So, the fair Eugenie would not have you. Well, I warned you, Andrew, but believe me, 'tis just as well. I heard several unsettling rumors about the lady, and am more convinced than ever that it is not a suitable liaison. Not cut up over it, are you?"

"No, sir. But, unfortunately, the interview turned rather

unpleasant, and I fear I made the lady quite angry. She is determined to spread what she termed my *absurd* proposal throughout the *ton*." Standford shifted his gaze to the signet ring upon his left hand. Although he dreaded seeing the disappointment in his old friend's face, he gamely brought his gaze to bear on the duke's brown eyes.

"My boy, you do have a way of getting one's back up with that stiff manner of yours." The older man shook his head woefully as he stared at Standford. "If only your mother had survived, or your late grandmother had taken more of an interest in your upbringing. Your father was a fine man, and he did an admirable job rearing you. But, you have pride enough for ten and no idea how to court a lady!"

"I know it, sir. The truth is they scare the devil out of me. When I try to talk to a lady, I freeze inside."

The duke nodded. He'd observed his godson on numerous occasions. His natural reserve and unease with the ladies came across as haughtiness, hence the sobriquet Stiff-neck. He sighed, "Needless to say, some new scandal will come along to supplant you as the latest *on-dit* by week's end. My advice is to go about in Society as usual and ignore the gossip. Now then, what has the lovely Carolyn done that you need seek my advice?"

" 'Tis what I have done," Standford answered, grinning ruefully. "I hired a companion for her."

With a deep chortle Atherton asked, "What requirements did you give the agency? One small dragon who breathes fire in the face of any who would suggest a game of whist?"

"In truth, sir, I did not engage the lady from an agency." Standford shifted uncomfortably in his seat at the startled expression on the duke's face.

"Oh, then where did you find a matron who would hold any sway over the determined Carolyn? Newgate? Bedlam?"

"How gratifying that this damnable situation affords you a measure of amusement."

"You, my boy, need to find more humor in life's little follies. Believe me, you will live longer and enjoy yourself far more," the duke said sagely.

"But I am responsible for keeping my aunt from the suds, and it is becoming a full-time job." Standford rose before he continued. "As to this companion, Miss Whitney is the Pemberton's former governess. She was inadvertently dismissed because of . . ." The earl fell silent, uncertain how to explain his meeting with the lady.

The duke brought a jeweled finger up and covered his mouth with a pensive gesture, then asked, "Would this companion be young and pretty?"

"Not *so* young. She appears in her early twenties." Standford studied his dust-coated boots with fascination.

With a gentle smile, the duke added, "And not *so* beautiful?"

"I cannot say, sir," the earl replied stiffly. "I will tell you that Lady Pemberton completely misunderstood what she thought she saw. You know I went to offer for Eugenie, I—"

Atherton raised a slender white hand to stop the earl's explanation. "You have no need to explain yourself to me. I must say, however, that I begin to think there is hope for you yet, my boy."

"If you are insinuating I was taking liberties—" Standford's chin rose with wounded dignity.

"Good lord, Andrew, I would be the last to encourage any man to trifle with servants, no matter how elevated. You misunderstand me. I meant I have hope since you took the time to concern yourself with this woman's welfare. 'Tis not your usual style."

"The folly of a befuddled mind, I assure you, sir. But that is neither here nor there. It may all come to naught for Carolyn is determined to send her away. I had to threaten to cut off my aunt's funds just to keep her from throwing the girl out immediately." The earl felt the resurgence of the anger at the scene in his drawing room, and his hand gripped the back of the high-backed chair where he stood.

"Then I don't think you need worry that Carolyn will defy you, but I recommend you take your aunt aside and tell her of your act of kindness to the governess. It might help smooth the way for a more amicable relationship between the ladies."

As the duke finished speaking, a knock sounded at the door. The duke called, "Enter."

The door opened, and a tall gentleman dressed in the height of fashion strolled in. Beneath the dark brown locks, his deeply tanned face was moderately lined and bespoke an outdoorsman.

"Jamie, come in. I hoped you would get a chance to meet. This is my godson, Andrew Marsh, the Earl of Standford. Andrew, this is James Pennington, Viscount Hammond, my sister's boy."

The viscount raised an eyebrow and smiled at the term "boy" while he bowed at the earl. "Standford, my uncle has told me a great deal of you."

"I am sure little of it to my credit," the earl said, remembering the duke's criticisms.

"On the contrary, sir, my uncle sang your praises. Indeed, I was expecting someone ten feet tall and carrying a sword and shield to defend the Empire," Hammond replied, his brown eyes twinkling.

"Now, Jamie, you will put Standford to blush and all because I merely said he was want to do his duty in the House of Lords."

"I enjoy the responsibility, sir." Standford smiled at the duke before turning to Hammond. "How long do you plan to stay in England?"

"Permanently. I sold my plantation and returned to buy a house in Town and to set my late father's estate to rights. Once I have accomplished this my children will join me. I am widowed and hope to find a new mother for them."

" 'Twas a monstrous tragedy for Judith to die so young of the fever," the duke lamented.

"Aye, sir, but we have had two years to mourn and must

move onward. High time my boys were enrolled in a proper English school, and I must make arrangements for my daughter's coming out," the viscount said decisively.

"We can use good men in the House, what with the war. Do you plan to take your seat?" Standford liked Hammond's no-nonsense attitude.

"Most assuredly, but I must get family matters taken care of first."

Speaking about family reminded Standford of his own search for a countess. He could not postpone his own responsibility much longer despite his error with Eugenie. Mentally, he made a note to accompany Carolyn and Miss Whitney for the next week or so. He'd use the opportunity to smooth the relationship between the ladies and look for a prospective wife at the same time.

The duke rose and smiled at his godson. "You must forgive us, Andrew, but we are promised to friends at Brook's. However, if you are of a mind to, we would be pleased to have you join us. Perhaps a game of cards? It would do you good."

The earl realized Atherton was right. Worrying over the past profited no one. He would go home to change, then join his friends for some much needed relief. "I shall meet you at the club in an hour, gentlemen." Standford smiled, then bowed as he left for Cavendish Square.

"Mrs. Polk, please have the Green Room prepared for Miss Whitney," Carolyn instructed the plump-cheeked housekeeper standing before the ladies in the Rose Drawing Room. The woman's snug, black bombazine dress emphasized her large bosom and hips.

"Very good, madam. But Cook is threatening to go to bed with the megrims if you don't speak to her about the menu for the coming week."

"Oh, for heaven's sake, how did the woman manage before my arrival? Never tell me my nephew consulted with her several times a day because I shall not believe Karolyn warned the housekeeper.

"No, ma'am, I believe Cook simply enjoys having mistress in the house."

"Well, I would much prefer her to enjoy a good tipple, a game of cards and cease bothering me with menus already approved, but I suppose I shall have to placate her. Lydia, my dear, please excuse me," she murmured as she followed Mrs. Polk from the drawing room.

Left to herself, Lydia inspected the portrait which hung over the fireplace. Noting the somber countenance of the gentleman, she wondered if he were the earl's father or grandfather. The remote and forbidding look reminded her very much of the current earl, but she knew from personal experience there was a kind heart beneath that cold exterior. Did he show that side often, she wondered, and how tolerant would he be? Shocked to discover she would be residing in London, instead of some remote village as she'd imagined, Lydia realized she needed to tell the earl the truth about her father—before someone else did.

Her attention was suddenly diverted when the drawing room door flew open. An adorable little girl of some four or five years glanced at Lydia curiously. The child was dressed in pink with white lace pantaloons peeking from under the plain frock. Golden curls bounced at her shoulders and dark blue eyes were full of inquiry.

"Where is Mama? Chandler said she was here." The girl approached the sofa with hands tucked into the pockets of a mock white apron.

"If you are referring to Mrs. Trevor, she will return soon. Mrs. Polk had need of her. Are you her daughter?" Lydia asked with a friendly smile.

Nodding, the little girl curtsied with formality, "I am Miss Georgette Trevor. Are you a friend of my mama's?"

"Not precisely. I am Miss Whitney. Lord Standf me to be of assistance to your mother."

The blue eyes clouded with worry and a frown marred her pretty face. "Is Cousin Andrew at home again?"

"Yes, we returned a short time ago."

With a deep sigh, Georgette came to the sofa and sat down, "Do you like cats, Miss Whitney?"

Startled at the abrupt change in the conversation, Lydia still managed a smile. "Yes, I like them very much. I had a large grey tabby named Smokey when I was your age."

"I love cats. My cat's name is Boots. I had to leave him in Leeds because Mama said Cousin Andrew might dislike cats." Georgette pouted.

At a loss for words, Lydia said, "Oh, I see."

"I don't like Lon'nun, but Mama says she must find me a new papa. Why do you think it is taking so long?"

"Well . . . I think your mother wants to find the very best papa for you she can." When the face of Sir Jasper flashed in Lydia's mind she hoped for Georgette's sake that Carolyn was only amusing herself in that quarter.

"I miss Boots. Cook said he is the best mouser in the parish. I wish he might come for a visit to Town, as well."

"Perhaps he can. Why not ask your mother to persuade Cousin Andrew to allow Boots to visit? I am certain he can arrange it."

"Arrange what, Miss Whitney?" The earl stood in the open doorway of the drawing room. Neatly clad in an olive-green coat over buff pantaloons, he appeared much calmer than when she last observed him. However, he still wore his natural hauteur like a cloak wrapped about him. Only when his gaze fell on little Georgette, did his eyes soften and something very like a smile erased the sternness from his mouth.

The child, perhaps reacting to his imposing height and deep voice, drew closer to Lydia. She seemed frightened of the earl and reached for Lydia's hand.

Lord Standford did not miss the gesture and for an instant, Lydia thought she saw a flash of disappointment in his eyes. Did he truly wish to win over the little girl, or was she only

imagining it was so because *she* wished it. Gathering her courage, Lydia challenged him, "My lord, Georgette was just telling me how much she misses her cat."

"Indeed? Then Aunt Carolyn should have brought the animal along. Did you tell your mother you wished for your cat?"

Georgette cowered at Lydia's side, staring mutely at her large cousin.

"I believe, my lord, that her mother holds the impression you dislike cats."

"I cannot conceive where she had such a notion. I certainly have no objection."

"Then, would it be possible, my lord, to arrange for someone to bring the child's cat to her?" Lydia asked, her cheeks warm. She was ashamed of having thought, even momentarily, that the earl would deprive this lonely child of her pet.

"I am in communication with Carolyn's bailiff. It should be simple enough to arrange."

The earl's intent gaze traveled over Lydia's face. Her heart suddenly lurched, then she felt foolish at the strange sensation. To cover her unsettled emotions, she looked down at the child. "Do you hear that, Georgette? Lord Standford is going to have Boots brought down from Leeds for you. What do you have to say, my dear?" Lydia smiled at the child who had remained quiet throughout the conversation.

Georgette rose and curtsied to the earl. "Thank you, Cousin Andrew," she managed before rushing from the room as if chased by spirits.

Looking after the child, Lord Standford said, "She is a quiet little thing. Never know she is in the house."

"She is quite young, sir. Given a little time and gentle handling she will not treat you like a stranger." Looking at Standford's kind expression while he watched the fleeing child, Lydia realized there was quite a complex man behind the stiff manner.

The earl simply nodded his head before reverting to his

usual cold style. He glanced around the room and inquired, "Where is Aunt Carolyn?"

"Consulting with Mrs. Polk on household matters. Is there something I can do for you, sir?"

"No. I just wanted to see how you were getting on with each other. Are there . . . er . . . any problems?"

"We have come to an understanding, my lord, but there is another matter I should like to discuss with you." Having decided she must tell the earl the truth about her father, she wished to do so without delay.

"Can this wait until later, Miss Whitney? I do not mean to put you off, but I have an engagement with some friends."

"Of course, my lord."

With a nod of his head, the earl turned and left. Feeling disappointed and uncertain, Lydia sighed. Her job was not secure until the earl knew the truth from her own lips. It would be a disaster if he heard of it from someone else. She could imagine the disappointment in those azure-blue eyes.

Carolyn startled Lydia from her musings when she appeared in the doorway. "Well, my dear, Cook has been appeased. Shall we get you comfortably settled in your room? You must be tired after your early start from Pemberton. 'Tis certain you will enjoy being in Town again after being on a lonely country estate."

Knowing the pitfalls of moving among her father's friends, Lydia wasn't convinced she would enjoy being in London. As she rose and followed her mistress, she simply hoped she would get the opportunity to remain with Carolyn. All would depend on how his lordship handled the news that her father was one of Society's most infamous gamesters.

Three

Lydia, arms slightly extended to avoid a pin prick, stood in the middle of Carolyn's bedroom. The widow's abigail hovered behind her, awaiting Mrs. Trevor's approval on the alterations to the Clarence blue silk evening gown.

The surrounding floor was cluttered with open trunks spilling a colorful array of gowns previously discarded by the earl's aunt. She'd declared them overused after being worn only a few times during the current Season and consigned them to storage. Now they would be seen again as fashionable attire for Lydia.

"Millie, that is exactly right. The gown will look as if it were made for Miss Whitney when you finish. But however will we change the dress so that no one recognizes it as one of my old cast-offs?" Carolyn asked while she scanned the silk creation critically.

"Well, madam, I reckon we could take off all that white froggin' and replace it with the leftover silver ribbon I found in the first trunk. Mayhap a bow with long runners down the front and small bows at the sleeves," the plump maid suggested, after taking the spare pins from her mouth.

"Excellent, Millie. You are so clever with a needle. You will see, Lydia."

"It sounds wonderful, and the gown is beautiful. But . . . don't you think it perhaps too elegant for your companion?"

"Nonsense—as if I would allow dear Freddie's daughter to go about looking like a governess."

"But that is exactly what I was, Carolyn," Lydia protested.

The widow ignored the girl's candor. "That may be, but you are a Whitney, which makes you the Duke of Graymoor's granddaughter. One cannot expect so elevated a person to go about looking like a dowd."

Lydia's back went rigid. She'd had no inkling that Carolyn perceived the relationship. "Madam, my . . . grandfather," she spoke the word as if tasting something bitter, "does not acknowledge that I even exist. I would prefer that you do not mention the connection to anyone."

Carolyn looked closely at Lydia before nodding. "I completely understand, my dear. I never liked the crusty old fellow myself."

"I have not met the gentleman."

"Never—"

Before Carolyn could finish her sentence, the chamber door opened. Georgette Trevor, clad in a night dress, entered followed by her nurse.

"Muffin, are you ready for bed?" Carolyn asked as she bent down to kiss the top of her daughter's head.

"Might I stay and visit with you and Miss Whitney for just a short time, Mama?" The small girl smiled pleadingly up at her mother.

With a delighted laugh, Carolyn said, "Yes, if you promise not to get near the pins and sit quietly. We have much to do."

"I shall be good, Mama." Georgette crawled up on a yellow damask chair, one of the few not covered with discarded apparel. She placed the cloth doll she carried carefully beside her so Nella could watch, also.

"Nurse, why not go have a dish of tea with Cook," Carolyn kindly encouraged the older woman.

When she'd left, Carolyn returned to the work of selecting dresses for Lydia. Several already lay heaped on a nearby bed, including a willow-green, a pale pink, and a silver gauze confection. They were discussing the changes to be made to rework the gowns when a scratching sounded on the door.

Millie, three shades of ribbons draped around her neck, walked to the door and discovered the butler who peered past the stout abigail in search of her mistress. "Mrs. Trevor, Lord Standford would like you to join him in the library at your earliest convenience."

"Thank you, Chandler. You may tell him I shall be there momentarily." Turning back to Lydia, Carolyn said, "I must see what Andrew wishes. Will you take care of Georgette until Nurse returns?"

"Gladly," Lydia replied.

"Millie, that will be all for the night. You may go after you put the unwanted dresses back in the trunks. Bess can attend me tonight."

Lydia watched Carolyn throw her daughter a silent kiss before leaving. Turning so Millie could undo the dress, Lydia stepped behind a screen and removed it. Quickly donning the worn grey silk which buttoned up the front to her neck, she came out and gave the blue gown to the maid.

The abigail, busy repacking the trunks with the unchosen outfits, thanked her and placed the blue silk on the stack to be altered.

Lydia took a seat near Georgette, who looked up and innocently asked, "Are you poor, Miss Whitney?"

Millie frowned at the child, but Lydia smiled and replied, "I am not exactly poor, but I am very low on funds. That is why I must work for a living, my dear."

"I heard Mama tell the housekeeper that Papa left us with our pockets to let. Cappy said that means we have no money either," Georgette stated innocently.

Knowing Mrs. Trevor would be deeply embarrassed by Georgette's confidences, Lydia tried to steer the conversation away. "Who is Cappy?"

"He is the stable boy at home. He said Cousin Andrew was sending him to work for the squire down the road. I wish he wouldn't go." The girl looked sad while she fussed with the doll which now sat in her lap.

Lydia was starting to understand why Georgette seemed afraid of her cousin. First there was the misunderstanding about the cat, which she suspected was inadvertently Carolyn's fault. Then the dismissal of old employees from the girl's home for reasons of economy. The earl was trying to help the Trevors but the child was too young to understand the necessary changes.

Aloud she said, "I think Lord Standford is trying to assist your mother to keep the estate. It is very expensive to run a property. I am sure should your mother remarry, you will see Cappy again." Lydia hoped she was right, for it was difficult enough for the child to have lost her father. All this uncertainty was surely adding to her unhappiness.

"Mama told the housekeeper it looked like she would be forced to tread the boards to support us."

Lydia sighed, wondering if Mrs. Trevor had any idea how much her daughter overheard. Smiling, she reassured Georgette. "No doubt your mama was upset. I am very sure she did not mean it."

"What does one do with those boards, Miss Whitney?"

"Why don't you call me Lydia, my dear?"

"I would like that, Miss Lydia." The child smiled back.

"Don't you be askin' Miss Whitney so many questions," Millie said while she gathered up the gowns to be altered and opened the door to leave. Coming up the hall was her mistress. She held the door, allowing Mrs. Trevor to enter the room with Nurse following behind. "I'll be getting to work on these, Mrs. Trevor."

"Yes, excellent, Millie. Don't stay up too late." After the abigail left, the widow turned to her daughter. "Well, Muffin, it is time you were in bed. Give me a kiss."

Georgette climbed down from the chair and ran up to hug her mother. When the child clung over long, Carolyn gently said, "All will be well, my dear. Don't worry. Mama will take care of things." She soundly kissed her daughter and coaxed a smile from her before the girl left the room with Nurse.

Lydia eyed her mistress with respect for the obvious care and affection she bestowed on her child. "You must be quite proud of Georgette."

"Yes, she is my life. She is the true reason why I came to Town," the widow said earnestly when she came and sat down by her companion.

Lydia hoped the surprise she felt was not registered on her face. She knew the child would have been happier in Leeds. "You came to Town because of Georgette?"

With a sigh, Carolyn's lovely mouth drew downward. She stared toward the large windows where pale yellow drapes were drawn to shut out the darkness. "In truth, I have come to marry. I must secure Georgette's future. Dear Sydney was ill so long before he died, but I did not realize the seriousness of our situation until his will was read. There are almost no funds for my Muffin to have the simplest luxuries or even a Season. Without a reasonable portion, she will have no chance to wed. There is just enough to live modestly, according to the solicitor and Andrew." Tears filled her pale blue eyes.

"Then you can ill afford a companion, Carolyn." Lydia's stomach tightened, knowing she was encouraging the widow to be rid of her.

"True, my dear, but Andrew hired you and it is he who will pay your salary. I would not have agreed, except it frees him to go back and forth to his estate without worrying about me."

Relieved her job was secure, Lydia asked the question which had worried her when the widow spoke of her reasons for coming to Town. "Won't the earl provide for you and Georgette?"

"He offered, but we are not his responsibility and I shall manage without his help." The widow held her head high and spoke heroically, but she ruined the effect by adding,

"Besides, he would forever be looking over my shoulder, criticizing my choices and my expenses. I will not have it. Marriage is preferable."

"But, Carolyn, surely a husband would do the same."

"My dear," the widow said with a wicked grin, "when a gentleman is in love, he is usually quite . . . malleable. 'Tis *not* the same at all."

"Do you truly wish to remarry?"

"I have thought of other ways that I could help recover the estate, but marriage seems to be the most reliable. I am determined, however, that it must be a love match. I am sure it is just as easy to love a nabob as a handsome, penniless lord."

"No doubt." Lydia suppressed a smile. She was glad Carolyn was not marrying only for money. Despite the lady's volatile nature, she liked the widow and her small daughter and wished them both to be happy.

"Well, my dear, are you looking forward to being in the social whirl again? Going to balls and seeing old Town friends?"

"I am afraid I have been gone from London so long I know little about what is happening. My mother died when I was quite young so even before my father's death I did not move much in Society." Lydia hoped few would remember her or her infamous father. Her *friends* were mostly gaming companions of Lord Frederick's.

"After one ball, you will meet a great many of the *haute ton*. In fact, Andrew just told me he wished to host a dinner on Wednesday night. Most of the gentlemen of his acquaintance are rather older, but it will be a nice way to ease back into Society for you."

Lydia felt a wave of nervousness. The earl's friends were more likely to remember her father than the ladies of the *ton*. With tepid enthusiasm, she said, "How nice."

"I told my nephew we were redoing some of the my old gowns for you. As a man, he, of course, did not realize we must outfit you properly, and was actually pleased at my frugality. Oh, my dear, I insisted you be called my goddaughter. I will not have some of the Society hostesses treating you like a potted plant as some are want to do with companions."

Lydia would have been flattered by the widow's concern for her, but she suspected Carolyn did not want the term companion associated with one so young as herself. Nevertheless, Lydia had suffered enough slights as a governess to know she would receive equal treatment as a companion. Being called a goddaughter suited them both, and certainly the small deception could harm no one. "Thank you, Carolyn. 'Tis exceedingly kind of you."

"Now that we have taken care of that, my dear, I did want to hear more about life with your father. You actually went into some of the gaming dens on St. James?"

Feeling uncomfortable with the subject, Lydia answered briefly, "Yes, when I was younger."

"Was it terribly exciting?"

"Not to a ten-year-old."

"And how did your father manage to get such a nickname as Faro Freddie?" Carolyn pursued.

"He always managed to walk away a winner when he played the game despite having to give half to the bank. Sometimes the sums were small, but to a gambler a win is a win." Lydia sighed when she remembered the hard times due to short funds. Her father was addicted to all forms of gambling. Fate had decreed his vice to be his source of income.

"And he *always* won when he played Faro?"

Lydia failed to note the glitter in Mrs. Trevor's eyes, and answered innocently, "Yes, always by the end of the game."

"Did he employ some trick or special strategy—a system, perhaps?" the widow asked breathlessly.

Lydia looked closely at her mistress. Having been questioned by many gentlemen about her father's accomplishment, she was leery of inquiries about his play. However, there was little reason to worry about telling the widow how her father succeeded at the game. No genteel lady would go to the gaming hells. Mrs. Trevor could never attempt to use Lord Frederick's method. "In truth, the wins he attributed to intuition."

"Intuition? What ever does that mean?"

"He said that a feeling would come and he would just know what the cards would be before they were turned up. My mother's Scottish maid called him *fey*," Lydia explained.

Frowning, Carolyn repeated, "The maid called him Fay? Hopefully the saucy girl was dismissed for her impertinence."

With a laugh, Lydia said, "No, *fey*, meaning intuitive."

Clearly not understanding, Carolyn got to the matter most important to her. "Never mind about troublesome staff— what about this intuition business, was it the same with the other games?"

"I asked him once about whist and he said he merely memorized the cards and counted them as they were played; it required no intuition only an excellent memory. But he played whist only when there was no Faro or Hazard table. The method did seem to work."

"Why how clever and simple," Carolyn said. "I am surprised more gentlemen do not use such a method."

"I believe that once my father saw anything it remained in his memory indefinitely. I think that is not true with most people."

"You may be right. Lord Frederick must have had a special gift." Carolyn fell silent, sure she would be able to use the memory trick. Did she not remember every word of the poem that dear Sydney had written her so many years ago? The difficulty would be finding an opportunity to put her plan into action. Andrew would try to thwart her at every turn. A cold fish like her nephew could never understand her need to recover their funds for her child. With a determined sigh, she vowed to risk anything for the sake of dear Muffin.

Standford sat perusing the *Times* in the sunny breakfast room at Marsh House. He patiently awaited the arrival of Aunt Carolyn and her companion, wishing to speak with the ladies about their plans for the week. He was curious to see what his aunt had done to transform the governess into a fashionable young lady.

Having already dined, he drank a second cup of coffee while he read the latest news from the peninsula. However, this morning, it failed to hold his interest. As soon as he heard the sound of female voices, he folded the paper and gazed expectantly at the door.

Carolyn opened the portal, then halted on the threshold. "Andrew, I am surprised to find you lingering over breakfast, but you are just in time to see the new Lydia. Millie and I have been very busy, indeed. She will take the *ton* by storm." She stepped into the room as she spoke.

Lydia followed hesitantly, uncertain how Lord Standford would react to the change in her appearance. She had argued with both Carolyn and Millie about dressing her hair in such a fashionable style. The women insisted that cutting the front would soften and enhance her natural beauty. Secretly pleased with the results, she still doubted that her employer would think she looked a proper companion.

"I assured Lydia that you gave your permission for us to improve her appearance, but she is resisting us yet. Pray, tell her you have no objection to her being fashionably attired," Carolyn insisted while the earl observed Lydia.

Standford sat with his hands gripping the edge of the polished table. He stared at his aunt's companion. He'd thought the girl passably pretty before in her drab costume with the proper hair style of her station. But due to his aunt's intervention, Miss Whitney was now a stunning beauty.

Silvery tendrils of hair framed her perfect oval face. Tawny eyes stared at him with a touch of trepidation, awaiting his reaction. A pale green muslin morning gown outlined a decidedly feminine figure. As his gaze moved over the young woman he'd brought into his household, the earl felt a masculine stirring deep within him that jarred his aristocratic composure.

Clearing his dry throat, he stared at the girl for a moment longer. He managed to utter, "Very nice, Miss Whitney." He turned his disturbed gaze upon his aunt. Searching for something to say, he spoke in an unsteady voice. "Were you planning on attending the Washburns' ball on Friday?"

"We are. Do you wish to act as our escort?" Carolyn asked, looking back at Miss Whitney to admire the changes.

"I was planning on going . . . if you need someone . . . I would be glad to act as escort." Standford felt like he was babbling.

The ladies came forward and took their seats at the table. While a footman poured coffee, Carolyn said, "That would be delightful, Andrew."

Risking a glance at the beauty, the earl noted that Miss Whitney's gaze was locked on her cup. Deciding he needed to distance himself from the enchanting vision, he rose. "Very well, I shall join you on Friday. Until this evening, ladies."

Lydia looked up at the closing door. She'd detected some strong emotion in Lord Standford when she entered the room, and feared he was displeased with her stylish appearance. He'd hired her to be a companion, not to have a Season at his expense. Her appetite completely fled. " 'Tis as I said, Carolyn. The earl does not like my changed appearance, nor think it suitable for a person in my position."

"You mistake the matter. He said you looked very nice, so don't worry, Lydia. You will make an excellent companion regardless of how you dress, I am sure." Carolyn looked across at the despondent Lydia and smiled. In truth, the widow suspected Andrew liked the change too much for his own peace of mind. Dear Lydia just might be the one to unsettle his staid and proper life.

"Good morning, my lord," Rupert Farlow said as he pushed the glasses up on his nose and watched the earl enter the library. The secretary's gaze fell to the earl's hand absently fingering the single fob hanging at his waist. "Is there a problem, sir?"

"Yes, Farlow. I hired a companion for my aunt, and now I begin to doubt the wisdom of such a move." Standford came to sit behind the desk where his secretary had stacked the correspondences to be answered.

"If you are unhappy with the female, sir, I recommend you send her packing," the frail young man advised in a no-nonsense voice before he went back to sorting the documents for the earl's perusal.

"Not unhappy . . . merely uncertain if she is quite capable of watching Carolyn."

"Have you fully explained what you expect her duties will be?"

"I must do so today." The earl examined the top sheet before him without really seeing it.

"Should you decide she will not suit, I can arrange to place her with a good agency here in Town and find a replacement at the same time." Farlow's tone held little sympathy for the unknown companion.

Standford felt a strange emptiness in his chest at the thought of Miss Whitney's departure. He must be over-tired. Aloud, he said, "I must be fair. First, I shall explain to her about my aunt. Would you go to the dining room and tell the young lady I would like to see her at ten?"

"Yes, my lord," Farlow said, a touch of disapproval in his voice.

After the secretary left, Standford pondered why the girl

affected him so strongly. Probably because Eugenie had wounded his pride so badly at Pemberton. He would have to be on his guard. Hadn't he made up his mind that only a proper lady would do for his wife? He knew little of Miss Whitney, good or bad—only that a mere governess left him speechless at the sight of her.

Rising, the earl walked to the fireplace and stared at the burning coals. Confusing thoughts swirled in his head. Mayhap Farlow was right. He could make certain Miss Whitney obtained another position and find an older woman to deal with Carolyn. Someone with the wisdom of age.

The door opened and closed with a snap when Farlow returned from his errand. "Miss Whitney said she would be here promptly at ten, sir."

The earl noted the secretary's flushed face. "Are you feeling well enough to work today, Rupert?" Standford remembered the young man had been ill only recently with an inflammation of the lungs.

"Me, sir? I am fine. It is just a little warm in here." Farlow bent over the stack of papers he'd abandoned to run the earl's errand.

Coming back to his desk, the earl took a seat. "Perhaps you are right about sending the girl away. Do you think you could quickly find a replacement?"

"Well . . . er . . . I may have been unduly hasty, my lord. Miss Whitney seems capable and your aunt is quite taken with her, my lord."

Standford gazed up at his secretary in astonishment. Good lord, Farlow was smitten after one encounter with the lady.

Eyeing the flushed secretary for a moment, the earl sighed with resignation. "Very well, if she wishes to stay after I explain the situation to her, I shall allow her to remain, but I must be certain she can handle Aunt Carolyn."

Having made his decision, the earl drew the stack of papers forward and got to the business at hand. The pair worked intently for over an hour. They had gotten through almost half of the documents when the clock on the mantel began to chime the hour.

The last gong still reverberated in the room when a scratching sounded at the library door. Standford watched his secretary rush to the door as if he pursued footpads who'd stolen his money. The young man bowed low when Miss Whitney flashed him a hesitant smile.

The earl, having risen, came around the desk. "Miss Whitney, this is Rupert Farlow, my secretary."

"We met in the breakfast parlor, my lord."

"Rupert, I would like to speak with Miss Whitney privately. You can work in the morning room for now. Make certain that letter goes to Mrs. Trevor's bailiff." While the secretary gathered some documents, the earl spoke to the pale young woman. "Do you and Aunt Carolyn have plans for this morning?"

"We are planning to take Georgette for a walk in the park, my lord." Lydia nervously twisted her lace handkerchief while she stood before Lord Standford. Aware of his unsettling gaze, she felt a tingling in the pit of her stomach. She wished she'd eaten something, but their earlier encounter had left her too unsettled to break her fast. She remained uncertain why she was summoned, but feared the worst after his abrupt departure.

"I shall only keep you for a few moments." The earl waited until the door closed behind Farlow before he continued. He walked to the windows behind the desk and stood peering out at the new spring growth on the plants. "I fear that I was not entirely forthright with you when I offered you a position as companion. The truth is my aunt has a propensity for getting into trouble."

Apprehension swept through Lydia while she watched Lord Standford clench his hands behind his back. What dark secret lurked in her congenial mistress's life? "I shall do my best to assist Mrs. Trevor in any way possible."

"Thank you. You will have a full-time task, I suspect. I

have spoken to my aunt until I have all but lost my breath. She will not heed me. She is quite convinced that she can turn around the losses to her late husband's estate single-handedly."

"I know she is planning to remarry for that very reason, sir."

Looking back at Miss Whitney, the earl's gaze fell to the creamy white expanse above the green bodice. He gritted his teeth in frustration at the direction of his thoughts. Bowing his head, he stared at his gleaming boots before saying, "If she would but concentrate on that task, I would not have needed to hire you. No, I fear she has another plan for restoring the family fortune."

An alarming thought came to Lydia as she stood near a rosewood table which held a bowl of hothouse roses. She reached out to steady herself on the well-polished surface while echoes of last night's conversation repeated in her head. She'd told Carolyn her father's memory trick.

Please let it be something else, she prayed.

With a deep sigh the earl again looked out at the garden. "My aunt, Miss Whitney, is a determined gamester."

The full horror of what she'd told Carolyn appalled Lydia. The smell of the flowers became oppressively sweet to her, the library became unduly warm. The room swirled alarmingly.

The sound of a loud thud caused Standford to turn in the direction he'd studiously avoided looking for the past few minutes. To his startled amazement, the beautiful Miss Whitney lay unconscious on the Oriental rug.

Four

"What is all the noise, Andrew?" Carolyn Trevor swept into the library in search of the din which had disturbed her in the breakfast parlor. An ornate gold lorgnette was clasped in one dainty hand and a letter in the other.

"Someone at last. Why can I never find a servant when I need one?" Andrew turned to face his aunt. He was using a folded newspaper to fan the unconscious Miss Whitney, who lay on the room's only sofa.

Carolyn gasped. Pointing her ornamental glasses at Standford, she indignantly demanded, "What have you done to Lydia? Were you berating her in that highhanded way you have? I will not have it."

"I was not berating her," Standford replied tersely. He resumed fanning the unconscious young woman, and added defensively, "We were but speaking of you and her duties."

Clucking softly, Carolyn laid the letter and the lorgnette on the nearby table. She took one of Lydia's cold hands in her own and sat beside the supine girl. "Standford, do stop flapping that paper around as if you were warding off insects. You are doing the dear girl no good."

The earl laid the newspaper on his desk. He mutely stared at Lydia's pale face.

"She would have only coffee this morning, poor child. No doubt that is the cause of her fainting. Please, go find Chandler. Have him bring Millie to me with my vinaigrette." Carolyn rose as she watched Standford hurriedly leave the room.

He seemed surprisingly disturbed. Since her arrival on the scene, the taut look had left his face, but he'd gone too meekly to do her bidding.

Looking at her companion, Carolyn wondered if it was really the lack of food that precipitated Lydia's faint.

Moaning, Lydia moved her head slowly back and forth.

"Yes, dear, you must come out of your swoon and eat something," the widow murmured encouragingly as she patted the girl's face gently.

"Must tell . . . truth . . . father a gamester," Lydia mumbled disjointedly.

"No, my dear, pray do not do anything so foolish," Carolyn beseeched, suddenly gripped by a sense of urgency. "With such an admission, Standford would turn you off. It would not matter to him that you did not game yourself. He is too stiff-necked to see the way of things."

While the girl continued to mutter the same daunting phrase, Carolyn did her best to soothe her, but she thought rapidly. She did not want Lydia to be sent away merely because Standford foolishly believed his aunt to be addicted to gaming.

Pooh! She'd surely won as much as she lost since she came to Town. Her nephew, however, acted as if she was about to be hauled away to debtors' prison. Well, she would not allow Standford to punish this innocent because of his misguided duty and rigid principles.

Watching Lydia slowly return to consciousness, Carolyn worried the girl would blurt out the truth when Standford returned. He must be sent away and kept away until she had sufficient time to persuade Lydia it would be foolish to confess the truth about her father.

When the door opened, Standford ushered in Millie with the viniagette. "Chandler was in the alley accepting a delivery from my wine merchant. However, I found your abigail."

Grabbing the small silver box from the plump servant, Carolyn said, "Very good, Andrew. Now leave us and Millie and I shall see that Lydia retires to her room after she eats. Millie, please go to the kitchen and bring a tea tray. Make sure Cook sends toast and preserves, as well."

The earl preceded the maid to the library door. Carolyn sighed with relief. The danger had passed. Now she could concentrate on her companion without worrying about what the befuddled girl might say. She bent down and waved the pungent container beneath Lydia's nose.

At once the young woman tossed her head to avoid the unpleasant scent. Her eyes opened but seemed unfocused.

"Lydia, 'tis I, Carolyn. Can you hear me?"

Watching her companion regain alertness, Carolyn's heart froze. The young woman's tawny eyes had locked on a point beyond where Carolyn stood. Glancing over her left shoulder, she was appalled to discover Andrew directly behind her.

Lydia uttered, "My lord . . I must . . ."

Impulsively, Carolyn grasped the bowl of roses on the nearby table. Throwing the flowers to the floor, she dashed the water in Lydia's face.

"Are you mad, Carolyn?" the earl nearly shouted and would have rushed to Lydia had not his aunt blocked the way.

"The girl looked like she was about to faint again," Carolyn said. "Trust that I know how to deal with a lady in a swoon."

Lydia sat blinking at the pair in wide-eyed surprise. The cold water seemed to have left her speechless.

" 'Tis only water, Andrew, the child won't melt like sugar," Carolyn nervously added.

The earl watched the path the rivulets of water took with fascination. They slowly dripped from Miss Whitney's chin, pooling into a stream in the hollow of her throat, disappearing beneath the green bodice. As the dress grew wet, leaving little to the imagination, he averted his gaze.

To Carolyn's horror, Miss Whitney again opened her mouth to speak. Recklessly, she snatched a white lace handkerchief from her pocket and clamped it over the girl's parted lips. "Here let me dry your face, my dear. I had no idea there was quite so much water in that bowl."

Lydia's eyes widened in bewilderment as Carolyn hovered over her. She was effectively silenced by the lady's hand covering her mouth.

Pursing her lips, Carolyn tried to signal her companion to be quiet.

"I think her face is quite dry enough, Aunt," the earl said, frowning at Carolyn's handling of the young woman.

"Oh, Andrew, are you still here? Do run along to your club. 'Tis embarrassing for Lydia to have you see her so. Surely, you can finish your conversation with her later."

He hesitated, feeling somewhat responsible. "Are you all right, Miss Whitney?"

When Lydia nodded mutely, Carolyn slowly released her hold on the girl's now flushed face.

His features relaxing, the earl replied, "Very well, Aunt Carolyn, if you are sure Miss Whitney is recovered, I shall leave you ladies."

"Trust me, Andrew. 'Tis a mere trifle. Once she eats, all will be well."

"Then, I shall bid you good day."

Watching her nephew bow then leave the room, Carolyn took a deep breath. Sagging back into a high-backed chair, she said weakly, "That was a close one, my dear."

Lydia stared across at her mistress. She'd realized at the last moment that the lady was urgently trying to prevent her from blurting out the truth.

Sitting up slowly, she said, "You must realize, Carolyn, I do have to inform Lord Standford about my father. If he were to learn such information from anyone else, he would have a right to be quite angry, considering his reason for hiring me."

"So he did engage you to spy on me!" Carolyn said, outraged.

Although she was unsure why, Lydia felt a need to defend Lord Standford. "He did not ask me to spy on you, or report your activities. He merely stated that you . . . like to game. Therefore, I think it only fair to inform him about my father."

Carolyn managed a faltering smile. She realized Lydia would not be persuaded to remain silent out of concern for her own position. Other measures were called for. She lifted her brows and asked, "Did you inform your other employers about who your father was, my dear?"

"Only that I was Lord Frederick Whitney's daughter, but this is a—"

"Did Andrew ask for any references when he employed you?"

Lydia set her chin in a stubborn line. " 'Tis not the same situation. I would not have been going into Society and meeting all my father's old gaming friends. Under the circumstances, it would not be fair to withhold the information from his lordship."

Sitting forward in the chair, Carolyn confidently said, "Under the circumstances? I see, but, contrary to what Andrew may have told you, I am not some zealous gamester. I admit on several social occasions I have lost a little money. Very little, but you would think I had gambled away the family estate by the manner in which my nephew reacted."

"He appears quite concerned."

"Overly concerned, my dear." Carolyn waved her hand dismissively. "That is why I don't want you to do anything foolish like mention your father was Faro Freddie. Andrew might think you unable to keep me from gaming."

Watching the earnest look on Carolyn's face, Lydia realized she had an opportunity to repay the earl's kindness in offering her a position. "Very well, I shall promise not to tell Lord Standford who my father was unless he directly asks me, if you will promise no gaming."

A cry of relief broke from Carolyn's lips. She was genuinely concerned about Lydia's future, but she also knew that if she allowed Andrew to turn her companion off, the next one he engaged might be far less agreeable. "I promise you I will be good."

Individual lamps glowed softly on each green baize table in the gaming room at Brooks, casting an unheathly pallor on the faces of the gentlemen at play. Standford paused in the doorway, scanning the room for the Duke of Atherton among the gathered card players seated at the various tables. Several gentlemen waved a greeting to which the earl nodded his head before he spied the duke at a distant table intently eyeing the cards in his hands.

Sauntering toward his godfather, Standford stopped briefly to exchange a few words with acquaintances from the House of Lords. Presently, he arrived at the table where the duke was seated with two swells, both clad in garishly hued coats and collar points so high they could not turn their heads.

Tossing his cards disgustedly upon the table, Atherton said, "My luck is out today. I think I shall find another sport to amuse me."

"Then join me in a glass of claret, Your Grace." Standford clasped his friend on the shoulder.

"Andrew, you are late, my boy. Had you been earlier you could have won all my money instead of Worthy and Morton."

The two gentlemen mentioned rose while they collected their winnings from the table. Worthy drawled, " 'Twas a pleasure to play, Your Grace."

Standford took one of the seats vacated by the departing men. "Whatever possessed you to play with those sharps?"

"Boredom does strange things to one's judgment, I suppose. Tell me, what kept you? Hammond is late, as well."

Flipping one of the cards over idly, the earl answered, "Carolyn's companion swooned this morning just as I was telling her of my aunt's propensity for gaming."

"Devil take it, Andrew, what did you imply? That Carolyn was cavorting in the hells on St. James? The lady merely lost some pin money at whist."

The earl's brows drew downward in a frown. "Money she can ill afford to lose. But I am sure it was nothing I said that caused the young woman to faint. Leastwise, Aunt Carolyn thought it was because Miss Whitney failed to eat breakfast before the interview."

"Keeping a miserly buffet these days? You need a countess to arrange these things, my boy." The duke grinned at his godson.

"You do like to paint my soul black of late. Aunt Carolyn said the young woman was just nervous, being new at the post and such. However, you are right about my needing a countess." Standford sank into thought, wondering how he should go about seeking a possible wife.

"You will need to start going to all these infernal balls and routs if you are looking for a wife. Can't abide the things anymore but I found my Annabelle at the Ashbys' first ball of the Season all those years ago. Mark my words, Andrew, when you see the right lady your heart will tell you, if you will but listen." The duke's eyes gleamed as he fondly recollected the long-ago memory.

"Balderdash, marriage is a contract. Love is of no consequence," Standford stated decisively.

Atherton gazed with knowing eyes at the earl. "Your father did you no good by failing to remarry after Diana died. You would not say such about marriage if you knew how much he loved your mother."

A loud altercation erupted between two gentlemen at another table, sparing Standford the need to make a comment. While they watched the dispute escalate, shouts could be heard placing bets on which could best the other at Gentleman Jackson's. The quarreling pair agreed to move the dispute to the ring and a large crowd followed the twosome out of the gaming room.

With a lull in the noise as the roisterous group exited into St. James, the duke asked, "How do you plan to look for a wife, my boy, if love is to be no part of it?"

"Well . . . I was hoping . . . Her Grace might be of some assistance." Embarrassed, the earl dropped his gaze back to the cards scattered on the green baize.

A look of sadness passed over the duke's face. "Andrew, you know Annabelle and I shall do all in our power to aid you even if we don't agree with your method. Do you wish her to make you up a list of eligible young ladies who are making their bows this Season?"

With a wry grin, Standford rushed to say, "Nothing that formal, Your Grace. If she could just tell me the names of some of the chits, I can take it from there."

"Annabelle will never do anything halfway, my boy. We dine with you on Wednesday night. I am certain she will have a list for you of at least ten or twelve prospective brides."

"Thank you, sir. I do appreciate your help."

"Tell me, do you have any specific qualifications for these gels? I know Annabelle will ask." Atherton rose while he queried the earl.

Rising, Standford mused over this for a moment before he replied, "I believe she must be well bred and possessed of a suitable portion, sir. Yes, pedigree and portion are all that matter."

Having nervously anticipated the earl's dinner party, Lydia was surprised to discover that the invited group consisted of only three individuals. He introduced her to the Duke and Duchess of Atherton, an older couple near sixty, who stood as godparents to Lord Standford, and their nephew, Viscount Hammond. A likeable man in his forties, he immediately drew Carolyn's notice.

Small the gathering might be, but the group proved most

congenial. Lydia forgot her fears as they sat down to dinner, and after the first remove, she felt entirely at ease.

Gazing to her left, Lydia observed the earl in animated conversation with the duchess. He was speaking earnestly of his current efforts to repeal the Corn Laws. Lydia watched with interest as the earl relaxed his customary formal manner.

This evening was the first time she'd encountered Lord Standford since their disastrous meeting in the library on Monday. She suspected that he'd avoided her after she'd so missishly fainted, no doubt thinking her a weak and silly creature. Her cheeks warmed as she remembered her foolish behavior. The blush deepened when she caught the Duchess of Atherton's gaze resting on her face with interest.

While the group at the opposite end of the table listened to Lord Hammond's harrowing tale of his voyage to England, Lydia covertly studied the earl under her lashes. Tendrils of chestnut hair curled in artful disarray at the edge of his smooth forehead. He owned a generous mouth and an aquiline nose in a face that hinted at strength of character. She suspected such a man would never understand her father's weakness for games of chance. She suddenly felt grateful that Carolyn had prevented her from confessing all.

Apparently having heard enough about corn prices and the small farmer's plight from the impassioned earl, the duchess changed the subject during a lull in his discourse. "Andrew, your aunt tells me you are promised to the Washburns' on Friday."

The earl frowned slightly. "Yes, Your Grace."

"I own myself pleased. You have spent far too much time with politics and your clubs since you came to Town. You need to practice your gallantries."

"I should gladly do so, Your Grace, if most young ladies possessed your charm. Unfortunately, it seems to me so many ladies have more hair than wit, and engage in such pointless chatter, it drives me to distraction."

The duchess laughed. "Not pointless, Andrew. I suspect the ladies have been flirting with matrimony in mind. How lowering to think their efforts all in vain. Really, my dear, you must strive to be more gallant." She slanted a glance at Lydia, and added, "Most young ladies long for sweet words and compliments. Is that not true, Miss Whitney?"

Lydia looked up from her plate. "I cannot say, Your Grace, never having heard such speeches. But I do recall a gentleman who made a vast impression on me by the simple recitation of a poem."

"Poetry, ah I agree, my dear. What lady's heart would not be touched if a gentleman were to recite, 'She is beautiful and therefore to be wooed, She is a woman, and therefore to be won.' "

"Poetry," Lord Standford said disdainfully. "Surely you are not suggesting that *I* should go round spouting couplets to a lady."

"Heavens no, Andrew. I would sooner expect Prinny to practice economy than such a miracle. I was merely agreeing with Miss Whitney," the duchess replied, a smile turning up the corners of her mouth.

Lydia watched as the earl glared at his godmother, but the teasing kindness in her look finally melted the frosty mask on his face. He confessed, "I have not the knack for pretty speeches. 'Tis too undignified. I dare say I am a hopeless case in matters of courting."

"Never say that, Andrew. The reason for your silence is that you have yet to meet the lady who touches your heart, and therefore inspires a gift of poetic praise. Use some of that wit and eloquence that I have heard in the House of Lords—just on a more personal level. You will set all the ladies' hearts aflutter. Is that not true, Miss Whitney?"

"To be sure, Your Grace," Lydia answered, remembering how often her heart misbehaved in the earl's presence without his paying her any pretty compliments. She caught his gaze as he shifted uncomfortably in his chair. He was clearly unhappy being the subject of the duchess's forthright style of speaking.

"Ladies," Carolyn said, intruding on Lydia's musings. "Shall we retire to the drawing room and leave the gentlemen to their port?"

Lydia followed the duchess and her mistress abovestairs to the Rose Drawing Room. Taking a seat across from the older women, she sat quietly as befitted her position. She knew herself to be in elegant company and prayed the years would treat her as kindly as they had these two gracious ladies.

The duchess, who she knew must be nearing sixty, retained much of the beauty that had made her a reigning belle. True, her hair had greyed, but she wore it in a coronet that added to her regality. And one could not fault her figure, still as slender as a girl's in a pomona-green gown. But it was her kindness, Lydia thought, that drew people to her.

". . . do you like living here in Cavendish Square?" the duchess was asking Carolyn.

"I suppose, but I would have much preferred a small establishment of my own." Carolyn, looking youthful in pink silk with a burgundy over-dress, sounded pensive when she glanced about the large room.

"To be sure, my dear, but Standford is always one to get his own way," the duchess responded before turning her attention to Lydia. "I understand from the duke that you are to be companion to Mrs. Trevor."

Before Lydia could respond, Carolyn interrupted in a huff. "Oh, that Andrew. I told him that we are to call Lydia my goddaughter for I am much too young for a companion, and now he is out telling tales."

"Never fear that I shall not keep your secret, Carolyn. Andrew spoke to the duke in confidence and neither of us indulges in Society tittle tattle." The duchess reached over to give Carolyn's arm a reassuring pat.

"Oh . . . I beg your pardon . . . I did not mean to imply . . ." Carolyn stammered in embarrassment.

"I know you did not, dear. Now, Miss Whitney, tell me something of yourself. I feel you look quite familiar." The duchess's gaze scanned Lydia's face as if she searched for the clue to her identity.

A wave of anxiety swept through Lydia at the statement. She knew her Grace to be quite close to the earl and she'd promised Carolyn not to reveal her father's identity. Nervously fingering the long silver ribbons on her blue dress, she answered, "I grew up in London, Your Grace. My mother died when I was quite young and my father followed her last year. I was engaged as a governess when I first met Lord Standford. He offered me the position of companion to his aunt when I had to leave my former post."

" 'Tis the eyes I recognize, my dear. They are quite lovely and distinctive," the duchess replied, her brow puckered in thought.

Carolyn nervously laughed. "Oh my, I often think I know someone, then discover later I was mistaken." Clearly, she longed to keep Lydia's connection to Faro Freddie a secret.

Lydia knew she'd inherited the Whitney eye color, and was also aware that the duchess had watched her closely all evening. It would not do to deny her kinship to this astute lady. Perhaps if she skipped a generation, Her Grace would not associate her with the notorious gamester in the family. "I am told the color runs in the Duke of Graymoor's family."

"You are one of Graymoor's grandchildren?" At Lydia's nod of assent, the duchess added, "You must pardon my surprise, but I am astonished to find you employed when your grandfather is so wealthy."

With a brittle smile Lydia answered, "My father married against my grandfather's wishes and was disinherited. He gave little thought to his younger son's plight. I do not stand on terms with the gentleman."

"Men can be quite foolish about matters of the heart, my

dear. Here is Standford asking the duke for a list of eligible young ladies to court and his only requirements are what he calls 'pedigree and portion' as if love were of little importance." The duchess pulled a small square of paper from her reticule as she spoke.

Staring at the small piece of vellum, Lydia felt a strange churning in the pit of her stomach. She put the feelings down to curiosity about the kind of lady the duchess would think right for Lord Standford.

"I cannot say I am surprised Andrew would approach it so," Carolyn lamented. "I fear he is quite full of his own consequence. He feels the honor of being a countess is all that is required to sway the ladies."

"Some people are uncomfortable in social situations. I fear my godson is one of those. 'Tis unfortunate that his natural wit is lost behind all that hauteur."

Looking doubtful, Carolyn said, "I should think a list is just the kind of old-fashioned style that would best suit Andrew."

"That is because the pair of you spend more time in argument than in real discussion. I fear you have not come to truly understand your nephew. But let us ask Miss Whitney. My dear, what do you think of the earl selecting a bride from a list?" the duchess inquired as she smiled at Lydia.

"For myself, it would be unthinkable to marry without love. My father gave up much for the woman he loved and he said he never regretted it for a single day," Lydia said.

Carolyn nodded her head in total agreement, but the duchess's face was inscrutable. Feeling foolish, Lydia admitted, "I know that Society's views are quite different, Your Grace."

"Yes, 'tis true, my dear, but it has been my experience that in marriages of money and breeding, the partners are in general miserable. I am determined that shall not happen to dear Andrew despite his plans. I believe I know what type of wife he needs, and she will not be found on some list of heiresses."

Carolyn reached out for the bit of paper the lady held, "Then what have you written on the list, Your Grace?"

The duchess laughed as she relinquished the vellum sheet to Mrs. Trevor, "I gave him what he asked for, dear Carolyn. 'Pedigree and portion' were the duke's exact words I believe. These ladies will be neither intimidating nor enticing. Gels with little to recommend them *but* their money and breeding. Hopefully, Andrew will come to realize he wants and needs much more."

Lydia watched with fascination while Carolyn perused the list, then burst into laughter. Before she could comment on the duchess's choices, however, the doors to the room opened to admit the three gentlemen. Carolyn quickly handed the paper back to Her Grace and rose to greet the men.

Lydia stared at the earl's elegantly clad figure when he joined Hammond and Carolyn. She would not be surprised to hear he was betrothed to a lady selected by his godmother quite soon, she thought with a sigh.

The conversation became quite general in mixed company and Lydia found herself liking the earl's friends. She sat listening to the debate on the continuing war and was duly impressed with Lord Standford's knowledge and ideas on the subject.

When the tea tray was brought in, Lydia found herself seated beside the duchess. In a hushed voice the ducal lady said, "I hope you enjoy your post with Carolyn, Miss Whitney. I know it is her intent to allow you to go about as if you were having a Season, but please be careful."

Leaning closer to the lady, Lydia asked, "In what way, Your Grace?"

"Carolyn is delightful in many ways, and she has very good intentions, but I fear little head for the realities of life. She rails against Standford for keeping a tight rein on her spending—and her beaus—but he means only to protect her. As you will learn, Carolyn is too often driven by emotion rather than reason. Despite her mature years, she has not yet learned to be ruled by her head rather than her heart. I know you will do your best to dissuade her from any foolishness, but if you should need someone to talk to, please feel free to visit me."

Lydia felt both comforted and honored by Her Grace's offer. She missed having her dear Bertie in whom to confide. She would like to reassure the duchess that she'd received Carolyn's promise to behave. But that would involve matters Lydia thought better left alone, at least until she was more comfortable with the Duchess of Atherton. With an air of earnestness, she said, "I would be honored to call, and I shall do my best with Mrs. Trevor, Your Grace."

The duchess nodded and nothing more was said, but later Lydia noticed Her Grace having a private *tête-à-tête* with Lord Standford. The small square of paper changed hands. The earl thanked her and pocketed the note without reading it's contents. Lydia was sure she again detected a devilish twinkle in the duchess's eye while the lady stared up at Lord Standford.

After the Atherton party departed and they were all comfortably settled in the drawing room, the earl said, "A most pleasant evening. I had not realized the difference having an excellent hostess makes. Thank you, Aunt Carolyn."

She smiled. "It was an enjoyable evening. Viscount Hammond is charming and 'twas good to see the Duke and Duchess of Atherton again." Carolyn covered her mouth to suppress a yawn.

"I hope you found the evening pleasant, as well, Miss Whitney. It did not tire you overmuch?" the earl asked, his blue eyes observing her with concern.

"Not at all, sir. I am sure I shall be able to keep pace with your aunt," Lydia said, intending to reassure the earl she was both capable and determined to fulfill her post.

"Well then, I shall bid you good-night, ladies. I am meeting Hammond at Brooks in half an hour."

Lydia felt wistful as she watched his elegant form disappear down the stairs. She wondered if he was planning on using the list the duchess gave him to look for a future countess at some function this very evening. She pushed the thought from her mind with a miserable sigh.

She told the earl the truth—she was not tired, not physically tired, but she was unaccountably low in spirits. She wished only to retire and sink into the blissful forgetfulness of sleep. But Carolyn wanted to discuss the evening and implored Lydia to come to her room.

"Is Lord Hammond not the most handsome man you have ever laid eyes on?" Carolyn demanded. "He is the first gentleman in London who has truly drawn my interest."

"I liked the viscount very much. Did he say why he returned to England and for how long?" Lydia asked as she watched Millie brush out Carolyn's curls before wrapping them tightly in papers for the night.

"Oh my, I did not think to ask, my dear. I was fascinated just hearing about the islands. He has been down there for over fifteen years. I was surprised to discover that he only recently met Andrew."

When the earl's name was mentioned, Lydia remembered the list. "If I am not being impertinent, may I ask what was so amusing about the duchess's list of names?"

Laughing, Carolyn answered, "I believe the Duchess of Atherton took Andrew too literally when he said he was interested only in pedigree and portion."

"I don't understand."

"She had five names on the list—every one a bonafide heiress with impeccable breeding." Carolyn smiled.

In a quiet voice, Lydia said, "I fear I don't see the reason for your amusement. It sounds like the duchess did exactly as Lord Standford requested."

Carolyn took pity on her and explained, "These ladies are all in their second and third Seasons. Even with fortunes to recommend them, they have been unable to secure husbands. I hardly think Andrew will take to any of them."

"That seems unkind of the duchess. I thought she was fond of Lord Standford."

"She is, my dear," Carolyn said, and chuckled. "I believe this is her way of showing my nephew that money and pedigree alone do not form a sufficient basis for marriage. Oh, I wish I could see Andrew's face when he meets his prospective brides."

Lydia felt surprisingly cheerful at this announcement.

"There is an irony here, my dear. In looking for quiet, proper misses, Her Grace chose ladies that remind me greatly of hounds. You see, my nephew has always been quite proud of the pedigree of the retrievers he keeps at his estate."

Lydia's eyes widened in surprise. "The duchess chose ladies who bear a resemblance to hounds?"

"Well, I would just say they own certain canine features—but he did ask for pedigree, my dear. Those on the duchess's list of eligible hopefuls have long noses, large ears, protruding teeth, and spotted faces. Just the things a hound fancier would associate with good breeding."

"I see," Lydia said thoughtfully—and she did. The duchess had wisely chosen not to inform the earl that his plan for a bride was foolish. Like many gentlemen, he might dismiss her advice on love as feminine sentimentality. Her Grace had decided on a more subtle approach, and hopefully one which might work.

Carolyn, with her hair neatly wrapped and under a lacy bedcap, turned and said, "I wish *I* had as much wisdom when dealing with Andrew."

"Perhaps when you are better reacquainted?" Lydia suggested.

"I am sure you are correct, my dear. He is nearly a stranger, since I have scarcely seen him since my own marriage. But I mustn't keep you up all night going on about my difficulties with my nephew." The widow rose and brushed a kiss on Lydia's cheek.

Bidding her mistress good-night, she made her way to her

room wondering if her presence would ease the discord between her mistress and the earl. She donned her nightrail, then settled into the large fourposter bed. Just before falling asleep, her thoughts returned to the conversation about the list of young ladies Lord Standford had requested.

Lydia knew in her heart she was inexplicably pleased the duchess hadn't intended for the earl to make an offer for one of the ladies on her list. He would have to look elsewhere for a countess. Perhaps even—how absurd of her, she mused, putting thoughts of the gentleman aside for the night. As if the proud Earl of Standford would ever look with favor on a mere companion.

Five

"Mama, the lace came loose from my Nella's bonnet," Georgette exclaimed, extending the doll and the tiny lace hat to her mother who sat by the window reading.

Lydia paused from the letter she was writing Bertie to glance across the small sitting room where the trio had retired for a quiet afternoon. Carolyn and her daughter made a lovely picture. Both were dressed in shades of blue, and the reflected light from the garden illuminated their blond curls.

"Muffin, I fear we shall have to wait until Nurse is well before it can be repaired. I am quite useless with a needle and thread," Carolyn apologized, putting down her novel.

"Is Nurse going to go away like Papa?" Georgette asked fearfully, clutching the toy to her breast.

Carolyn hugged her daughter. "No, my dear, Nurse just went to have a tooth drawn. She will be back to her old self on the morrow or the day after. 'Tis not like a real illness."

Thinking to distract the child, Lydia folded the completed letter, placing it in her pocket. She rose and came to the pair at the window. "Would you allow me to repair Nella's hat? I can teach you how to set stitches at the same time."

"Oh, yes, Miss Lydia." Georgette beamed up at her.

"Thank you, my dear." Gratitude shined in Carolyn's blue eyes when she smiled at her companion over the child's head. "Muffin, run up to the sewing room and bring down Nurse's mending basket. We shall have your Nella's wardrobe all the crack before you go to bed."

Georgette dashed from the sitting room, leaving the door ajar. Lydia came to her mistress and sat on the opposite settee.

"I must say I think the pink muslin is quite lovely on you. I shall have the maid look for other gowns in that shade for the hue is perfect with your flaxen hair," Carolyn said, smiling across at Lydia.

"Thank you." Looking down at the pink and white sprigged muslin that Millie had refashioned, Lydia felt her cheeks warm with pleasure.

" 'Tis fortunate we are both blonde and of the approximate same size. We can have all my old gowns refurbished for you when Millie has the time."

In a short while, the child returned with a large brown basket which she set on the floor by the yellow settee.

Patting the sofa, Lydia said, "Show me this bonnet and we shall pick the right color thread to repair the lace."

Georgette handed Lydia the tiny brown hat, then climbed upon the seat. Together they selected the correct shade of thread and the room fell silent as the child intently watched Lydia place the tiny stitches on the hat.

Carolyn watched the sewing lesson briefly, then with a sigh returned to her novel.

As Lydia snipped the thread after the final stitch, the butler entered. With mouth drawn downward, Chandler intoned, "Madam, you have a visitor."

"Who is it, Chandler?" Carolyn sat forward, eyes sparkling with anticipation.

"Sir Jasper Masten," the old man primly replied.

Disappointment flashed briefly on Carolyn's face before she said, "Very well, show him in."

Moments later, the door opened to reveal Sir Jasper in all his Town splendor. Lydia studied the man whom she knew Lord Standford disliked.

A portly gentleman, he wore a bright red coat over a garish yellow and green striped waistcoat. Lydia blinked at the vision and her gaze noted his buff pantaloons encased surprisingly thin legs for such a round body. The gentleman had brushed his thinning brown hair in a Brutus fashion over a broad forehead. The style did not suit him, serving only to emphasize how small and wide-set were his brown eyes.

The man strutted into the room as if he were on review in a military parade, Lydia thought, listening as he greeted Carolyn.

"My dear Mrs. Trevor, I hoped I would find you at home. We have missed your charming presence this past week. I had expected to see you at the Chadleighs'."

"Sir Jasper, how good of you to call. May I present my goddaughter, Miss Lydia Whitney, and you know my dear Georgette. We have been so busy getting Lydia ready for the Season, there simply has been no time for socializing." Carolyn rose and politely extended her hand to the visitor.

"Charmed, Miss Whitney," Sir Jasper said, raising his quizzing glass to stare at her fleetingly. Then he bestowed a lingering kiss upon Carolyn's hand.

"Sir Jasper," Lydia said, acknowledging the introduction with a slight nod.

"Dear lady, I have come to take you for an outing at the park. And now I see you surely need the amusement after all this business of gowns and fittings for the young miss."

"How kind of you, sir, but as you can see I am taking care of my daughter today. Unfortunately, her nurse is ill, and I simply could not abandon her to one of Standford's maids. They are not used to young children, you know."

"I shall not take no for an answer, my dear. An outing is just the thing you require and I have even brought my new curricle. I shall have my tiger put down the hood so all may see my luck in securing so lovely a companion. I am sure Miss Whitney will gladly take charge of your little girl," Sir Jasper insisted, winking broadly at Lydia.

Uncertain what Carolyn truly wished, Lydia hesitantly offered, "I shall happily entertain Georgette . . . if you would like to go for a drive."

"You truly don't mind?" Carolyn asked, showing an eagerness for the proposed outing.

"No, indeed. Remember, I have a great deal of experience with children. We shall get along famously. Please take your drive if that is what you wish." Lydia had sensed a certain restlessness in Carolyn over the past hour. Like many Society mothers, she was unused to the constant demand for attention small children made on their attendants.

"Then I shall just fetch my hat and pelisse." Carolyn kissed her daughter, admonishing her to be good. Thanking Lydia for her assistance, Mrs. Trevor left with Sir Jasper strutting beside her.

"My dear, you missed an excessively entertaining evening at Lady Halbrook's . . ." the baronet's voice trailed off as the door closed.

Georgette bit pensively on her lip for a moment after the door shut before she asked, "Do you think Mama will marry that gentleman?"

I hope not, Lydia thought, but she answered, "I don't know, Georgette. Why?"

"I don't like him. He walks like the cocks at the stables at Trevor House. I always 'spect him to crow instead of speak."

Struggling to suppress her amusement, Lydia only answered, "Nevertheless, he may be a very nice man. Now, does Nella have anything else which needs repairing?"

Lydia proceeded to fix a loose button on a tiny grey cloak and reattach a ribbon to a miniature dress. While she worked, Georgette sat by her side chattering about her former life in Leeds. They were looking over the remaining doll clothes when the door to the drawing room opened.

Glancing up, Lydia saw Lord Standford standing, cool and aloof, in the portal. Her pulse fluttered as he stood there looking devilishly handsome in a grey superfine coat over a grey striped waistcoat and pale grey pantaloons. His quiet elegance was in marked contrast to Sir Jasper's foppish excess.

"Good afternoon, Miss Whitney, Georgette. Where is my aunt?" he asked pleasantly when he entered the room and closed the door.

Hesitant to answer, knowing his lordship's dislike of the baronet, Lydia nervously fingered the tiny dress in her hand before replying. "She has gone for a drive, my lord."

"With whom?" A tiny crease on his lordship's brow now marred his handsome features.

Lydia swallowed hard, then lifted her chin to reply, "Sir Jasper Masten came to take her to the park, my lord."

Lord Standford's mouth thinned in displeasure. "You were engaged as a companion to my aunt, Miss Whitney." His gaze shifted to Georgette briefly before coming back to stare pointedly at Lydia. "Not as a nurse for my young cousin. You should have accompanied Mrs. Trevor with that . . . court card."

"What would you have me do, sir? Toss his tiger to the cobblestones and take his perch behind the curricle? I assure you otherwise there would be no room in Sir Jasper's vehicle."

As the pair glared angrily at one another, Georgette, innocently unaware of the tension between them, giggled. "I should very much like to ride on the tiger's perch."

The child's laughter eased the strain between the adults, and they looked at one another with contrition. Lydia felt her cheeks warm remembering her angry tone in responding to the man who temporarily controlled her fate.

Lord Standford glanced at his small cousin and his eyes softened. Teasingly, he said, "I fear your mother would have me drawn and quartered if I were so imprudent as to allow you to do such a thing. But I shall take you for a ride in the park if you like."

Eyeing her large cousin consideringly, Georgette seemed

to find him less frightening, for she replied, "Yes, I should like that very much, Cousin Andrew, but not today for I must wait for Nurse. She went to have a tooth drawn and I think that is not pleasant."

"Nurse will be fine, Georgette," the earl gently reassured her before turning back to Lydia, his manner again formal. "Please accept my apologies, Miss Whitney. It was unforgivable of me to be so harsh about such a trivial matter. I fear my worries about Aunt Carolyn have addled my thinking."

"I apologize, as well, my lord. I should not have spoken to you in such a manner." Lydia looked down at her hands which still clutched the small doll dress. She could ill afford to lose her temper no matter how unreasonable his lordship behaved.

A door closed somewhere in the house, then voices sounded in the hall. Georgette jumped up from the settee, dashing across the room. "That is Nurse. I must see how she is."

The earl appeared startled when the child rushed from the room. "Is there something seriously wrong with her nurse?"

"No, merely a toothache, but Georgette is very close to the woman. She has had a great deal of upheaval in her life this year. I think she feared Nurse might die as her father did." Lydia gazed up into Lord Standford's concerned face.

"By Jove, I never thought about how all this is affecting her. First losing her father, then moving to Town, and now her beloved Nurse ill. You were able to reassure her, were you not?"

"Yes, she knows it is a mere trifle and Nurse will be back on the job soon," Lydia reassured.

"Good. I am also pleased to see she does not seem so frightened of me as she was at first," Lord Standford said coolly as he abruptly shifted his gaze to the sunlit garden. Looking back at Lydia after a moment, he suddenly seemed to realize they were alone in the sitting room. "Miss Whitney,

I am glad for this opportunity to speak privately with you. I wish to make certain you understand exactly what is expected of you with regards to my aunt."

"I hope I am not lacking in wits, sir," Lydia replied stiffly. "I believe that my job is to see that Mrs. Trevor does not game."

"I did not mean to imply your understanding is in any way deficient. 'Twas only that our conversation was cut short by your . . . er . . . becoming ill which brought the interview to an abrupt end." The earl spoke kindly, despite his constrained manner.

Remembering the disastrous outcome of that meeting, Lydia was reminded of Carolyn's pledge. "But some good came from my swoon. Mrs. Trevor and I later spoke of her gaming and she has given me her promise not to engage in any games of chance."

Clearly, the earl doubted the earnestness of this statement for he raised one chestnut eyebrow. "Do not be taken in by the promises of a gamester, Miss Whitney. They often mean it at the time they pledge to no longer gamble, but their will to resist is not great. I see it daily in the clubs."

Having lived with a hardened gamester, Lydia was convinced Carolyn was not such. "Sir, I cannot believe that Mrs. Trevor is obsessed with wagering. She is merely trying to recover—"

With a dismissive gesture of his hand, the earl snapped, "I appreciate your loyalty, but you must allow me to be a judge of my aunt's character. I have known her considerably longer."

Angered at his highhanded dismissal, she merely replied, "As you say, my lord."

"I expect you to watch my aunt carefully at the Washburns' ball tomorrow night." With a nod of his head, Lord Standford moved across the room to leave.

"My lord," Lydia said to halt his exit. "Do you think Mrs.

Trevor is . . . interested in Sir Jasper as a prospective husband?"

"I certainly hope not. My own dislike for the man aside, Masten will never be brought up to scratch. He is merely amusing himself with a beautiful lady who shares his interest in gambling. He generally prefers gaming with women and selects one for the Season to be his flirt."

"Surely, there are other gentlemen after her hand?" Lydia queried.

"Being past the first blush of youth and possessing a child makes it difficult when looking for a husband. I fear Lord Digby is her only other serious suitor, and he still allows his mother the upper hand in all matters. I find him equally objectionable despite his fortune."

"But does Mrs. Trevor?" Lydia bravely asked.

"I don't know what Aunt Carolyn thinks. Unfortunately, my dear aunt neither confides in me nor listens to a word I say about gentlemen or money. I am hoping, Miss Whitney, you can succeed where I seem to be failing." So saying, the earl bowed and left.

Lydia sank into worried thought. She had Carolyn's promise not to game, but Sir Jasper might be difficult to thwart. Carolyn was obviously his chosen gaming partner for this Season and, as she'd witnessed earlier, he did not appear to take no for an answer.

On the mysterious Lord Digby, she would reserve judgment until they met. Mayhap the earl did not always know what was best for his aunt despite his arrogant assertions.

The earl had not mentioned Viscount Hammond, but Lydia was convinced that the gentleman was interested in the beautiful Carolyn. He might well prove to be an ally in keeping the widow from Sir Jasper and the tables.

Tomorrow night at the Washburns' ball would be a double test for Lydia. She must keep constant watch over Carolyn while avoiding those who might recognize her as Faro Freddie's daughter. It would clearly be a long evening.

Listening to the earl's footsteps ringing in the hall, Lydia vowed to do her best for Carolyn . . . and Lord Standford.

The following evening Standford surveyed the Washburns' ballroom with a jaundiced eye. Glitteringly arrayed ladies and fashionably clad gentlemen whirled about the dance floor. Surely, he thought, there is an easier way to find an appropriate bride than spending one's evenings making small talk with giggling chits under the watchful eyes of their ambitious mothers.

The earl had barely arrived when Lady Washburn brought Lady Clara Winchester, her niece, to him to partner during the first dance. Manners decreed that he stand up with the girl. The chit had little beauty and less conversation. He had been relieved to take her back to her mother.

Lost in thought while he stood alone against a tall white column, Standford wondered if he should merely take the list the duchess gave him and approach the parents of one of those girls for permission to pay his address.

A young woman near him emitted a rather high-pitched giggle, causing him to think better of the idea. There were certain characteristics even the list of exalted ladies might have that he would find objectionable. No, he must meet the prospective brides first.

The earl scanned the large room for his aunt and Miss Whitney. The ladies had disappeared into the throng while he danced with the wooden-like Lady Clara. Searching the crowd of dancers for Aunt Carolyn, he was pleased to observe her dancing with Lord Rosedale, a widowed baron from the north. She smiled up into the peer's bedazzled face with enjoyment.

The earl was finding his volatile relation as changeable as the weather. The lady was determined to plot her own course despite his warnings. He hoped Miss Whitney would prove more successful than he had been.

Thinking of Carolyn's beautiful companion, he curiously looked to see what became of the lady since she parted his company. Scanning the dancers while they moved down the room, he found she was not among the ladies who'd taken the floor. An odd circumstance, he thought, remembering how lovely Miss Whitney looked when she joined them in the Rose Drawing Room earlier this evening.

She'd been a shimmering vision in silver, with matching silver roses worked into her pale blond hair. When she'd shyly smiled at him, he'd suddenly longed to taste her pink lips. He'd chastised himself for so foolish a thought, then rushed the ladies out to the waiting carriage to cover his disturbing reaction to the alluring chit.

Staring at the dancers, the earl realized he must find his countess soon, which would effectively put a stop to these odd fancies about Miss Whitney. He'd set his course in a different direction entirely. He would not become bewitched by a mere companion.

Pushing the distracting thoughts of Miss Whitney from his mind, the earl walked toward the opposite end of the room looking for friends. He spied Hammond standing beside a sofa upon which sat the Duchess of Atherton, looking strikingly regal in dark red silk—and the lady who'd just dominated his thoughts.

"Good evening, Your Grace, Hammond," the earl said as he joined the company. He merely nodded at Carolyn's companion since they parted but thirty minutes past.

"Standford," the duchess said pleasantly. "I was just asking Miss Whitney whether you were present. You must convince her that she has your permission to dance. She thinks she must sit watch on dear Carolyn for the evening."

Feeling uncomfortably warm under his dark green coat at the censure in the duchess's voice, he said, "Of course you may dance, Miss Whitney, while my aunt is in the ballroom." He gave her a speaking look which he hoped she took to mean that Mrs. Trevor was to be kept away from the card room.

Intelligent gold eyes gazed back at him as Miss Whitney said, "I fully understand, my lord."

"Very good," the earl replied, then moved to stand beside the viscount to watch the dancers.

Standford's attention was drawn to a young gentleman determinedly making his way toward their party. He recognized the lad as the duchess's great-nephew the Honorable Arthur Landers. Light brown curls framed the boy's handsome square face and he'd inherited the duchess's green eyes. Correctly dressed in evening clothes, if somewhat haphazardly, the earl noted the boy's poorly tied cravat and wilted collar.

The callow youth had introduced some of his friends to Standford at Manton's shooting gallery earlier in the Season, where the sprig had marveled at the earl's skill with a pistol. Their paths rarely crossed again since the younger man possessed a large set of rowdy friends.

"Good evening, Aunt Annabelle. You are in looks this evening," Arthur Landers gallantly stated, bowing to the group. "Lord Standford, Uncle James." He then looked expectantly at the lady beside his uncle.

The duchess smiled and made the introductions. "Miss Whitney, this young rascal is my great-nephew, the Honorable Arthur Landers. Arthur, this is Miss Lydia Whitney who is goddaughter to Standford's aunt, Mrs. Trevor."

The young man gallantly bowed. " 'Tis a pleasure to make your acquaintance, Miss Whitney."

The duchess noted a blush came to the girl's cheeks as she politely responded and she sought to distract her nephew. "Tell me, Arthur, what brings you to such a staid event as the Washburns' ball? Have you tired of boxing the watch or have you no one to get into mischief with?"

"We have not been in so much trouble, Your Grace." The young man spoke to his great-aunt but looked nervously at his uncle, who corresponded regularly with his father. "His

Grace told me he did much the same as a young sprig on the Town."

"Knowing your uncle, it was probably much worse," the duchess said. "Where are those two pups who are usually at your heels?"

"I must amuse myself for a few weeks. They are out of Town, but both should return quite soon. I came here because Lord Washburn's son is an old friend from Eton."

"Yes, I believe Lady Washburn did mention she knew you," the duchess replied. "Well, my boy, you have done your duty to me so go amuse yourself."

Relieved, Arthur turned to Lydia. "Would you do me the honor of standing up with me for the next dance?"

"I should be delighted," she replied with a demure smile.

Lord Standford, who'd watched the exchange, frowned as Landers took a seat on the settee beside Miss Whitney. The earl suppressed a sudden and nearly overwhelming urge to grab the young man by the back of his wilted collar and toss him out into the street.

Puzzled by the disturbing emotions Landers engendered, the earl turned to engage Hammond in small talk. Thinking to keep his aunt from gaming, he suggested to his friend they make up a party for the opera for the following evening. The viscount happily agreed.

"I hope you will stand up with me for another dance, Miss Whitney," Arthur Landers stated while the last strains of the music died away.

"I would be delighted," Lydia answered, smiling at the engaging young man. The nervous tension she'd experienced over attending the ball eased. After nearly an hour, she'd seen no one she recognized from her youthful excursions into the gaming hells, and none had claimed to know her. Perhaps her fears of being exposed were groundless.

Glancing around, her gaze locked with a pair of piercing

azure-blue eyes staring in her direction. Lydia was surprised at the look of displeasure on Lord Standford's face. It appeared he had taken an instant aversion to Mr. Landers, and his stare followed them as they danced. She wondered if the earl truly disliked her partner, or if he'd been merely placating the duchess when the lady insisted Lydia dance.

"Where shall I take you, Miss Whitney? Back to my great-aunt or to Mrs. Trevor?"

Startled from her musings, Lydia rapidly searched for Carolyn. How could she have forgotten her responsibility? Worried, she said, "I *must* find Mrs. Trevor."

Arthur's brows rose in surprise at the urgency in Lydia's voice. "Is there some problem, Miss Whitney?"

"No, I merely wish to speak with her for a moment," she prevaricated, hoping she sounded less urgent in tone.

"Do wait until I introduce you to my friend, Matthew. He will forever be in my debt for such a kindness." Mr. Landers began to lead her toward a group of fashionable young men.

Lydia, after spotting Carolyn in a conversation with Viscount Hammond near the door to the hall, relaxed and willingly accompanied her partner to his friends. After the lengthy introductions, the young men drifted into talk of the latest mill.

Glancing around the room, Lydia noted Lord Standford had ceased glowering at her and was in the company of a tall young lady whose hair was so full of white feathers, Lydia could barely discern her exact hair color. She wondered curiously if this was one of the ladies from his lordship's list, then promptly dismissed the worrisome thought as Lord Devere, the Earl of Washburns' oldest son, invited her to dance.

"You are new to London, Miss Whitney?" the young man politely inquired while they moved to take their place in the set.

Lydia faltered a moment at the dangerous question before answering, "Yes, Lord Devere. Indeed, this is my first ball."

"Then I am honored that you chose to grace my mother's house. There has been a decided dearth of beautiful ladies this Season. Arthur and I were lamenting the matter the other night at the opera." Devere, a handsome young man with dark eyes and hair, smiled with open admiration at Lydia.

"But were you speaking of eligible young ladies or the ones who adorned the stage? I am sure there are any number of beautiful ladies here this evening," she teased.

"None as lovely as you, Miss Whitney," Lord Devere answered with such a besotted look, Lydia felt her cheeks warm.

Hoping to distract the young man, she asked, "Speaking of young ladies, can you tell me who Lord Standford is dancing with?"

Lord Devere turned to gaze with interest at the couple at the bottom of the set. "Oh, Lady Margaret Collins. Surely you are not calling her a beauty," he said, a shudder of horror running across his face.

"I was merely curious." Lydia's scrutiny intensified when she suspected the girl was from the duchess's list.

Lady Margaret appeared to be in her twenties. She stood nearly as tall as the earl, but looked taller due to the massive feathers. Now Lydia could see thin brown hair curling about the lady's lean face, the locks drooping from the heat.

Lord Devere warmed to the subject as he continued to gaze at the earl and his partner. "Whatever can Lord Standford be thinking to stand up with Lady Margaret? If he is not careful, her mother will have the banns read. It was a near thing when Lord Brandon stood up with her last Season for a dance at the Applebys' ball. Even ten thousand a year has not helped to fire off such a Long Meg."

"But it is only one dance," Lydia protested. Her brows rose while she watched the tall lady peek flirtatiously at the earl who looked every bit as stiff as his nickname suggested.

"Yes, but Mrs. Howell is spreading the tale of a marriage offer she rejected from Standford. All Society is agog with the news and believe him to be seriously looking for a wife. Depend upon it. Lady Margaret's mother will have heard the *on-dit*."

"I think his lordship is well able to take care of himself," Lydia stated coldly at the unwelcome news.

"True. But then 'tis most people's opinion that Old Stiff-neck is no prize either, regardless of the title and money," Lord Devere answered, smiling. Suddenly appearing to realize his jest had gone awry by Lydia's frown, he apologized. "I am sorry, Miss Whitney. I forgot you are staying with Lord Standford and his aunt. Mother's forever saying my wagging tongue will get me into trouble."

Lydia distractedly shook her head. Her thoughts were on the earl and the news that Mrs. Howell had made good on her threat. She hoped some new scandal would come along quickly to push Lord Standford's humiliation from the minds of the *beau monde*.

After the dance, Lord Devere passed Lydia to her next partner, Mr. Eastman, and her worries about the earl were momentarily forgotten. Lord Standford seemed to have disappeared from the ballroom when Lydia searched for her party at the end of the dance with the shy young Eastman. Thankfully, she spied Carolyn chatting with friends.

Time seemed to move fleetingly by. The only disappointment for Lydia was that Lord Standford did not offer to stand up with her. 'Twas just as well, she thought, for her heart hammered if he so much as smiled at her.

Lord Devere soon arrived to take her down to supper. She remained separated from Carolyn and the earl while they dined. Gazing across the room as she tasted the lobster patties, she noted the tender look on Carolyn's face when she spoke with Lord Hammond. It was clear to Lydia her mistress was forming a tendre for that distinguished gentleman.

Lydia was delighted with both her first ball and Carolyn for keeping her promise not to game. Continuously surrounded with partners, it seemed each time Lydia looked for her mistress she had been either dancing or conversing with some handsome lord.

The fact that Sir Jasper Masten was not present greatly relieved much of Lydia's worry. She had come to believe that Carolyn was being led into gaming by this rather questionable baronet.

When the strains of the orchestra were heard in the ballroom, the company began to exit the dining room. Carolyn paused a moment for a brief word with Lydia.

"Are you enjoying your first ball, my dear?"

Feeling lighthearted, Lydia replied, "Oh, yes. I could dance all night."

"I quite agree. Especially if one has the right partner." Carolyn gazed at the tall figure of Lord Hammond awaiting her near the doorway.

"Ah, my dear Mrs. Trevor, where have you been keeping yourself all evening?" a deep voice spoke behind the ladies.

Lydia turned to discover a rotund gentleman, dressed in a moss-green coat, partially covered with a napkin tucked at his throat. The white square was covered with stains of wine and mushroom sauce. He clutched a plate piled high with slices of ham and roast beef with one hand and extended his other.

Resigned, Carolyn gave the man her hand. "Lord Digby, I did not know you were present."

A loud creaking noise sounded when the baron bent to kiss Carolyn's fingers. Lydia suppressed a giggle, and Carolyn rolled her eyes above the man's bowed head. The gentleman obviously wore a corset. Her amusement fled when a pair of small, dark eyes turned to gaze at her.

"Who is your lovely friend, my dear?"

"Lord Digby, may I present my goddaughter, Miss Lydia Whitney."

Lydia said all that was polite, but she found herself thoroughly agreeing with Lord Standford. The oafish baron was not the person for Carolyn, and from the reaction of the widow there was little doubt of her lack of interest. Lydia was glad when her next partner arrived at her side to escort her to the ballroom. She left Carolyn to her corpulent suitor.

Later, having just completed a second dance with Mr. Landers, Lydia stood beside a large window and plied her fan. A group of young ladies and gentlemen she'd met during the evening were gathered about her chattering.

Arthur and Devere stood on either side of Lydia, telling tales of their adventures in Town. Suddenly Arthur said, "I say, there is Gravely, entering late as usual. Would he be your cousin, Miss Whitney? But of course he must be. You both have much the look of the old Duke of Graymoor."

Lydia's heart lurched with fear when she gazed across the ballroom at her relative. She had never actually met her cousin, but Bertie had once pointed him out as the Duke of Graymoor's carriage had traveled past. The fair-haired young fop surveyed the company with a bored expression. His golden-brown gaze paused briefly at their group.

She noted Standford entered the ballroom behind her newly discovered cousin. Lord Gravely drew the earl's attention and they fell into conversation.

Lydia knew little of her father's family and finding her young relative in Town completely unnerved her. Feeling her knees begin to tremble, Lydia realized it would only be a matter of time before Lord Standford and, indeed, all Society knew her to be Faro Freddie's daughter.

The Earl of Standford suddenly started across the dance floor. He was coming straight toward Lydia. Whatever had Lord Gravely said to the earl? She felt a knot tighten in her stomach when his blue eyes glared at her with some indefinable emotion.

Six

Devil take it, this is a dreadful evening, Standford thought, pausing at the entrance to the ballroom. First, he'd made the mistake of having his hostess, Lady Washburn, introduce him to Lady Margaret Collins, one of the prospects on the Duchess of Atherton's list. He'd danced with the insipid lady, then found it nearly impossible to get rid of the plain chit. He'd managed to foist her upon Hammond before making his escape into the foyer.

Then Lord Washburn had arrived from the card room and dragged him aside on the pretext of discussing the coming vote on the Corn Laws. A mere pretense, for he spent the entire time questioning Standford about Miss Whitney. It was evident to all present that Lord Devere, Washburn's heir, was smitten with an unknown young woman, much to his parents' consternation. That Washburn had abandoned his game of whist was sufficient proof that he was apprehensive about his son's marked attentions to the lady.

Knowing little of Miss Whitney's family history, Standford had been at a loss for words. He merely reassured Washburn there was nothing to be concerned about. The earl resisted an urge to tell Washburn that Devere was little more than a fribble without a serious thought in his head.

Escaping at last from what he considered an inquisition, Standford returned to the ballroom. The entrance was blocked by several late arrivals. Standing behind them,

Standford gazed over their heads, searching the room for his aunt.

"Ah, Standford, late as well?" Lord Gravely inquired, looking up to see the earl. His long white fingers fussed with the intricately tied cravat above a Spanish blue evening coat.

"No, Gravely. I am rarely late to any event. I was merely speaking with Lord Washburn."

"Well, my valet is forever making me late. The man simply cannot tie a cravat to suit me," Lord Gravely said in a bored tone, surveying the assembled crowd.

"Then I suggest you replace the man with one who is more competent. Pray, excuse me." Walking away, Standford barely spared a glance for the simpering fop, for the earl suddenly realized his aunt was nowhere to be seen.

Spying Miss Whitney near a large window with two hand-some young men at her side, anger surged through him. Had he not employed the young lady to keep his aunt from gaming? Yet there she stood with no apparent thought about her mistress as two cubs fawned over her.

Striding across the dance floor, Standford kept his gaze locked on the provoking chit. Even in his irritated state, he noted how beautiful she looked with her cheeks flushed from the heat of dancing.

The lady's wary gaze was riveted on him while he approached. Halting in front of the trio, he said, "May I have a word with you in private, Miss Whitney?"

Guiding her some distance from the group of young people, he tersely asked, "Where the devil is my aunt?"

"Aunt?" Miss Whitney seemed surprised by the question.

"Yes, you do remember Mrs. Trevor? She is the lady I employed you to take care of. Or have these gentlemen so taken your fancy you have completely forgotten your post?" He spoke more harshly than he'd intended. The thought that Miss Whitney had succumbed to the charms of one of the young bucks present filled him with an unreasonable surge of anger.

Stains of scarlet appeared on Miss Whitney's flawless complexion, but she met his accusing gaze unflinchingly. "Mrs. Trevor was here but a moment ago. I have her promise not to game and I believe she will keep her word. She cannot have gone far, sir. I shall find her at once."

"*We* shall find her, Miss Whitney. I believe it must be time to take our leave, and we shall do so once our party is together. Shall we look in the card room?" Standford firmly took her arm and guided her across the floor to the hallway, trying determinedly to ignore the soft ivory shoulders just above his grip.

As they made their way through the throng, a gloved hand suddenly clamped upon Standford's arm, halting their progress. "There you are, Lord Standford. I have been searching all over for you."

The earl bestowed his most frigid look upon Lady Collingwood, a matron of rather large proportions. Dressed in a dark orange gown with matching turban which sported no less than three feathers, she reminded him of some exotic bird. The earl distractedly thought that both the Collins ladies were a menace to the plumed creatures of the Empire.

Hovering behind the countess, Lady Margaret was regarding him with a bovine gaze of adoration. He felt a chill run down his spine at the determined look in the mother's eyes.

"You must forgive me for intruding on you and your companion. I have not had the pleasure," Lady Collingwood said, eyeing Miss Whitney curiously.

"May I present my aunt's goddaughter, Miss Lydia Whitney? Miss Whitney, this is the Countess of Collingwood and her daughter, Lady Margaret," the earl said through tight lips.

"Delighted, Miss Whitney," the countess said in a patently false voice.

"Lady Collingwood, Lady Margaret, I am honored," Miss Whitney replied in a flat tone.

"Would you excuse us, dear," Lady Collingwood said condescendingly to Miss Whitney, drawing Standford toward her ample person. "I must have a few words with the earl."

Looking up at him with an enigmatic expression in her golden eyes, Lydia said, "I shall find Mrs. Trevor, sir. We shall await you in the front hall."

"Why, I believe I saw her going toward the card room earlier, dear," Lady Collingwood offered.

"Or perhaps the ladies' retiring room, madam. They are in the same direction," Miss Whitney countered before walking away.

"Odd sort of gel your aunt has for a goddaughter. 'Tis no crime to go to the card room, after all. Is that not so, my dear?" the countess said, bringing her daughter into the conversation.

"Yes, Mama," Lady Margaret replied, batting her eyelashes at Standford in a foolish manner.

"I must say I find all that blonde hair makes Miss Whitney look rather washed out, don't you, Standford?" Lady Collingwood asked, watching the departing lady.

Ignoring the question, the earl said, "You wished to speak to me, Lady Collingwood?"

"Yes, dear boy. I have just learned from Lord Hammond that you are to take a party to the opera tomorrow to hear Catalini. My daughter adores the soprano, but alas since the theater is charging three hundred guineas a year for a box, Lord Collingwood has simply refused to pay such an exorbitant fee. Is that not so, my dear?"

"Yes, Mama." Lady Margaret now raised her open fan, coquettishly looking over the top at the earl. Standford stared with fascination as the lace fan barely missed the lady's long nose with each flick of Lady Margaret's thin hand.

"I fear we must throw ourselves on the mercy of our many friends for a visit to the Royal Italian Opera," the countess hinted broadly.

Wishing Hammond were near so the earl might throttle him for his loose tongue, Standford sighed. Manners demanded he ask the ladies. Looking at the mother's expectant face, he decided he would make sure the duchess accompanied them, as well. She too must suffer the Collins ladies since she'd recommended the chit. "Would you and your daughter care to join my party tomorrow night?"

Drawing her hands to her large bosom in delight, the countess gushed, "You are too kind, Lord Standford, but then I was just saying to Margaret earlier that you are everything a gentleman should be. Is that not so, my dear?"

"Yes, Mama," Lady Margaret intoned, smiling with obvious pleasure at the invitation. Her head nodded in approval, sending a shower of tiny feather parts floating in the air.

"We shall have a delightful evening, I am sure," the countess purred.

Standing in the doorway of the card room, Lydia's gaze scanned the tables for Carolyn. She desperately prayed that her mistress had kept her promise and not come to play, for Lord Standford would be furious.

"Lydia, my dear," the Duchess of Atherton called.

Turning, Lydia smiled warmly. "Yes, Your Grace."

"Are you looking for Carolyn? I suppose Standford sent you to search the card room." The duchess sighed as she walked up to stand in the doorway. "He and Carolyn are always want to think the worst of one another."

"It is difficult when complete strangers are suddenly living under the same roof, Your Grace. They somehow manage to misunderstand the other." Lydia spoke from experience as she thought of her former employers. She had been misjudged by both.

"True, my dear, only time and patience will resolve their differences. Now, I came to inform you that my oafish greatnephew stepped on Carolyn's lovely gown, tearing the flounce. She is in the retiring room repairing the damage."

The tight feeling relaxed in Lydia's chest when she learned

that Carolyn had been true to her promise not to game. Knowing her mistress's lack of sewing skills, Lydia suspected the lady might need assistance. "Thank you, Your Grace. I shall go and see if I might be of some help. Shall I see you later?"

"No, my dear, I intend to get one of these idle relatives of mine to take me home. I must be up early for I have a great deal to do. You know, of course, that Hammond's family arrives from the Indies next week." The duchess turned to survey the ballroom in an effort to discover the viscount or her great-nephew.

"Lord Hammond's family?" Lydia was stunned at the carelessly dropped information. Hammond was a married man. Why ever would he trifle with the widow's affection in this cold-hearted way? Carolyn would be devastated for she was clearly captivated by the handsome peer.

"Did he not mention his family is expected? How like a man!"

"I—I don't believe so," Lydia replied haltingly.

"They were the reason he went to the Indies. His father was a foolish man and Hammond had to fend for himself. He knew he would likely inherit a load of debts and a rundown estate in Devonshire. So, he took them down to make his fortune, and he did that very well. He has returned a wealthy man."

"How nice," Lydia said weakly.

"Yes. 'Tis good to have him back and soon Felicity and the boys will be here, as well. I must go now, my dear. Bring Carolyn round for tea one morning." The duchess drifted toward the ballroom looking for her escort.

Lydia walked slowly toward the retiring room in deep thought. Were Carolyn's affections truly engaged by Lord Hammond? She had spoken often of the viscount over the past few days and there was a certain look in her eyes when they rested upon the gentleman.

Lydia realized she knew little of the ways of Society. Bertie had once hinted that widows often dallied with gentlemen who they did not intend to marry when Lydia's father had kept company with such a lady. Perhaps she was worrying needlessly. Carolyn might simply be enjoying her freedom. Surely she, who'd spent so much time with the gentleman, knew the viscount was married.

Entering the room set aside for the ladies, Lydia discovered Carolyn seated by a branch of candles, needle and thread in hand. "May I be of assistance?"

"Lydia, you have arrived just in time to save me. I am simply hopeless with stitchery," Carolyn confessed with a smile.

"Then, allow me to do that for you." Lydia crossed the room and took the needle before she sat on the sofa beside Mrs. Trevor. Flipping the gown's hem inside out, she held the flounce in place and began the repair work. She mentally struggled with what to say to Carolyn about Lord Hammond.

"Have you heard? Andrew takes us to the opera on the morrow," the widow said.

"I have never been to the Royal Opera. My father never could abide all that shrieking, as he called it." Lydia welcomed the distraction from her worrisome thoughts.

"My dear, he can never have heard Catalini. The singer's voice is nothing short of amazing. Her tone is rich, yet—"

The door to the retiring room flew open and Lady Collingwood and Lady Margaret entered, interrupting Carolyn's effusive praise of the Italian diva. "Mrs. Trevor, just the person I wished to see." The ladies sat on the sofa opposite the one where Lydia and Carolyn reposed.

"Lady Collingwood," Carolyn said weakly.

"Your dear nephew just insisted that Margaret and I accompany him to the opera tomorrow night. It was most gracious of him considering he just met my little Margaret."

Carolyn's eyebrows rose when the countess called her daughter little. Then she gave her companion a quick glance.

Lydia was sure she detected a slight tremor as Carolyn's shoulders shook with suppressed laughter.

Lady Collingwood appeared oblivious to her audience's reaction to her statement and continued to chatter. "He would have it no other way once he learned of her love of Madame Catalini. We shall all have such a grand time."

"Why, that does not surprise me, Lady Collingwood. Standford is known for his easy, open manner," Carolyn replied.

Lydia looked up from her sewing to stare at her mistress in amazement. The earl was known for the exact opposite. Whatever could Carolyn be about?

"I believe he has an estate in Suffolk," the countess stated slyly. "Margaret and I do so love that part of England. We travel through the county on our way to visit my sister in Norwich. Perhaps we have seen his estate. What is it called?"

Carolyn, who'd developed a strong interest in finding something in her reticule, answered with studied nonchalance, "I believe it is called Crosswell, Lady Collingwood."

"And what is the style of architecture? Margaret is a great student of building styles. Is that not so, dear?"

The younger lady's eyes widened in surprise at her mother's statement, then she blandly replied, "Yes, Mama."

"Oh, I know little of such things. I only find the estate rather dark and forbidding. The chimneys smoke dreadfully and Standford cannot be made to update the furnishings. Wants everything left that his dear departed mother installed." Carolyn looked at Lydia, and her mouth twitched while she struggled not to smile. Then she occupied herself with a small mirror she drew from her reticule, tucking honey-colored curls back in place.

"I am sure that he will give his wife free rein—"

An exaggerated sigh escaped Carolyn's lips. "The only thing given free rein at Crosswell are those cursed hounds. One cannot escape them morning, noon, or night."

"My, my . . ." Lady Collingwood clucked her tongue in disapproval.

With a wicked twinkle in her eye, Mrs. Trevor continued. "Yes, and here in Town he is always bringing the oddest creatures home to tea. Whoever he is with at the time, be it peer, coachman, or actress, he brings them along to Cavendish Square. Lydia and I scarcely know what to expect from one day to the next."

Lady Collingwood's gloved hand fluttered nervously up to cover the shocked opening of her mouth. Determination to see her daughter wed appeared to win out, for she stoutly said, "The earl merely needs a wife who will not allow such foolishness. Is that not so, Margaret?"

"Yes, Mama," the daughter replied, seemingly unconcerned by Carolyn's outrageous information.

"I seriously doubt there are many who could make Andrew do anything he did not wish," Carolyn said, a hint of steel in her voice.

"My dear," Lady Collingwood stated knowingly, "most ladies can get their way if they simply use the correct method. I have trained my Margaret well. She knows that successful marriages do not come to the timid."

Lydia experienced a tremor of fear for Lord Standford. The Collins ladies had the earl in their sights. With a huntress like Lady Collingwood, he might not escape capture.

The earl called for a footman to bring their wraps while he waited for Aunt Carolyn and Miss Whitney. He warily scanned the milling crowd in hopes of avoiding Lady Collingwood and discovering the whereabouts of the duchess. He was determined to take her to task over the inclusion of Lady Margaret on his list of possible brides. What on earth could she be thinking of? Both the girl and her mother were intolerable.

The throng of ball guests parted and Hammond, with the

duchess in tow, came toward Standford. He greeted his godmother warmly, then asked, "Has Hammond conveyed my
invitation to attend the opera on Saturday night?"

"He mentioned it," Lady Atherton gazed at Standford with
amusement.

"I *very much* hope you plan to honor us with your presence," the earl said, insistently.

"Jamie, my boy, would you excuse Andrew and me for a
moment. I believe the earl has a matter he wishes to discuss
with me." The duchess's eyes sparkled in enjoyment.

The viscount said, "Yes, Aunt Annabelle. I shall just have
a word with Arthur. Signal when you are ready to leave." He
looked curiously at Standford before turning back toward
the ballroom.

"Now, Andrew, what has occurred to overset you?"

"I don't mean to complain, Your Grace, for it was exceedingly kind of you to draw up a list of eligible young ladies . . ."

"But," she prompted, a devilish gleam of amusement in
her eyes.

"How could you include a . . . a . . . a milk-and-water
miss like Lady Margaret with a termagant for a mother on
a list of eligible young ladies?" Standford asked, exasperated.

"My dear boy, when you believe marriage is not an affair
of the heart, what can it matter? Lady Margaret is exactly
what you asked the duke for—a lady of pedigree and portion.
I hear she will bring ten thousand a year with her."

"But the lady has no address, no . . . beauty . . ."

"True, however, she will most likely produce large,
healthy sons." The duchess placed a gloved finger over her
lips as if struggling not to smile.

"With equally large noses? I prefer my sons not to be able
to tell me what is being served for supper three estates over."
Standford suddenly smiled in spite of himself at the absurd
notion.

"Is that not just like a gentleman to see the disadvantages

of the matter? Do but think what a blessing it would be to have a son who could pick up the scent of the fox by himself after the hounds had lost the trail," Lady Atherton teased.

Standford shouted with laughter, causing people to stare at his unusual burst of levity. "You are incorrigible, Your Grace. You must at least come to the opera with us. 'Tis only fair that you suffer that woman's incessant chatter and her daughter's foolish poses along with the rest of us."

"If you took her so much in dislike, why did you invite the dreadful woman to accompany you?"

"I fear good manners overcame my repugnance," the earl replied with a sigh.

"Well, my boy, be advised by me. Someone like Lady Collingwood's stamp can be relentless. Keep your guard up, or your good manners may lead you to a betrothal. Of course, Lady Margaret does meet both your requirements—excellent bloodlines there and she has a substantial income." The duchess raised her hand and signaled Lord Hammond while she spoke.

"I know well what is due the earldom. My father spoke—"

"Andrew, I mean no disrespect to the late Lord Standford, but he became a bitter man after he lost your mother. He closed his heart to the world because he never wanted to be hurt in that way again. Unfortunately, he made the mistake of trying to protect you in the same manner, insisting that love was not important. Do not pursue this marriage of convenience you are set upon. Look for love, my boy. 'Tis the difference between merely existing and truly living."

Hammond arrived with Carolyn on his arm and Miss Whitney trailing behind as the duchess finished speaking. "Are you ready to leave, Aunt Annabelle?"

"Yes, I must get my rest, for we are for the opera on the morrow, which promises to be splendidly amusing. Sleep well, ladies. Come along, Jamie, I believe that is our carriage at the door."

The viscount bowed low over Carolyn's hand, and spoke

in a voice which barely reached the earl. "Until tomorrow evening, dear lady."

Looking past Hammond, Standford was surprised to see Miss Whitney frowning at the pair. Whatever could have caused such a look of dismay?

Tawny eyes showed glints of distress as she looked up from the parting couple to the earl. Were the shadows in those beautiful eyes because of unhappiness? A sudden chill ran through Standford. Had the chit developed a tendre for Hammond, like Carolyn?

Miss Whitney's gaze trailed the viscount and his aunt out to their carriage, but there was no look of longing on the beautiful face. If Standford was not mistaken, it was one of distaste.

Some minutes later when the footman announced the earl's carriage, he gestured the ladies ahead. Settling into the carriage with his back to the horses, the earl decided to satisfy his curiosity about his aunt's disappearance. "You ladies were a long time in coming. What kept you?"

Pulling her cape tighter against the chilled night air, Carolyn said, "Why, your very dear friend, Lady Collingwood. She came to the retiring room to discover all she could of your situation. It would not do to have Margaret housed beneath her station. I believe I helped you by fabricating Crosswell into a gothic horror."

Standford frowned. "I suppose I should thank you, Aunt Carolyn. Do I need fear what other tales you created on my behalf?"

"Oh, I blackened your character as best I could. I knew you would not mind after seeing which way the wind was blowing with the Collins ladies. It was most diverting to watch their reactions."

"I am glad I was able to provide you with an amusing evening at my expense. I believe it was equally entertaining for the Duchess of Atherton." The earl wondered with bemusement how his very serious pursuit of a wife had become such a comedic effort to his family and friends.

Tapping her fan upon his knee, Carolyn asked, "Whatever possessed you to invite that old harridan to the opera?"

"The countess placed me in a position where it would have seemed churlish not to invite her and her daughter. I believe we can survive one night."

"As long as you are sure it shall only be one night," Carolyn replied, before turning to Miss Whitney and prattling about the ball.

Standford fell silent, allowing his aunt to dominate the conversation as the carriage rumbled back to Cavendish Square. Moving past one of the gas street lamps, the earl clearly saw something was bothering Miss Whitney as she glumly stared out the window into the briefly illuminated darkness. Was her sadness caused by his aunt or Lord Hammond, the earl wondered?

When they arrived at Marsh House a few moments later, Carolyn attempted to stifle a yawn while the footman removed her cape. "I declare I could sleep until Sunday, I am so tired. Shall we retire, my dear?"

Miss Whitney hesitated before answering. "I believe I shall get a book from the library to read, for I am still rather excited and cannot fall asleep in such a state."

"Very well then. I shall see you in the morning, Lydia," Carolyn said and headed for the stairs.

The earl walked over and opened the library door for the young woman. "May I direct you to the book you would like? Tell me your interest."

"Perhaps a novel?" Distracted, Lydia entered and paused in the center of the room gazing around at the shelves of books.

"I have a single copy of that Radcliffe woman's work called *The Italian*," the earl suggested as he walked toward a shelf near a large window.

"That will do, my lord."

As he retrieved the book and brought it to her, Miss Whitney stood deep in thought staring at her gloved hands.

"Is there some problem troubling you?" the earl asked gently.

Her gaze flew up to his face, and she took a single half-step back. "N-no, Lord Standford. I am merely overtired." Taking the book from him she said, "Goodnight," then quietly turned and left him.

He watched her retreating form. She'd been wary, and it was clear she did not wish to confide in him. But could he blame her? He'd overreacted on several occasions of late and the young lady had been witness.

With a frustrated sigh, the earl walked to his desk and poured himself a brandy from the decanter left by Chandler. Sitting in front of the dying fire, he sank into thoughts of the duchess's advice about love and marriage.

Some twenty minutes later, with no clear decision about heeding the Duchess of Atherton, the earl made his way up the stairway. Abruptly, he halted in startled surprise.

Coming toward him in a pale pink wrapper was Miss Whitney. Her silver-blonde hair tumbled from beneath a frilly white bedcap. The candle she held flickered almost to darkness as she walked up the hall.

"Oh, Lord Standford . . . I thought you already abed, sir." The young lady tugged the delicate garment tightly about her.

The earl felt a sudden surge of desire rush through him as he stood watching the dancing light of the candle on the porcelain skin of her throat. He'd never known a longing this strong for anyone or anything. What magic was this unknown woman working on him?

Shocked by the strength of his desire, he gruffly snapped, "Why are you wandering the hallways in your bedclothes?"

"I went to speak with Carolyn, but found her already asleep, my lord." Miss Whitney's golden eyes grew larger at his harsh tone.

"Oh," the earl said tightly, feeling foolish for allowing his emotions to get so out of control. "Very well, goodnight, Miss Whitney." He moved aside, resisting the urge to stroke her silken curls as she walked past to her door.

Looking back, the lady softly called, "Sleep well, my lord."

Watching the door close behind the alluring beauty, the earl growled, "Not likely, Miss Whitney."

Seven

Scurrying down the stairs holding the skirt of her lilac muslin gown, Lydia stopped short on the last step at the sight of the earl's secretary. Of all the mornings to oversleep, she thought with dismay.

Loitering near a polished table in the front hall, Mr. Farlow seemed to be awaiting her. His eyes lit and he stepped forward eagerly when he saw her. "Good morning, Miss Whitney," he said, pushing the glasses up on his nose and smiling shyly.

"Good morning, sir."

"I have a message for you. In fact, I have two. The first is from Mrs. Trevor. She and Miss Georgette went to Gunter's to treat themselves to ices with Nurse. The morning is yours to do with as you will."

The news that her mistress was safely occupied sent a calming wave through Lydia. Carolyn was not likely to get into mischief with her daughter at her side. "Thank you, Mr. Farlow."

The secretary gazed at Lydia like an adoring pup. When the silence lengthened, she cleared her throat, then gently encouraged him. "And the other message?"

A slight flush rising in his pale cheeks, Farlow added, "Oh, yes, Chandler said there is a visitor awaiting you in the rear morning room."

"A visitor?" Lydia was expecting no one and certainly not before the proper hours.

"Yes, a Miss Bertha Armstrong." Farlow began to shuffle the papers he'd been clutching in his hands as if he suddenly remembered his own morning tasks.

"Bertie!" Lydia almost shrieked the name. "Thank you for being the bearer of such joyous news, sir." Without further conversation, she rushed around the startled secretary to the small room at the rear of the hallway.

Opening the door, Lydia discovered her beloved Bertie standing in front of a door which led out to a pretty garden. The lady, who always had a fondness for growing things, was closely inspecting the earl's plants through the glass.

"Bertie!"

She turned at the sound of Lydia's voice and surveyed her with mock severity. "Well, my dear, you have been quite the traveler since we last met."

"Yes, indeed, but not of my choosing." Lydia studied her former governess and cherished friend. Bertie looked much the same as always. A tall woman in her fifties, she was lean without being frail. Her plain face was angular beneath light brown hair, streaked with grey. Amber eyes reflected a mixture of wisdom and practicality. She was dressed in a much-worn, navy-blue gown which gave her a cold and forbidding appearance. But Lydia knew the lady too well to be misled. She closed the door and gave Bertie a hug.

"I certainly did not expect to find myself in London when I left for Mrs. Brisby's employ."

Holding her former student away from her after the embrace, Bertie asked with a frown, "I have worried much about your present post, not being acquainted with Lord Standford. Are you quite happy, Lydia?"

"Yes, for I could not ask for a better position than acting as Mrs. Trevor's companion. She is kind and good-hearted, if somewhat unpredictable. I am to go about in Society as her goddaughter. But we will speak of that later. Is the tea still warm, or shall I order another pot?" After feeling the silver pot, Lydia rang for a servant.

When the maid arrived with fresh tea and scones hot from the oven, Lydia and Bertie settled onto a gold damask sofa for a comfortable coze.

Handing her visitor a cup, Lydia said, "I know you are not fond of traveling by stage. Why ever have you journeyed to Town? Surely not just to inspect my situation?"

"I came as soon as your letter arrived informing me of your new position. There is such exciting news that I would have walked all the way from Hertfordshire to bring it to you, my dear." Without waiting for Lydia to respond, Bertie continued, leaning forward with eagerness at what she was to impart. "I received a visit from Mr. Karling this week."

"My father's man of business? Do not tell me there is some old gaming debt that we did not pay." Lydia felt a rush of apprehension, for her funds were nearly depleted.

"Tut, tut. Do you think I would tell that old coin-pinching goat where you are if that were the reason?" Bertie sat up straighter at the implied insult.

"Of course you would not, for I know how well you protected me this past year. But you did tell Mr. Karling my direction. Why does he wish to see me? He assured me our business was finished after Lord Crawley got the hundred pounds my father lost at the race track." Lydia made no mention of the fact that she'd had to sell every last piece of jewelry she owned, with the exception of a small heart locket, to discharge the debt. But then her possessions tended to come and go over the years according to her father's run of luck.

Taking Lydia's hands in her own, Bertie said, "My dear, I have the most wondrous news. Your uncle, Angus Mackay, died." Realizing what she'd just said, Bertie frowned. "I did not mean it was wonderful he died, but only that he left you a comfortable inheritance."

"I had an Uncle Angus?" Stunned by Bertie's amazing announcement, Lydia's brows drew together while she searched her memory for such a person.

"Mr. Karling says he was your mother's older brother. He went to sea when he was but a lad and worked his way up to captain and owner. You are the last surviving relative on your mother's side and all is left to you. My dear, you shall be able to resign your position and might never work again if you invest your new funds wisely," Bertie said, decisively nodding her head.

Surprised delight was immediately replaced with a sense of disappointment. Lydia was startled at her reaction to her friend's announcement. While the news of a secure income pleased her, she did not want to quit her post. She'd come to care about Carolyn and Georgette and, she admitted to herself, Lord Standford.

"Is the sum so very great, then?" Lydia turned her head and gazed out the door into the garden, watching a newly emerged butterfly search the foliage for a flower.

"In truth, I do not know, but Karling left a card with his direction. He said you may send word and he will call any morning that is convenient. I received the impression your circumstances would change considerably. He suggested he could engage a residence for you in Town if you so wish, which certainly indicates a considerable bequest." Bertie removed a card and held it out to Lydia.

Absently taking the white vellum, Lydia's mind whirled. Despite the windfall inheritance, abandoning Carolyn at present was unthinkable. The impetuous lady would no longer be bound by her promise not to game.

Lord Standford's azure-blue eyes came unbidden to her mind. Had he not come to her rescue after she was unfairly discharged by Lady Pemberton? She could not repay his kindness with such a backhanded turn, she argued with herself. She would remain at Cavendish Square until Carolyn was safely wed.

Taking Bertie's hands, Lydia said, "I am delighted with the news, but I think I shall remain in my present position for yet a while. Mrs. Trevor has been more than kind to me, and I do not feel right leaving her before the Season is complete."

Bertie looked at Lydia sharply. Clearly the announcement that her former charge would remain in her post was not what she expected. She stared down at the half-eaten scone on her plate, then looked back at Lydia and wisely said, "Mayhap that is best, my dear. That will give you time to meet with Karling and ascertain the extent of your good fortune. He will be able to find you a suitable house and companion for I cannot leave my cousin, who is ill at present, without someone to help with the children. I asked a neighbor to sit with her while I came to Town."

"I shall have no companion but you, dear Bertie. Once Carolyn is married, I can come to you in Hertfordshire. We shall decide then if it is to be London or some lesser town where we can set up house." Lydia suspected she would not want to be constantly in Town after the Season. By the little Season both Carolyn and Lord Standford were likely to be wed. She would be forever meeting the earl and his new countess, whoever she might be, and that gave Lydia a strangely uncomfortable feeling.

"Very well. Now you must tell me why—" the older woman began.

Muffled voices sounded in the hall and the morning room door opened to reveal Lord Standford. He looked very handsome in a dark brown coat over a tan brocade waistcoat and tan pantaloons. The sight of a stranger caused him to halt at the door. "I beg your pardon, Miss Whitney. I was not informed that you had a caller."

Rising, Lydia ignored the foolish flutter of her heart. "Do come in, sir. I should like to introduce you to my former governess and friend, Miss Bertha Armstrong."

His lordship came and stood before the women, giving them a formal bow. "I am honored to meet you, Miss Armstrong. Are you making a long stay in Town?"

"No, my lord. I came only for the day to visit Lydia." The older woman's knowing gaze took in every detail of the earl.

Lydia was surprised by Lord Standford's strangely light mood considering his brooding demeanor in the hall outside her bedroom last night. She'd thought him annoyed with her, but perhaps she was merely suffering from a guilty conscience. It still troubled her that she had not disclosed her family history.

"Then I shall not interrupt your reunion but a moment." Turning toward the door, the earl gestured to a dark-haired man dressed in a rumpled duffle coat who hovered in the hall outside holding a wooden crate. The earl pointed to a small table, saying, "Place the box there, Brigman."

"Aye, sir. Will that be all, milord?" The swarthy man peered at the ladies curiously while he gently set the crate on the table.

"Yes, Brigman. I daresay you had your hands full with this parcel. Go to the kitchen and Cook will find you something to reward your efforts." The earl spoke to the man, but stared at the box.

"Aye, sir. 'Twas a prodigiously long journey with this 'ere cargo, but ol' Brigman is up to any rig what you ask, milord." The servant then bowed to his master before swaggering from the room.

Lydia was curious about the contents of the wooden box.

"Come, Miss Whitney, Miss Armstrong. I hoped to find Georgette here, but Chandler tells me she is out with her mother and Nurse. Therefore, I shall let you be the ones to see this surprise since you, Miss Whitney, were responsible for it." The earl gestured them forward.

The ladies walked toward the small brass-inlaid table. Lydia looked a question at Lord Standford. His handsome presence seemed to befuddle her thinking.

Without a word, the earl quickly removed the top of the box. There, sitting in the bottom, hunched down with an indignant look on his face, was an extremely large, black and white cat.

"Good heavens," Lydia uttered in amazement. "Is this Georgette's much longed for Boots?"

"Yes, and by Jove, he is the largest cat I ever beheld," the earl said, glancing up at Lydia, disbelief evident in his attractive face.

Laughing, Lydia said, "Georgette did say her Boots was the best mouser in the parish."

"Then I must say there cannot be a rodent left in Leeds, for it looks as if this fellow ate them all."

Lydia felt a strange sense of loss when the earl centered his attention on the cat. What madness possessed her? She followed his gaze to the huge feline, who now peeked over the edge of the box at his new surroundings.

"He is a very fine fellow," Bertie said admiringly.

The earl's gaze again settled on Lydia. A gentle smile played about his mouth. She smiled back at him with pleasure at his kind gesture to his little cousin. His blue eyes darkened with some emotion while he looked at her, then he straightened and his customary mask of formality fell back into place. "Georgette deserves to have her cat. Circumstances have denied her much else of her former life."

Looking at Lord Standford's suddenly staid countenance, Lydia was exasperated. She longed to shake him out of this stilted behavior. A thought flashed into her mind. She reached into the box and struggled to remove the heavy animal, who protested loudly at this rude handling. Dropping the cat unceremoniously into the earl's arms, she said, "We must all make friends with Georgette's pet or he will run away looking for more familiar surroundings."

The earl stared down at the animal as if it were a three-day-old fish. "Miss Whitney . . . I know nothing of cats."

"Then now is the time to learn, since you will be sharing a residence with this feisty fellow, my lord," Lydia said, watching Boots dig the claws of his white-booted feet into the earl's coat, slowly working his way up to the gentleman's shoulder. "Hold him with one hand, and stroke him with the other."

Lord Standford awkwardly petted the cat's back when Boots settled with his paws perched on either side of the earl's neck, his large black head pushed under the man's chin. "Like this?"

Shocked by a sudden desire to be in Boots' position, her arms wrapped about Lord Stanford's neck, Lydia could not answer the question.

"Exactly, Lord Standford," Bertie said, looking at Lydia curiously.

Pushing her disturbing thoughts aside, Lydia avoided Bertie's penetrating look and said, "You have made a friend for life. Boots will likely seek you out when he is looking for companionship and Georgette is not in the house."

"I am sure my man, Hadley, will be thrilled at my newfound friendship." There was a touch of humor playing around the earl's mouth, as he stopped stroking the cat to brush at the black and white hairs clinging to his brown morning coat.

When Boots began to meow plaintively, the earl stroked him again. Looking up, eyes twinkling, he asked, "Shall I have to continue to pet the beast until Georgette comes back?"

"No, my lord, I suggest you give him to one of the servants to place in Georgette's room. The cat will settle down once he feels comfortable." Lydia's heart misbehaved while she watched the smile soften the gentleman's features.

"Miss Armstrong, it was a pleasure to meet you. I hope you will allow me to provide you transport back to your home. Tell Chandler when you are ready to leave and the carriage will be brought round for you. Boots and I shall bid you ladies good day." With only a slight bow, the earl left with the clinging feline.

The door barely closed behind the earl before Bertie reprimanded her former pupil. "Lydia, whatever possessed you to shove that cat at Lord Standford?"

Feeling like she was ten again, Lydia defended her action. "Just when I think the earl will unbend and be congenial, he suddenly draws back into his stiff and proud manner. I was just trying to shake him out of that pose. Do you know that everyone in Town calls him Stiff-neck behind his back?"

The older woman's eyes studied her with grave concern. "What can that matter to you, my dear?"

Lydia turned and walked over to the glass door looking out on the small garden. "Because I know from experience that behind that very proud manner, Lord Standford is a kind and compassionate man. Unfortunately, few are allowed to see that side of him. 'Tis unfair Society so misjudges him."

Bertie stared at Lydia for a long moment before saying, "Shall we take a turn about the garden and enjoy the flowers while you tell me all about Mrs. Trevor and Georgette and ... how you came to be hired as companion for the lady."

Lydia agreed and they exited the morning room. With her arm locked in Bertie's, they strolled the small gravel circle which was cut in the garden. When they arrived back at the house, the ladies took a seat on a marble bench while Lydia continued her tale of how she thought she was hired for an older lady in the country, and instead found the beautiful Carolyn in London. She blushed when she mentioned her agreement to keep her past a secret from the earl in exchange for a promise by Mrs. Trevor not to game.

Bertie sat turning a leaf she'd plucked from a nearby plant for a few moments after Lydia finished. "I cannot like that you did not tell his lordship at once about Lord Freddie, but at least some good came from the omission by securing the lady's oath. But Lydia, do not deceive yourself, for often gamesters cannot help themselves."

Lydia gave a mirthless laugh. "I well remember my father's promises, Bertie. I shall be vigilant, but I don't think it is the same with Carolyn. She is only trying to make enough for Georgette's future to be assured. I think if she were to marry, she would give up gambling completely. I believe she did not game before her husband died."

"I hope you are correct," Bertie stated skeptically. "So, the pretty widow is looking for a husband?"

Lydia sighed. "Yes, unfortunately I believe she has formed a tendre for Viscount Hammond."

Tossing the leaf she'd held to the ground, Bertie asked, "But is that not good?"

"Last night at the ball, I learned that his wife, Felicity, and his sons are coming from the West Indies to join him." Lydia glanced up at the sky, watching the white clouds drift past. "I don't know if Carolyn is aware that he is married. Should I mention the matter to her?"

Bertie frowned, then shook her head. "My dear, as yet you know little of the passions of a grown woman. I have told you before, Society does not frown on a discreet dalliance. I would advise you to do only what the earl wants. Keep the lady from the gaming tables. Otherwise she might think you are censuring her conduct."

"Yes, you are right." Lydia knew Carolyn had enough of that from the earl, she didn't want to do so, as well.

Behind the ladies, standing unobserved at the open drawing room door was Carolyn Trevor. Her mouth felt suddenly dry and her knees began to shake.

Hammond married! That could not be possible. An emptiness overwhelmed her when she accepted the truth of the situation. Along with that realization, another followed rapidly. She was in love with the viscount and he was lost to her forever.

In a daze, Carolyn backed away from the open door, too emotionally distraught to speak with Lydia and her friend. She needed to find some place were she might think and find comfort, but she knew there would be little solace found.

* * *

We'd Like to Invite You to Subscribe to Zebra's Regency Romance Book Club and Give You a Gift of 4 Free Books as Your Introduction! *(Worth $18.49!)*

If you're a Regency lover, imagine the joy of getting 4 FREE Zebra Regency Romances and then the chance to have these lovely stories delivered to your home each month at the lowest prices available! Well, that's our offer to you and here's how you benefit by becoming a Zebra Home Subscription Service subscriber:

- **4 FREE Introductory Regency Romances** are delivered to your doorstep
- **4 BRAND NEW Regencies** are then delivered each month (usually before they're available in bookstores)
- Subscribers save almost **$4.00 every month**
- Home delivery is always **FREE**
- You also receive a **FREE monthly newsletter**, *Zebra/ Pinnacle Romance News* which features author profiles, contests, subscriber benefits, book previews and more
- **No risks or obligations**...in other words you can cancel whenever you wish with no questions asked

Join the thousands of readers who enjoy the savings and convenience offered to Regency Romance subscribers. After your initial introductory shipment, you receive 4 brand-new Zebra Regency Romances each month to examine for 10 days. Then, if you decide to keep the books, you'll pay the preferred subscriber's price of just $3.65 per title. That's only $14.60 for all 4 books and there's never an extra charge for shipping and handling.

It's a no-lose proposition, so return the FREE BOOK CERTIFICATE today!

With the ease of a noted whip, Standford guided his phaeton out into the traffic at Hyde Park Corner. The Duke of Atherton sat beside him in contented silence after a successful visit at Tattersalls. Concentrating on his driving while he made his way up Park Lane, the earl was equally mute.

When they rounded the corner approaching Curzon Street, the earl noted numerous carriages halted in the roadway. There was clearly some accident ahead on Park Lane. He reined in the matched bays to a walk and idly stated, "I hope one of those cow-handed whipsters cluttering the streets these days hasn't locked wheels, causing harm to someone."

The duke squinted while he peered into the afternoon haze at the distant commotion. "No, I would say some fellow has managed to tumble some furniture from a fourgon into the street. Take Curzon Street to South Audley and we shan't be delayed in reaching Grosvenor Square."

With a gentle flick of his wrist, the earl returned the phaeton to a quick pace. Turning onto Curzon Street, he questioned the duke about the horses just purchased. "What are you planning for Silverton's greys?"

"I bought them as a gift for Hammond's eldest boy. He must be taught to handle the ribbons when the family gets settled in Town. Those greys are a prime set of goers."

"Yes, they are well ribbed-up. I am surprised Silverton is parting with such cattle."

"Alas, the lad is all to pieces. 'Tis unfortunate, but often the way with these green fellows who come to Town. I keep warning Arthur to stay out of the gaming hells. Many a fortune is lost on the tables." The duke folded his arms across his chest while he watched the earl handle the team.

Slowing for the turn on South Audley, Standford countered, "Try being responsible for one as headstrong as my aunt who has almost no fortune to lose."

"No, thank you. Arthur is more than enough trouble to keep away from the leeches. But now that you have the beautiful and sensible Miss Whitney to watch your aunt, you should have little to worry about."

The earl raised one eyebrow in surprise. "You seem surprisingly impressed with my aunt's companion on such short acquaintance."

Atherton turned to give Standford a piercing look. "I find Miss Whitney to be everything most pleasing in a young woman. Don't you agree?"

Standford shrugged stiffly, not wanting to voice his confused thoughts on the young lady.

"Besides, I don't think you need worry about Carolyn much longer. I believe my nephew is quite taken with the lady. Surely Miss Whitney can keep her out of mischief until James comes up to scratch."

The mention of Miss Whitney's name had distracted Standford. Why did he behave like a gapeseed in her presence? His mind went back to his meeting with the lady in the morning room. He'd almost forgotten himself and reached out to touch her porcelain skin while he stood staring into her beautiful face. Hopefully the duke was right about Hammond offering for his aunt. The sooner Carolyn was wed, the sooner Standford could be away from Miss Whitney's dangerously enchanting presence.

Pushing thoughts of the beauty from his mind, the earl attended his driving. The congestion of carriages on South Audley was great due to the accident on Park Lane. The earl slackened his pace. While the phaeton slowed for a crossing pedestrian, a nattily dressed Lord Washburn hailed them. On his arm was a lady unknown to the earl.

"Afternoon, Your Grace, Standford. Were you able to get Silverton's cattle at Tattersalls?" Lord Washburn eagerly queried.

The duke turned in his seat to face the pair on the street, surveying the lady on Washburn's arm. "That I did. I must thank you for the tip that the lad would sell them."

" 'Twas nothing, but I am forgetting my manners. Allow

me to introduce my companion. Lady Halbrook, may I present the Duke of Atherton and Lord Standford."

"A pleasure." The earl lifted his beaver hat briefly, before he settled into studying the woman while the old friends talked. The name was familiar, but he could not remember what he knew of the woman.

Lady Halbrook was an attractive woman in her thirties. Her figure was elegant beneath a crimson walking dress. Raven hair peeked out of her red high-crown bonnet. Dark brown eyes stared back at him with a boldness that irritated the earl for some unexplainable reason.

While gazing at the woman's attractive face, the earl wondered why he did not experience the same tightening in his chest he felt when he looked at Miss Whitney. Surely it was because of this lady's somewhat brazen demeanor.

Interrupting his musings, Lady Halbrook cooed, "Lord Standford, I hope you and the duke will honor me this evening. I am having a small card party for a few select friends."

"We must regretfully decline, Lady Halbrook. I have engaged a party to go to the opera this evening."

"Then perhaps another evening. 'Tis No. 57 South Audley. I am home most evenings." Lady Halbrook smiled seductively at the earl, implying an invitation to more than mere cards.

There was a moment of uncomfortable silence at the woman's open lure. Lord Washburn cleared his throat before gruffly saying, "Mustn't keep you gentlemen. I am escorting her ladyship back to her house before I meet Matthew at White's."

The pair moved away from the carriage and the earl put his vehicle in motion, glad to be away from the couple. Beside him, the duke chuckled briefly before saying, "The lovely baroness had best watch her step around Washburn. His lady wife could put an end to those select card parties if she wished with just a few words to her Society friends."

"Why should Lady Washburn care if he attends a private

card party? I hear he loses regularly at White's." Standford edged the phaeton carefully around several wooden crates that had fallen into the cobblestone street.

"I see you have not heard about Lady Halbrook's parties. Let me warn you, Andrew, to keep Carolyn away from the baroness. The play at her house is deep and could rival the meanest hells on St. James. It is a particular favorite with the lady gamesters for they can experience all forms of gaming not usually seen at a fashionable party."

Standford felt a momentary wave of fear causing him to tighten his grip on the reins. Had his aunt met Lady Halbrook? He did not think so. He must remember to warn Miss Whitney to be especially vigilant where the baroness was concerned.

Easing his grip, he realized that for this evening he knew Carolyn would not game, for they were going to the opera. He must remember to speak with Miss Whitney before Carolyn came down. The thought of the coming meeting made his pulse beat stronger.

Carolyn lay in her darkened room that afternoon, a damp cloth over her eyes. There was no fever, no chills or physical pain, only the grinding ache in her heart because she had fallen in love with Lord Hammond. She had not even realized it herself until she overheard Lydia's conversation about the viscount. The news he was married had taken the breath from her.

With supreme effort, Carolyn had made it to her own room before collapsing on her bed in tears. Millie arrived later and Carolyn pleaded a severe headache. Settled into bed, she managed to get rid of her abigail after an appropriate amount of the woman's nursing.

How could she, a woman of the world, make such a foolish mistake? Removing the cloth from her forehead and staring into the fading light, Carolyn's mind continued to go over all the talks she and Hammond had shared. He was full of tales of the Indies, plans for renovating his run-down estate in Devon, and the latest *on-dits*. The viscount had listened to her own problems with compassion and concern. But never did he mention a . . . wife.

Turning her head to brush a tear from her cheek, Carolyn saw the miniature of Georgette which always sat by her bed. She picked up the tiny portrait and drew it to her chest. "Oh Muffin, whatever shall I do now? I gave my heart to a gentleman I can never marry. There can be no other to take his place."

A scratching sounded at the door before a click, then Lydia's whispering voice in the darkness. "Carolyn, are you awake?"

With a hurried effort to dry her eyes, Carolyn tiredly answered, "Yes, my dear. Come in and light a candle."

While Lydia lit the branch of candles on the bedside table, Carolyn noted how lovely the girl looked. There was a suppressed excitement about her; clearly she was enthusiastic about going to the opera this evening.

"Millie said you were ill. You should have called me. I am here to help you." Lydia brushed strands of hair from around Carolyn's face while she gazed down at her, shadows of concern in the depths of the tawny eyes.

" 'Tis only a headache," Carolyn said. "I want you to go to the opera tonight and enjoy yourself."

"I could not leave you here alone and ill."

"Nonsense, my dear. I shall have a light supper and go to sleep early. You would only be lonely and bored. I insist you go. Besides, someone must protect Andrew from Lady Margaret and her mother."

Carolyn noted a soft pink blush covered Lydia's cheeks at the mention of her nephew. Was her companion developing a tendre for Standford? Her own heart ached too much to worry about Lydia's emotions tonight.

"I want you go to the opera. You must tell me all about it tomorrow, when I am fully recovered."

"Are you sure?" Lydia asked hesitantly.

"Yes, run and get dressed. You will enjoy Catalini." Carolyn gestured her to go with a weak smile. She wanted to be alone tonight.

"I shall come to see you in the morning."

After the door closed behind her companion, Carolyn pondered her present situation. There could be no thought of marriage now. She would not endure a loveless marriage when her heart was engaged to another. There were other options to recover her fortune.

Clearly she would have to return to her original plan to win a fortune at the tables. But what of her promise to Lydia? Staring at the flickering light of the candles, the conversation in the library replayed in her mind. Her companion had asked her to promise not to game—

Carolyn bolted up in bed, causing the miniature to tumble to the blanket. She suddenly realized she had promised to be *good*, not to cease gaming. A slight nagging of her conscience told her it was one and the same, and she was splitting hairs. Lydia had agreed to keep silent about her past if Carolyn would cease gaming, and in response, Carolyn had said she would be good. She shrugged the thought aside.

No doubt Lydia would be disappointed, but Carolyn knew she must resume her gaming for Muffin's sake. Fate was telling her that gaming was the answer by sending Faro Freddie's daughter to her. She knew his memory trick now and she would use it.

The decision made, Carolyn placed Georgette's picture back on the bedside table and rose. She took the branch of candles to the small writing desk against the wall. Pulling out a sheet of paper and a pen, she nibbled at her lower lip thinking what she must say. Dipping the pen in ink, she began her letter with *Dear Sir Jasper.*

Eight

After leaving the duke at his residence, Standford jumped down from the phaeton in front of his Cavendish Square town house. Handing the reins to his tiger, he said, "That will be all, Willis. Inform Jacobs to have the town carriage ready for this evening."

"Yes, milord," the freckled-faced youth answered before remounting the vehicle and driving off toward the mews.

The earl, about to place his foot on the bottom stair to ascend, halted at the sound of his name being shouted. Turning, he discovered Lord Gravely hailing him from down the street. Standford struggled to keep the distaste he felt from showing while the town tulip briskly advanced toward him.

Gravely, dressed in an ostentatious blue coat sporting lemon-hued buttons and pantaloons in a delicate yellow, drew wide-eyed glances from passersby. His waistcoat was marigold in color with blue stripes and his white-topped Hessians, which proclaimed his dandyism, sported large gold tassels.

"Lord Standford, I must request a moment of your time on a matter of some urgency." Gravely halted directly in front of the earl, nervously fingering the lion-headed cane he carried. His usual bored expression was gone, replaced with one of uneasiness as his thin lips twitched. He removed his black beaver hat, exposing pale blonde hair glistening with Russian oil.

Curious what the idle saunterer wanted with him, the earl

politely asked, "Shall we adjourn to my library, Gravely? Or is this a matter easily finished here?"

"As 'tis a delicate affair for my family, sir, I would much prefer the library," Gravely stated while glancing up and down the street as if worried some gossipmonger might happen past.

Some minutes later in his library, the earl gestured for the dandy to be seated before going to a lacquered table which held a brandy decanter and glasses. "Tell me, sir. I confess I am at a loss to know what this urgent business could be."

The dandy sat quietly staring at his boots while the earl poured out two glasses, then accepted the amber liquid Standford offered. Taking a sustaining drink, the fop answered, "I just heard the most disturbing rumor from your friend, Mr. Arthur Landers and his rowdy companion, Devere. Those cubs lack Town bronze. Imagine wearing Belcher ties to Angelo's for fencing."

"Have you come merely to discuss the fashion *faux pas* of a couple of greenlings?" Standford asked, sweeping Gravely with a scornful gaze.

"No . . . no, I came to hear the truth from you of this farrago of nonsense Landers and Devere spouted, my lord."

Lounging back in his seat as the dandy appeared to have trouble getting to the point, Standford took a sip of brandy. His patience wearing thin, he raised an eyebrow while tapping a finger on his glass. "I am not in the habit of verifying idle gossip, Gravely. I leave such matters to the scandalmongers."

Angrily jumping to his feet, the fop retorted, "I shall know the truth before I leave this house, my lord."

"What foolishness is this? What truth do you think I know?" The earl rose and stood before Gravely, rigid with indignation at the man's belligerent tone. His already considerable dislike for the man grew steadily.

"I understand, sir, that you are housing Lord Frederick Whitney's daughter, a circumstance most peculiar for a bachelor, I might add. My grandfather, the duke, will not stand for it. The girl is the product of a *mesalliance* my uncle foolishly entered into. We shall not allow her to trade on the Whitney name to push herself forward into Polite Society."

Standford's fingers tightened around the glass he held. He felt as if he'd taken a blow at Gentleman Jackson's. Miss Whitney, the granddaughter of the Duke of Graymoor, the daughter of Lord Frederick Whitney! Not an impoverished miss as he'd assumed by her circumstances, but a connection of one of the oldest and wealthiest families in the *ton*.

Receiving this startling information, the earl at once perceived the family resemblance to Gravely. His pale blonde hair and golden brown eyes were almost identical to those of the young woman he'd hired. How little Standford really knew about her, despite her effect on him and his aunt's affairs.

With deliberate slowness, the earl turned and placed his glass on the mantel. Trying to gather his wits, he simply said, "I was not aware Miss Whitney claimed such a kinship."

"So," Gravely said, with a snicker. "The baggage didn't tell you she was Faro Freddie's daughter. Can't say I boast much on that connection, either."

The vague memory of Lord Frederick bent over the Faro table at White's flashed into the earl's mind. Dread filled Standford's heart at the dawning realization. The younger son of the Duke of Graymoor had been one of the most notorious gamesters in Society and Miss Lydia Whitney was his daughter. Even so, the insult to the young woman by this sniveling cad made the earl's blood boil.

Turning back to Lord Gravely, who'd casually tossed out the slur, Standford felt a strong urge to plant a facer on the man's smirking countenance. "I see little for the young lady to boast of about the family relationship in total, sirrah."

The nasty smile fell from Gravely's face. "You come close to crossing the line, Standford. I . . ." The dandy faltered when he looked at the earl's grim demeanor.

The insult was obvious, but the fop was clearly not willing

to fight a duel with a reputed crackshot like Standford. "Well, perhaps I . . . er . . . misspoke about my uncle's daughter." Gravely backed up a step. "I am not personally acquainted with her since my grandfather disinherited Uncle Frederick before the girl was born."

Stepping forward to tower above Gravely, the earl bit out, "Then I suggest you not speak of Miss Whitney. I assure you she is not drawing attention to her connection to the duke or yourself. You may tell Graymoor there is no need for his concern. She is a goddaughter to my aunt."

The man nervously edged back from the earl. There was a slight clink when he placed the unfinished glass of brandy on a marble-top table which he brushed past. Continuing to back toward the door, he spoke with more courage now that a greater distance separated him from the earl. "The duke shall watch her conduct closely. As head of the Whitney family, he retains the right to send her from Town if she behaves in an unsavory manner."

"If Graymoor has something to say about Miss Whitney, I suggest he come here himself." The earl turned his back on Gravely in dismissal.

Moments later Standford heard the door click shut. In a shocked stupor, he dropped into the gilt-armed chair beside the fireplace. What madness had almost caused him to force a duel on that sniveling fop?

The beguiling Miss Lydia Whitney, of course. What a fool he was! He'd hired the daughter of a hardened gamester to keep his aunt from gambling.

The beautiful face of the young woman came to him. There was a sudden aching around his heart when he perceived what his duty demanded he do. How had he made such a mull of things?

With a feeling of excitement, Lydia fastened the pearl drops to her ears. Taking her hand away, she gave herself a last appraising look in the mirror. The mauve silk gown with puffed sleeves and small pearls trimming the bodice suited her very well.

The earbobs swayed gently when she turned her head to admire Millie's work on her silver-blonde hair, which was piled in a cluster of loose curls on top of her head. The abigail had worked matching mauve-colored spiraled ribbons among the ringlets.

Scurrying footsteps sounded in the hallway, stopping outside her door. Lydia turned in expectation. Before a knock could be heard, the soft sobs of a child penetrated the oaken portal.

Lydia rose and hurriedly threw open the door. A teary-eyed Georgette peered beneath a long embroidered cloth which hung from a narrow table in the hall. Dropping the fabric with unmistakable disappointment on her tear-stained face, she caught sight of her mother's companion and cried, "Miss Lydia, Boots is missing. Nurse left the door of my room open and he runned away while I napped."

Nurse could be heard muttering at the far end of the hall about annoying beasts. She peeked in the linen closet in search of the missing pet.

"Don't worry, Georgette, I am sure we shall find him. He is merely curious about his new home." Taking the child's hand, Lydia took her handkerchief and gently brushed the tears away. She chatted soothingly to the girl while they worked their way along the corridor softly calling the cat and looking in each room. Nurse followed some distance behind, conducting her own search.

After fruitlessly exploring several empty chambers, they neared the end of the corridor. Lydia hesitated to go any farther, for she knew the last room belonged to his lordship. She felt a strange sensation in her stomach at the thought of meeting him in his private quarters.

Nervously peering down the hall, Lydia saw a shaft of light emanating from his door. A feeling of relief washed over her. He was not likely to be within if it were open. Perhaps they could safely search his room and be gone before he came to dress for the evening.

Tugging Lydia's hand, Georgette pulled her forward. "There is another chamber to look through. We must see if Boots is there."

"Yes, my dear, we must hurry—"

"Is there something I can do for you, miss?" Hadley called from behind them.

With gratitude, Lydia turned to the aged valet advancing toward them. He appeared to be returning from the laundry, for three snowy white cravats hung starched and ironed on his arm.

"Yes, Mr. Hadley. Georgette's cat escaped from the upper floor and we wondered if the animal might not have gotten into his lordship's room."

"Cat? I've seen no such creature, but they're rather sly things I believe. Forever popping up and scaring a body. Can't abide them, myself. All those hairs and their devilish claws create havoc with one's clothing," the valet stated.

"That may be true, Mr. Hadley, but such things count for little with a child," Lydia returned, with a smile. "Perhaps you will allow us to look for the animal in his lordship's room?"

"You think he might be in there?" Hadley's bushy grey brows rose in horror at the possibility. He increased his ambling gait to almost a trot, passing Lydia, who turned and followed close behind.

When the old man reached out a trembling hand, pushed the door open, and groaned, she curiously peered over Hadley's shoulder. To her dismay, she saw Boots immediately. The large feline lay upon a black superfine coat which rested on the bed awaiting his lordship's arrival.

Georgette edged past Lydia, then cried with delight, "Boots!" She dashed forward, climbing upon the bed beside her mischievous pet.

The large black and white cat turned to look at his owner, giving a soft pleasurable purr from deep in his throat. With supreme feline contentment, he began kneading his claws into the black fabric of his lordship's jacket.

Hadley staggered back against the open door, his hand pulled at his constricting cravat. He choked out, "Good heavens. 'Tis ruint . . . his lordship's new evening coat is ruint."

Eyeing the valet's pale countenance, Lydia became alarmed. His wrinkled face looked as grey as his hair. "Mr. Hadley, you must sit down. I am sure the coat will be fine once it is brushed."

Taking the cravats from the protesting old man, Lydia led him to a straight-backed chair near the door. She carefully laid the neckcloths on the nearby dresser. Picking up a sporting periodical, she moved to fan the obviously shaken Hadley.

The valet took a deep breath, then straightened. "Most kind of you to worry over an old man, miss. You've got a good heart. I shall be better soon. 'Twas just the shock of seeing the . . . animal in the earl's chamber."

Scanning the room quickly, Lydia discovered a decanter of brandy and several glasses on an elegant little rosewood table in the corner. She quickly poured a glass for the valet and returned. "Drink this, sir."

With a quivering hand, the old man obeyed. It was but a matter of moments before the color returned to his face. "You are most considerate, Miss Whitney and I very foolish."

Before Lydia could respond, Nurse appeared in the doorway. Spying the errant creature on his lordship's coat, she called, "You naughty beast. No good ever comes from allowin' animals in the 'ouse." She pulled a large white handkerchief from her pocket and rushed at the cat. "Scat, scat, you bothersome creature."

Too late, Lydia realized the woman's intention. Boots darted from the bed in fear and raced out the door. "No!"

was all she or Georgette had time to shout in unison before the cat disappeared again into the hallway.

To explain her abandonment of the valet, Lydia called back, "We must catch him before he gets downstairs. Should he get out of the house he might disappear forever."

"Go ahead, miss, I'm sharp-witted again," Hadley reassured her in a stronger voice.

Lydia dashed for the door. At an unladylike pace, she ran through the portal and straight into the arms of Lord Standford.

"What the devil . . ." the earl began in confusion, his arms encircling her.

Staring into the startled eyes of Lord Standford, Lydia was very aware of the feel of his hard masculine chest pressed against her and the muscular arms that held her. Gazing up at his handsome face, she suddenly wished she could forget about the troublesome cat.

"Miss Lydia," Georgette exclaimed urgently. "This is no time for greeting my cousin. Boots will get away." The child bolted past them, blonde ringlets bouncing wildly in her headlong dash down the hall.

Lydia stepped back from the earl, a blush warming her face. "I apologize for my unseemly haste . . . but the cat must not be allowed out, my lord."

The earl stood rigidly, making no comment. He stared back at her with dazed blue eyes.

Knowing she had no time to explain, Lydia turned and rushed after the child and the cat. She was not surprised at his stiff manner, for she was behaving like a hoyden. For the first time she realized she no longer need worry about being dismissed. She was a woman of means due to the inheritance from her unknown uncle.

Turning the corner, Lydia hastened down the carpeted passageway. She came to a sudden halt and looked up to discover Boots sitting at the top of the stairs leading to the nursery, casually cleaning himself. Georgette sat beside him, crooning endearments and stroking his large black head.

Short of breath, Lydia edged to the foot of the stairway. With a sigh, she wondered what Lord Standford must be thinking of her unladylike behavior. What did it matter if the earl disapproved of her? Deep inside her a small voice whispered, it mattered a great deal.

Standford watched the fleeing Miss Whitney, then suddenly remembered he wanted to speak with her. Raising his hand, he snapped, "Miss . . ." but she'd already disappeared around the bend in the hall.

Abruptly, Nurse darted out of his bedchamber door and ran past him. She managed a slight bob of a curtsey and backed away quickly saying, "Pardon me, my lord." The woman offered no explanation, merely ran down the hallway as fast as her short limbs could carry her.

"Fiend seize it, Hadley, what the blazes is going on here!" the earl shouted, entering his room in search of his man.

The valet stood calmly beside the bed vigorously brushing a black evening coat. Looking up, he sedately said, "Ah, you're early, my lord. I fear we must select another coat for this evenin'."

"Coat! Devil take the coat! What is all the commotion here?"

"Are we a bit mumpish this evenin', sir?"

"Hadley," Standford growled through clenched teeth, "I am never mumpish."

"As you say, my lord. Perhaps the Spanish blue coat is just the thin' to improve your mood for the evening."

"Hadley!" the earl snapped, coming near the end of his patience.

"Oh, about the bit of uproar in here, my lord, it was caused by Miss Georgette's cat." The aged attendant took the black coat to the wardrobe and hung it up. He returned with the lighter hued garment. After laying it upon the bed, he approached his master and removed the earl's jacket as if nothing out of the ordinary had occurred.

"Just how did that involve Miss Whitney?" Standford allowed his gentleman to do his job while continuing to question the old man.

"I believe she was assistin' the young miss and her nurse in searchin' for the . . . missin' animal. Miss Whitney's a very kind young lady, sir. I'm sure you'll come to like her immensely once you get to know her." Hadley shook the coat and laid it aside, then donned white gloves in preparation for removing his lordship's boots without leaving prints.

Standford sat on the edge of a brown damask chair and extended one leg. "I am not going to have that opportunity. I learned her father is a hardened gamester and I intend to dismiss Miss Whitney in the morning. She should have told me she was Faro Freddie's daughter. It is clear she is *not* the person to be watching my aunt."

Removing the dusty Hessian, Hadley stood up and frowned at the earl. "You're goin' to fire the young miss because of her father?"

The earl shifted uncomfortably in the chair, staring at his stockinged foot to avoid the old man's knowing eyes. He was never sure why Hadley could always make him feel like a wayward lad again. "The proper thing would have been for Miss Whitney to tell me who her father was."

The valet took the boot he held and walked over to the wardrobe, placing it carefully on the floor. He meticulously began to remove his gloves, walking toward the door.

"Upon my soul, Hadley, where are you going? I must be ready before the opera begins."

"To pack my belongings, sir."

"Come back here and remove my other boot. What tomfoolery is this?"

The old man slowly turned to Standford, keeping his eyes

downcast at the Oriental rug. "My lord, I haven't told you before, but my father was shot as a poacher."

Narrowing his eyes suspiciously, the earl asked, "Why have I never heard of this?"

Hadley brought his piercing brown gaze to bear on his master before saying, " 'Tis somethin' I am not proud of, sir. No doubt Miss Whitney feels much the same about her own father's failings. I, for one, don't believe the sins of the father should be visited on the child, and so did your own father, else I wouldn't have been hired all those years ago."

Standford slumped back into the chair and stared at the old man. "You think I am being too stiff-rumped about this matter, don't you?"

Pulling the gloves back on, Hadley was suddenly the perfect Town valet. He returned to kneel before the earl. " 'Tis not my place to say, sir."

"Balderdash! When have you not spoken your mind?"

Hadley removed his lordship's other boot, a smile tugging at the corners of his mouth. "The Quality are prone to look at thin's different from ordinary folks, but to my way of thinkin', sir, Miss Whitney deserves a fair chance. Besides, she could do no worse than you have, beggin' your pardon, sir."

"But—"

"I know you've got strong notions of propriety, but the young miss is just tryin' to make a livin' like the rest of us. Will you deny her the opportunity to prove herself?"

Untying the knot in his cravat, Standford wondered if his rigid sense of what was right and proper was getting in the way of what was fair. In truth, he'd not questioned Miss Whitney about her past. He'd taken her on with the assumption that Lady Pemberton would not hire someone with a scandalous background. There had also been the matter of his feelings of guilt at having contributed to her dismissal.

In all fairness he had not informed her beforehand of his aunt's problem, so how could he judge her harshly?

"Very well, Hadley. In the interest of fair play, I shall ignore Miss Whitney's tainted ancestry." He failed to add that he would be watching the young lady closely.

Rising to finish the task of changing, a thought occurred to the earl. He would enjoy defying the arrogant Duke of Graymoor and his mealy-mouthed grandson by continuing to permit his aunt to sponsor the girl.

Hadley eyed his master thoughtfully when he heard what he was sure was a wicked chuckle.

"There's a reply to your message, ma'am," the abigail said, closing the door to Carolyn's room.

Pulling the cold compress from her puffy eyes, Carolyn sat up. "Let me see it. Don't dally." Breaking the seal, she quickly scanned the note. "I shall need my pale blue sarsenet gown this evening, Millie."

"But, ma'am, the earl and his party left for the opera 'alf an 'our ago. Moreover, you mustn't be thinkin' about goin' out in the cool night air with that 'eadache."

"Headache, pooh!" Carolyn slid from the bed with a renewed determination to secure Georgette's future despite her own heartbreak. She hurried to her dressing table to see how much damage she'd done her curls. "I am feeling much better and do not wish to spend an evening blue-deviled about my problems. Hurry, girl, I cannot keep Sir Jasper waiting."

Some thirty minutes later, she leaned close to the mirror in the Rose Drawing Room to assure herself her eyes were no longer red-rimmed. With a sigh, she realized she looked her usual self. No one would be able to tell her heart was truly broken.

Idly walking to the windows which looked out on the small garden, Carolyn stared into the darkness. She wondered how Hammond had reacted this evening when told that she was not to accompany them to the theater. Had he been disappointed? Had he worried about her? Had he given her any thought?

Feeling her throat tighten, she knew she must cease these useless thoughts. The married man must be pushed from her mind. The door opened behind Carolyn, causing her to paste a smile upon her face before she turned.

"Sir Jasper Masten, ma'am," a sour-faced Chandler droned, before leaving them alone.

"My dear, Mrs. Trevor, you are looking charming this evening." Sir Jasper strutted to her, unaware that his pea-green coat gave his face a sallow look. Taking Carolyn's hand, he pressed a kiss on her glove. "I must tell you I was surprised, but delighted to receive your note."

"Oh my, sir, 'tis some time since we were together. I hope you do not think me too forward to suggest you act as my escort." Carolyn smiled with an effort. She was not in the mood to play the coquette. "Standford arranged a party for the opera and I simply could not spend my evening at such a trifling entertainment."

"You have something more active in mind, my dear?" Masten's eyes glittered with anticipation.

Twining her arm into his, Carolyn looked up through her lashes. "I was sure that a sporting gentleman like yourself might have some suggestions."

Straightening, Sir Jasper preened for a moment at the compliment. "Why I am up to every rig in Town. What shall it be, the Barkingdales' rout, the Hanleys' masked ball? No, I have it, what do you say to an evening at Lady Halbrook's private gaming party?"

Putting her finger over her mouth pretending she was thinking, Carolyn dropped her hand, then said, "I am not in the mood to play for chicken stakes at some polite card party."

"My dear, Lady Halbrook's is not for timid gamesters. She allows the game to go as deep as the player wishes." Sir Jasper's face wreathed into a smile.

"Excellent, for I am feeling quite lucky this evening. Perhaps I will try my hand at Faro. She does have a Faro table, does she not?" Carolyn asked, worriedly.

"Faro! Yes, she does, but I have never known you to play the game before."

Walking to the sofa, Carolyn retrieved her reticule from where she'd placed it upon entering the room. "There is a first time for everything, sir. Shall we go? I must return before the . . . that is . . . I want to be home early. I always like to get up in the morning to spend time with my dear Georgette."

Extending his arm, Sir Jasper cooed, "I am at your service, dear lady. I think that this shall truly be a night that you will remember."

Carolyn suppressed a sigh. She hoped the baronet was correct about the evening and that luck was indisputably with her. She longed to take Muffin and be gone from Town and her painful dilemma.

Nine

The large black town coach emblazoned with Lord Standford's coat of arms drove slowly up Haymarket Street, joining the line of vehicles proceeding toward the King's Theater. The carriage moved in fits and starts while each arriving transport paused to unload passengers.

With her back to the horses, Lydia stared out the window while they awaited their turn to join the ladies and gentlemen outside the theater. Seated next to Lady Collingwood, Lydia attempted to ignore the lady's inane chatter, but in the close quarters of the vehicle that proved impossible.

Across from Lydia, Lord Standford sat in stony silence. Handsome in a dark blue coat over snowy white waistcoat and pantaloons, his chestnut hair reflected glints of red in the passing glow of the street lamps. Throughout the trip to the opera house he'd been politely remote, except when the countess spoke directly to him.

"La, sir, I always say you cannot entrust all the responsibilities of your household to a housekeeper. Too many of these fashionable young wives have no notion of how to go about managing their affairs properly, is that not true, Margaret?"

"Yes, Mama," Lady Margaret replied blandly.

"I know what is spent at Collingwood Place down to the last farthing. I can assure you, sir, I taught Margaret how to run a large household, as well," the grey-clad countess droned beside Lydia.

"Very wise," the earl said with little enthusiasm, turning to stare out at the passing buildings.

"Yes, I think so. But my Margaret's accomplishments don't stop there. She excels in all of the feminine arts. I knew where my duty lay in preparing her for the ultimate role any woman can aspire to. She will make a superior wife." Lady Collingwood paused and stared across at Lord Standford expectantly.

"To be sure, my lady," the earl tepidly responded.

Lydia glanced curiously at the young lady under discussion. Dressed in a yellow striped silk gown trimmed with layers of Belgium lace, Lady Margaret's skin appeared sallow in the dim carriage light. Her brown curls peeked out from under a surfeit of yellow feathers. White-clad fingers laced together in her lap, her expression was one of contentment while her mother continued to blatantly puff her off.

Why, the young woman was not even put to the blush by her mother's shockingly cow-handed matchmaking, Lydia thought. With disgust, she realized that she preferred to be on her own than to have a parent like Lady Collingwood.

"Mayhap you will tell us, sir, what *you* are looking for in a young lady?" the countess simpered while she tapped her fan impatiently in the palm of her hand. Clearly her temper was beginning to rise at the gentleman's cool responses.

"I?" Lord Standford raised one dark brow. "Madam, I am not presently looking for a young lady."

With a titter, Lady Collingwood reached across the aisle and tapped the earl's knee sharply with her fan. "You cannot fool me, my lord. All eligible young men are looking for wives. I have heard rumors—"

"Lady Margaret," Lydia hastily interrupted the countess when she realized what the foolish woman was about to say. "Do you enjoy riding?"

Startled brown eyes looked up at Lydia. A sudden spark of interest appeared in their depth and the young woman pronounced, "Miss Whitney, I enjoy the sport above all else."

"Such an exaggeration, Margaret," the countess snapped. "You will have his lordship thinking you are one of those horse-mad females who are such bores in polite company." Changing the subject, Lady Collingwood began a discourse on the latest *on-dit* while the others fell silent.

Lydia became aware of the earl's penetrating gaze resting of her. Gamely returning his look, she could not make out what emotion dwelled in his shadowed eyes. She'd wanted only to spare him Lady Collingwood's painful reminder of his humiliation at Mrs. Howell's hands. Surely he would not take offense at her trifling attempt to divert the ambitious countess.

The carriage started forward again after a brief stop, and the illumination of a street lamp gleamed brightly into the coach. Lydia noted the slight upward curve of his lordship's full mouth when he turned to stare out the window. Was it possible he appreciated her verbal ploy? A warm feeling surged through her at the thought she'd pleased him.

At last the lumbering vehicle drew up in front of the crowded theater. While the liveried footman lowered the stairs, Lydia spied the Duke and Duchess of Atherton waiting near the doors, conversing with friends. At their side stood a very tall young man with a shock of red hair and ill-fitting clothes who gestured with his hand while he spoke with the pair.

The duchess graciously acknowledged Lord Standford's party with a welcoming wave. Then, Her Grace led the awkward young man forward to greet them, the duke trailing behind.

Lord Standford exited the carriage, then turned and offered Lydia his assistance. When his large hand took hers, she felt a strange rushing of her blood from her fingertips to her toes. Glancing into his blue eyes, her heart jolted at the intense look she saw. There seemed to be only he and her in the world.

The moment was quickly lost when behind her Lydia over-

heard Lady Collingwood's fan snap as the woman reprimanded her daughter. In a loud whisper, the lady ordered,
"I absolutely forbid you to speak of horses again this evening, Margaret."

"Yes, Mama," the girl replied blandly.

Lydia was certain the earl heard her ladyship when his
hand tightened briefly on hers and an annoyed glint sprang
into his eyes. Had he developed an affection for Lady Margaret, or was he merely exhibiting his kind nature for another?

Pushing the worrisome thought from her mind, Lydia
stepped to the sidewalk and was greeted by the duchess. "My
dear, you look captivating this evening. We shall have all the
young bucks paying our box a visit."

Politely dismissing the flattery, Lydia moved forward to
allow the other ladies to step down.

The countess exited the coach. "La, Your Grace, I declare
you look younger every time I see you," the countess toadied.
She took a single step forward, her ample girth blocking
Lord Stanford's path to Lady Margaret.

Seeing a young lady alighting without assistance, the red-
haired gentleman stepped from the opposite side and gallantly offered Lady Margaret his hand.

A bright flush appeared on her cheeks, but she gladly accepted the support. Suddenly her foot caught in her mother's
voluminous grey skirt, sending her headlong into the stranger's
arms.

Lydia watched as Lady Margaret's startled brown eyes
gazed up into smiling green ones. Feeling like an intruder
on a very intimate moment despite the public realm, Lydia
glanced away.

"Ah, my wee lass, you must take care when using stairs."
The young man's voice held a pleasing Scottish lilt.

Glancing at the earl, Lydia smiled, but that gentleman's
attention was riveted on the statuesque pair. He raised an

eyebrow at the astonishing statement, while eyeing the young stranger curiously.

The duchess grinned at the towering young man who still held the tall lady. "Grierwood, I see you have made Lady Margaret Collins's acquaintance already."

"Aye, and a fine lass she is, Your Grace." The young Scot dropped his hands after assuring himself that the *lass* was soundly on her feet even as he continued to stare at the rosy-cheeked miss.

Lady Collingwood's face took on a rather severe look while she stood watching Lady Margaret's fascinated gaze rest on the unknown gentleman. "Won't you make the introductions, your Grace?" she said sternly, edging between the young man and her blushing daughter.

"Delighted to, Lady Collingwood. I should like to present my dearest friend's son, Lord Grierwood, heir of the Duke of Kinnell. He just arrived for a visit from Edinburgh. You have perchance heard of the Ross family? They are famous for their fine racing thoroughbreds."

"A duke's heir," the countess repeated, a predatory grin lighting her round face while she conspicuously stepped back and nudged her daughter forward. "My Margaret is a neck or nothing rider, my lord. Everyone in the country envies her seat on a horse."

A distinct twinkle leapt into Grierwood's green eyes. "I like a bonny lass who is a goer."

Lady Margaret fluttered her eyes, then smiled up at the young man with a genuine interest.

The duchess finished the introductions.

"Where is Lord Hammond?" the earl asked, searching the crowd for his missing friend.

"Gone to Portsmouth to greet his arriving family," the duke announced, eyeing Lady Collingwood's machinations with a slight frown. With a little shrug, he seemed to dismiss the matter and continued to speak with the earl. "Should be back in a few days. And where might the lovely Mrs. Trevor be?"

"My aunt is feeling unwell this evening. A good night's rest is all she needs to come about, she says." When the empty carriage moved away from the theater, the earl suggested, "Shall we adjourn to my box?"

Stepping forward, Standford started to escort his guests, but the red-haired Scot was before him offering an arm to Lady Margaret and her beaming mother. The ladies latched onto the gentleman like a pair of limpets.

As the earl watched the Collins ladies enter the opera house, Lydia found his expression unfathomable. She was curious if the obvious attraction between the pair in front distressed him.

The duke quickly joined his wife, whispering earnestly to her while Grierwood led the way. Her Grace gave a soft laugh at whatever the gentleman said.

Lydia found the earl beside her, arm extended. The thumping of her heart became nearly uncomfortable when she gazed up into his clear blue eyes. Her fingers tingled where they rested on the earl's arm and she forced her gaze forward to suppress her reaction.

The party made their way up the stairs. To distract herself from her strange sensations, she politely inquired, "Do you enjoy the opera, my lord?"

"Why, yes, Miss Whitney. And you?"

"I cannot say, sir, for this is my first visit." Lydia looked about her at the many paintings which cluttered the walls they passed.

"First?" The earl sounded shocked.

Looking at Lord Standford, Lydia replied, "My father was often short of funds, sir. The opera was a luxury we could ill afford."

His sculpted face suddenly became brooding as his brows flattened and his mouth drew downward. "Did you have a difficult childhood, Miss Whitney?"

"Difficult? No, my lord, I would say . . . unusual, but I had a loving father and that made up for a great deal. I think it was very hard for him after my mother died." Lydia nervously dropped her gaze to the floor. She was angry at herself for foolishly bringing up her father and her background.

The earl's voice held a gentle tone when he answered. "I am told my father missed my own mother a great deal. Unfortunately, I do not remember him as loving."

The admission was surprising. Lydia's gaze was drawn to the disturbing man at her side. She discovered Lord Standford staring at her with a kind but questioning look on his usually rigid face as if he expected her to exchange another confidence.

The look completely unnerved Lydia, causing her to tighten her grip on his arm and simply nod. His statement about his father explained much about what turned him into the stiff and proud man he showed the world.

Standford stared at Miss Whitney. Her golden eyes had shuttered from him at the subject of her father. Feeling a sense of disappointment that she'd not confided in him, the earl allowed his gaze to linger. He wanted her to trust him enough to tell him the truth about her father. But her beautiful profile was all he saw, for the young lady turned away to avoid his gaze while she feigned an interest in her surroundings.

Perhaps Hadley was right about the girl. She was not forthcoming about her father out of a sense of embarrassment, not deceit. He felt a need to reassure her, but realized it would likely make her feel more uncomfortable.

Arriving at his box, the earl pushed his troubled thoughts of the young woman aside. Once the party settled in the chairs, Standford stood quietly in the rear taking stock of his evening. Things were looking up considerably from what he'd expected—at least as far as the insipid Lady Margaret and her mother were concerned.

Was the duchess matchmaking with the inclusion of Lord Grierwood in their party or had his arrival in Town been a mere coincidence? He doubted his godmother would tell him, but she was still encouraging him to make a love match.

An instant fascination seemed to have developed between the tall pair. Even Lady Collingwood, presently directing all her attention to her new prey, had seen the young man's attraction. The earl could hear the lady rhapsodizing about her husband's fine stables and her daughter's devotion to riding—a topic she had forbidden but minutes ago.

Standford knew he owed the duchess a word of thanks for bringing the young Scot along to divert the tenacious Lady Collingwood and her eternal matchmaking. He truly wished the girl luck with the flame-haired suitor from the north.

Now he could be finished with the list the duchess had given him. She'd deliberately chosen girls who, while fitting his requirements, were unacceptable in an effort to convince him he must look for love. She planned her lesson well, he thought. She was quite the wise lady, knowing that he would dismiss her lectures on the subject out of hand.

Love. Was she right? Perhaps, but he still felt a strong sense of duty to his title. What lady could he love, while remaining true to his father's standards?

He allowed his gaze to roam, and it came to rest on Miss Whitney. He admired the slender white column of her neck. Then he chastised himself for allowing such thoughts. Why did he spend so much time in thought about Miss Whitney? He'd already decided only a *proper* young lady could be his countess. How could the daughter of a notorious gamester be considered?

Crossing his arms over his chest, the earl glumly fell into musings about Miss Whitney and her strange effect on him. The blonde beauty was happily conversing with the duke and duchess. He noted she frowned each time she glanced back and saw his aloof demeanor.

Perhaps he should visit his estate, he thought. That should clear his head of worries of both his aunt and the enticing

Miss Whitney. Deciding he would leave on the morrow, a knock sounded on the door of the box.

A smiling but hesitant Lord Devere entered. "Good evening to you all," he stated cheerfully, but had eyes only for Miss Whitney.

"Well, young man, where is my rascal of a nephew?" the duke turned and asked Arthur's friend.

The lad blushed brightly before stuttering out, "I-I believe he . . . is slightly foxed, Your Grace. D-Didn't think you would wish to see him so. Stayed in the pit."

While the duke turned to search the area before the stage for his relative, Standford took a closer look at Lord Devere. The earl strongly suspected the sprig a trifle disguised himself. His cravat was askew and his eyes slightly shot with red. What was the young whelp doing showing up in this condition?

Clearing his throat, Devere hesitantly asked, "Miss Whitney, might I have a moment of your time in the hall? There is a matter I should like to discuss."

Frowning, Standford said, "The opera is about to begin, Devere." Unconsciously, the earl's hand fingered his fob in agitation at the object of the lad's mission.

Eyeing the earl, the young man nervously tugged at his white waistcoat. "I know, sir. But I really *must* speak with the lady. I have . . . er . . . an urgent message."

Before Standford could question him further, Miss Whitney rose, a questioning look on her face while she excused herself. "I shall only be a moment, Your Grace."

"Take your time, child." The duchess smiled at the departing pair, then addressed the earl. "Andrew, come have a seat by me."

Pushing his concerns about the young man aside for the moment, the earl took the seat beside the duchess. Perhaps he was only imagining the lad was foxed.

The duke, giving up on finding his drunken nephew in the crowd below, turned and gazed at Lady Collingwood and her daughter. "Well, my boy, it would appear you will need to use Annabelle's list again for I fear the heir to a dukedom with a superior stable has the upper hand."

Eyeing the duchess, the earl arched one eyebrow. "I believe the list was intended as a lesson about the importance of love, was it not, Your Grace?"

"Was I so very obvious, my dear? Can you forgive me for such a trick? I meant it for your own good," the duchess replied kindly.

Standford reached across and took her gloved hand. "I know you did, Your Grace, and I shall try to heed your advice."

The duke took his wife's other hand, drawing it to his lips. "My wise Annabelle." He kissed the gloved surface, then added, "You will not regret your decision, my boy."

Suddenly, thinking it had been a long time since Devere had taken Miss Whitney into the hall, Standford looked back at the closed door of the box.

The duchess noted the glance and smiled. "Why are you glowering at the door? Are you worried about Miss Whitney and Devere?"

Forcing his face into a neutral mask, Standford said, "I am concerned, Your Grace. Devere seems a bit on the go. Do you think Miss Whitney will be safe in the fellow's company?"

"Matthew is a gentleman. I feel certain he knows how to conduct himself with a genteel young lady," the duchess said nonchalantly.

"Yes," the earl responded with a hint of derision as he looked over the balcony. "I see the other young swells of the *ton* are on their best behavior this evening, as well."

Her Grace raised her opera glasses to peer at the hoi polloi in the pits. The area was rife with fashionable young men vulgarly mauling the Haymarket ladies who'd come to display their feminine wares for the highest bidders. "Gad, sir! Are you comparing dear Lydia to the Fashionable Impures?"

Shocked the duchess misunderstood him, the earl turned to stare at her. "No, Your Grace. I meant that in Devere's condition *he* might not remember the difference."

Her emerald-green eyes held a strange twinkling quality when the duchess replied, "Then you must do what you think best, Standford."

Stepping in the hall with Lord Devere, Lydia was curious who would send a message to her. She allowed the young man to lead her down the passageway to a small alcove where they might be private. Folding her hands in front of her, she quietly waited for him to begin.

Devere scuffed his toe on the carpet before he started to speak. "Miss Whitney, I wish to apologize for a grave injustice I may have done you."

Lydia's hand seemed to flutter up to her mouth of its own volition. What could this pleasant young man have done which may cause her harm? "Go on, sir."

"Arthur and I popped down to Angelo's yesterday for some fencing. The lad's devilish quick with the blade. Hoping he can teach me to be as swift on my feet." Devere's eyes glazed as he appeared to drift to memories of Arthur's glories with an epee.

Losing patience with his distraction, Lydia encouraged, "Yes, yes, I am sure Mr. Landers is no end a good fellow with the sword, but you were saying . . ."

Bringing his gaze back to Lydia, the young man blushed. "Oh, yes, I fear we ran into your cousin, Lord Gravely."

"My cousin?" Lydia felt a knot form in her stomach.

"Didn't know your grandfather, the old duke, had . . . cut the connection. Never should have mentioned you were in Town and staying . . . with Standford. Thought Gravely would die of apoplexy right in Angelo's. Shabby fellow vowed to see you sent back to the country." Devere's tone became stronger and angrier as he told his tale.

"Did he now?" Lydia replied with a mixture of ire and disappointment at her cousin's reaction. The man had no power to make her do anything, she thought furiously. She dropped her hands back to her side after a moment. Why did she keep hoping that some member of her family might at least acknowledge her existence? She was clearly doomed for disappointment in her wish for familial ties.

Good heavens! What if he went to see Lord Standford? A chill ran down her spine. She would speak to Carolyn in the morning about what they must do.

Abruptly, Lord Devere grabbed her hand and began to shower kisses on her glove. "I shall not allow anyone to send you away for I fell in love with you at my mother's ball." Before she had time to react, he encircled Lydia's waist with his other hand, drawing her close.

At first shocked, she stiffened at his improper embrace. She quickly came to realize the young man was foxed when the odor of brandy wafted over her. Placing her one free hand on his chest, she tried to hold him at bay. "Please stop, Lord Devere, I am in no danger from Lord Gravely."

In the grip of strong passions, the young man ignored her statement. Instead, he pulled her close and forced a wet kiss on her protesting mouth.

Feeling like she might faint as the gentleman crushed her to him, Lydia swooned into Devere's chest. When he was suddenly jerked away from her, she nearly stumbled forward before regaining her balance.

Positioned with his hand on the round-eyed fellow's neck, Lord Standford barked, "Is this how you deliver a message, Devere?"

The young man's face became nearly as red as the ruby tucked in his crumpled cravat. "Intentions . . . honorable, sir. Want to marry the young lady."

Standford released Lord Devere and stepped back as if his hand was burned. Lydia noted his lips thinned and his brows came together. "Then I suggest you conduct a proper courtship, sir."

Devere backed away from the earl, bowing and weaving his way up the hall. "I shall, Lord Standford, behave a proper gentleman when next we meet. 'Pon my honor, sir."

Feeling nothing but relief to be rescued, Lydia smiled at the earl. There was no answering gesture. Instead, she saw a muscle twitch in his jaw before he stiffly said, "Miss Whitney, kissing gentlemen in public is not done, even if one intends on marrying the fellow."

A gasp escaped Lydia's shocked lips. An angry flush warmed her cheeks and her hands clenched into fists. "Do you think I encouraged that foolish boy to kiss me? Sir, do not take your bad humor out on me."

"Bad humor?" Chestnut eyebrows raised in surprise.

"Yes, you have been brooding all evening since you were cut out of Lady Margaret's affections by Lord Grierwood. 'Tis very ungallant, I must say." Lydia, lifting her chin, turned and left the speechless earl to return to the box.

The chattering voices at the party barely penetrated Carolyn's shocked stupor while she sat at a table in the refreshment room of Lady Halbrook's home. She'd abandoned Sir Jasper at the tables, declaring herself famished, but she'd left her plate untouched on the table before her.

How had she managed to lose nearly five thousand pounds in just a few short hours? Her fingernails dug into the palms of her hands while the sum echoed in her mind.

Dear God, Andrew was right. She was a foolish woman. A soft moan escaped her lips when she thought of having to face her staid nephew and tell him of her folly. She would be banished from Town and have to live under the rigid supervision of Standford for the rest of her unhappy life. "What have I done, Muffin?" she whispered to herself while tears welled up in her eyes.

A shadow fell across her. Blinking away the tears, she looked up and discovered Lord Digby, plate in hand, gesturing to the empty chair beside her. His cravat sagged limply about a straw-brown coat, and his large girth prevented his white waistcoat from meeting his pantaloons, leaving a bulge of lawn shirt exposed. "May I join you, my dear?"

Wanly she answered, "If you desire, sir."

The baron set the heaping plate on the table and lowered his bulk into the gilt chair, which protested at the excess weight. Surveying the treats he'd selected for himself, Lord Digby crooned, "Quite a run of bad luck tonight, dearest. Washburn informed me soon as I entered the room. I think your friend Masten did you no favor bringing you to Lady Halbrook's."

Watching pudgy fingers pop a small tart into his greedy mouth, Carolyn sighed. " 'Twas my own fault, sir. I cannot blame any other."

A large hand suddenly covered one of her own. Carolyn looked down to discover the baron's moist hand gently holding hers. Glancing up she saw only sympathy in the small brown eyes looking out of the round face, and again she felt like weeping.

"I would do anything to help you, dear lady. Please remember that my offer of marriage still stands. A husband would be honor-bound to pay his wife's debts."

Why couldn't she have fallen in love with Lord Digby, Carolyn wondered as the gentleman returned to his meal. Despite his slovenly appearance, he'd been only kind to her.

Carolyn knew she would never be happy without Lord Hammond. Why not accept the baron's offer? She would assure Muffin's future and he would gladly redeem her gambling losses. What did it really matter now?

Suddenly, sitting up straighter, Carolyn said, "Very well, Lord Digby, I shall consent to be your wife."

Pushing the plate aside, the baron quickly availed himself of Carolyn's gloved hands. Placing a kiss which smudged strawberry preserves on the back of each, he exclaimed, "You have made me the happiest of men. I shall call on Lord Standford on the morrow. We shall—"

"No!" Carolyn jumped from the chair. "I wish it to be an elopement." The earl had been disdainful of Digby on several occasions and he would question the rushed marriage. She was determined he never know about this disastrous evening at the tables.

Dropping the lady's hands, Lord Digby sat back in his chair in surprise. "Elopement? You wish to fly to Gretna Green?"

Seeing the shock in the man's eyes, Carolyn quickly amended, "Nothing so tawdry, sir. I have longed to be married on the continent. Italy, perhaps. You know we must travel with my child and her Nurse. 'Twill all be quite proper."

Digby appeared unconvinced of the wisdom of rushing off to Italy. Shrewdly, Carolyn added, "I hear that the Italians set a magnificent table . . ."

The baron's small eyes disappeared into tiny slits as a smile came to his face. "The marriage will be as you wish, my dear. When shall we depart?"

"Shall we say seven, sir?" Carolyn knew she would lose her nerve if she did not act quickly.

"Seven?" Lord Digby's eyes widened in horror. "I *always* breakfast at seven, my dear. Never miss a meal, my mother always says. First I must send word to my man of business to dispatch your debt, then I shall have a traveling coach just around the corner at eight on the morrow. Will that be soon enough, dear heart?"

With a sinking feeling in her chest, Carolyn struggled to smile at the gentleman. "Perfect, . . . Chester."

Ten

A fitful night was Lydia's reward for being cross with Lord Standford at the opera. Awakening just after ten, she lay in her bed remembering the uncomfortable silence between them the rest of the evening. Even now she got angry that he thought she'd encouraged young Devere.

Realizing she couldn't spend the day in thought about the earl, she decided to dress and see how Carolyn fared this morning. Quickly, she washed and donned a pale blue morning dress, then pulled her silvery blonde hair into a neat chignon at her neck.

Satisfied with the neat picture she presented, Lydia exited her room. In the hall, she discovered Boots, who meowed earnestly at her appearance. Lydia stooped to stroke his large head. "Did you escape the nursery again, old boy?"

The black and white cat began to rub against Lydia as if she were his beloved master. "Are you hungry? Is that what all this affection is about? Did Georgette go to the park and forget to feed you?"

Boots gave a throaty trill while looking up at Lydia as if he understood her every word.

"Follow me then and I shall share my breakfast with you, but first a stop at Carolyn's room." Rising, Lydia walked toward her mistress's door.

A sharp knock drew no response. Again she tried, listening intently, but only the noise of the meowing cat filled the hallway. With a shrug, Lydia reasoned that Carolyn was better and most likely at the park with Georgette.

"Shall we go break our fast, Mr. Boots?" The cat darted in front of her when she walked toward the stairs as if he knew the treat at the end of the journey to the breakfast parlor.

The pair made their way to the front hallway. Entering the breakfast parlor, Lydia was disappointed to discover the sunlit chamber empty. Somehow she'd expected, or was it *hoped*, to find the earl lingering over his coffee. She wasn't sure if she was relieved or disappointed not to have an opportunity to offer his lordship an explanation for her actions at the opera.

At the buffet, she crumbled bacon and poured a small amount of cream into a bowl for the cat who meowed impatiently for his meal. She placed the dishes on the floor for Boots. Silence reigned in the parlor as the feline devoured the food.

Not really hungry, Lydia placed a slice of toast on a plate and raspberries in a bowl. She took a seat and poured herself a cup of coffee, then while she ate, fell to pondering her strange behavior around the earl. Why did he exasperate her so with his stiff manners and overly proud bearing? Why was it so important to her that he understand about the unwanted kiss?

Before Lydia could arrive at an answer, a scratching sounded at the breakfast parlor door. Millie entered with a quick curtsey, carrying a letter. "Morning, miss. I've a note for you from Mrs. Trevor." Placing the slightly crumpled letter on the table, the maid stepped back, nervously wringing her hands while she awaited Lydia's response.

"Good morning, Millie. How is your mistress feeling?" Lydia smiled up at the servant, noting the girl avoided her direct gaze.

"Well, miss, I think you should be readin' Mrs. Trevor's

note and you'll know," the overwrought abigail replied with
a slight sniffle.

With a sense of foreboding, Lydia quickly opened the message with trembling fingers. A gasp of horror escaped her
lips as the contents of the note were read.

Carolyn had eloped!

The tear-stained letter was full of apologies for her unseemly behavior, but the widow informed her companion
that she was off to Italy with Lord Digby. She'd consented
to become his bride.

Digby! The matter became worse and worse. How could
Carolyn marry the baron when she'd vowed to Lydia to marry
for love? Had the widow argued with Lord Standford after
they returned last evening? This was strange conduct even
for the volatile Carolyn.

"Millie, does anyone else know Mrs. Trevor is gone?"

"Miss, I didn't even ken it until goin' to take the lady her
chocolate this mornin'. Packed herself, she did, and the little
miss and her nurse are missin' from the nursery." The maid
pulled a tattered handkerchief from the pocket of her apron
and began to dab her eyes. "Do you reckon his lordship will
be angry with me, miss, for not stoppin' Mrs. Trevor?"

"No, Millie." Lydia felt a knot form in her stomach at the
thought of telling the earl about his aunt. More than likely
Lydia would be the one blamed.

Forcing herself to think rationally, Lydia felt determination
form like a rock in her. She would not be intimidated by fear
of her undisclosed past this time, for unless they stopped
Carolyn, the lady would be doomed to a loveless marriage.

Rising with a forced calm, Lydia placed a soothing hand
on the agitated servant's arm. "Don't worry about his lordship. I shall be the one to inform him of Mrs. Trevor's departure and assure him no one was to blame."

A look of relief flooded Millie's features, and she gave a
slight curtsey. "Thank you, miss." The maid swiftly left the
room as if in fear of meeting his lordship.

Whatever would Lydia say to Lord Standford? She walked around the small dining table to the window where Boots sat on the marble sill, diligently cleaning his face. She remembered the conversation of several days before when the earl had disparaged the rotund baron. Would Standford save Carolyn from her impetuous flight?

Lydia truly hoped the earl would not be intractable and would consider what was best for his aunt. He *must* stop this disastrous elopement. The elegant widow would be miserable with the likes of Digby, despite his fortune.

Staring out into the garden, Lydia's thoughts reeled at the news. If Standford refused to stop the marriage, then somehow she would follow the pair herself. Mayhap she could reason with the impulsive lady. Why would Carolyn make such a rash decision?

Giving herself a mental shake, Lydia knew she must speak with his lordship at once. Carolyn must be stopped.

The breakfast parlor door suddenly opened, causing Lydia to turn with trepidation. She was relieved to discover only a red-faced Chandler, who stood stiffly in the portal looking like someone had wounded his sense of decorum. "Miss Whitney, Lord Washburn is here asking for Mrs. Trevor. Millie informed me madam is out, but his lordship demands to see you in her stead."

Not now, Lydia thought, but kept her exasperation from showing. "Very well, Chandler. Where is the gentleman?"

"I put him in the morning parlor, miss."

Taking Carolyn's letter from the table, Lydia folded it and placed it in her pocket. It wouldn't do to have the earl find it before Lydia had a chance to speak with him—which she must do at the first opportunity.

"Is Lord Standford presently at home, Chandler?"

"At present, miss, but I believe he intends to leave for his estate this morning."

"Please inform his lordship that I must have a word with him. The matter is most urgent."

One white eyebrow arched in surprise before the butler's face became a mask of propriety. "Very good, miss."

Quickly making her way to the small room at the rear of the hallway, Lydia resolved to send Washburn on his way. She or Lord Standford must follow the eloping couple or they would be aboard ship and married before anyone could convince Carolyn to think better of this plan.

When Lydia opened the door to the morning parlor, the large cat darted past her into the sun drenched room. The animal clearly missed Georgette.

Focusing her mind on the problem at hand, she turned her attention to the Earl of Washburn, who stood across the room examining a small painting on the wall. "My lord, I must apologize for my delay for we are at sixes and sevens here this morning. As you have been informed, Mrs. Trevor is gone. What can I do for you, sir?"

Washburn, dressed in a holly-green morning coat and tan buckskins, frowned at Lydia. Reaching into his coat he retrieved a clutter of small bits of paper. "I informed Mrs. Trevor last night I would be round this morning to redeem her vowels, for I am going to Bath on business. Now I find the lady conveniently not at home, Miss Whitney."

Lydia felt a sudden hollow feeling in her stomach. His lordship must be mistaken. Last night Carolyn was home ill. Was she not?

But the martial light in the elderly earl's faded brown eyes and the crushed notes in his hand told a different tale. "Lord Washburn, where did you game with Mrs. Trevor last evening? I did not think she went out."

"Met her at Lady Halbrook's. Sir Jasper brought her and they gamed the night away, all to my good fortune." The old earl smirked.

Her throat suddenly dry, Lydia rasped out, "What is the sum you are due, sir?"

"Four thousand six hundred pounds to be exact, miss, and I expect to be paid promptly."

Lydia's knees felt like they might give way as the gentleman named the sum. She longed to drop into the gold damask chair beside her, but she couldn't allow herself that weakness. Carolyn must be protected from scandal.

Squaring her shoulders for courage, Lydia fabricated an excuse. "I am sure Mrs. Trevor merely forgot the matter, your lordship. An urgent situation arose at her estate and she was required to leave before dawn to return to Leeds."

"This is no trifling sum, young lady. Do you expect me to believe the lady forgot her obligation?" Washburn scoffed.

Walking past the grey-haired peer while pretending to gaze into the small garden, Lydia allowed a silence to fall. Then she turned to look back disdainfully. "Do you actually believe the Earl of Standford's aunt cannot make good on her debts, sir?"

A flush appeared on Lord Washburn's wrinkled countenance. "I did not mean to imply—"

"Are you so short of funds you must dun a lady before noon of the next day then? I am sure Lord Standford will advance you a small sum, if that is the case." Lydia held her breath. The earl was the last person she wanted to know of this monstrous debt. He might wash his hands of his aunt and her finances.

Lord Washburn's chin rose as Lydia's barb appeared to wound his pride. "If Mrs. Trevor is away, I shall await her return for my payment. Inform the lady I called and shall again when I return to Town at the end of the week." He gave a stiff bow and exited the small sunlit room.

The door barely closed before Lydia collapsed into a chair near the window, dropping her head into her hands. What had Carolyn been about? She'd lost a small fortune. Lord Digby must have seen an opportunity and offered to pay the exorbitant amount in exchange for marriage. Dear Carolyn would have been frantic.

Feeling something brush her leg, Lydia lifted her head. Boots rubbed against her skirts. Dropping her hand, she stroked the animal's back. "Old boy, I fear matters are in a rare tangle."

And what of Carolyn's broken promise? Lydia wondered as a cloud covered the sun, taking the luster from the garden beyond the glass. She would not think of that now, only of convincing Lord Standford to go after his aunt and bring her back. She and Carolyn could worry about how to pay Lord Washburn once they had the widow safely back at Cavendish Square.

Realizing that Carolyn might be halfway to the coast by now, Lydia rose, rushing from the room. She must find Lord Standford.

Standford paused at the foot of the stairs, pulling on his driving gloves. "Do you have any messages for me to convey at Crosswell, Hadley?"

"Messages? No, just ask the head groom how that nephew of mine is doin' in the stables. I worry about that cub, him bein' so full of hisself and all." The valet stood two stairs above his master awaiting the earl's departure.

"A Hadley family trait?"

The valet did not raise so much as an eyebrow at the earl's teasing tone. Hadley was merely pleased that his lordship seemed to be coming out of the dark mood he'd been in since returning from the opera. Mayhap the message that Miss Whitney wished to see him had lightened his spirits. "Aye, that's what's got me on the fidget for the lad."

"Lord Standford!"

Miss Whitney practically shouted his name. The earl turned to discover her rushing from the rear hallway. The color was high in the young lady's cheeks and her white teeth tugged at her lovely lower lip while she hastened to him. She placed a slender hand on his slate-blue jacket.

"Mrs. Trevor has eloped, sir."

Somehow he was only cognizant of the lady's warm hand

on his sleeve. Then the words penetrated his bemused brain. "Eloped?"

Suddenly looking down at where her hand rested, Miss Whitney blushed. Withdrawing it, she placed her lovely white fingers at her throat. Appearing to have trouble with the words, she whispered, "Yes . . . with Lord Digby."

"Digby!" Standford growled.

While the full import of what Miss Whitney said whirled in his confused mind, Standford watched Hadley descend to the equally distressed young woman. Taking her by the arm the valet ushered her across the hall to the library. "I suspect a little brandy might calm you, miss."

Standford followed, wrath beginning to stir in his stomach. Why the deuce would his aunt elope? Carolyn had shown no interest in the baron whatsoever. He'd discouraged her from allowing the old pudding-bag to dangle after her when the stout peer began to show a marked interest, but she'd only laughed at the notion. There was some mystery here and he would get to the bottom of the affair.

Closing the library door, the earl barely missed the curious Boots who squeezed through the closing portal and joined them. The creature began to prowl the room, reminding Standford of his little cousin. "Did my aunt leave Georgette here?"

Taking the glass of brandy, Miss Whitney sat like over-starched linen on the edge of a chair. "No, she took her daughter and Nurse along."

"Why would she elope with Digby?" the earl angrily questioned.

Staring at the glass in her hand, Miss Whitney softly said, "You must ask Carolyn that question, my lord. I was not in her confidence."

Standford was baffled. He drew his gaze away from the pale-faced young lady sipping daintily from the glass of liquor and began to pace back and forth in agitation. His anger at his aunt so great, he could not speak at present.

After several moments Hadley asked, "What do you plan to do, my lord?"

"The woman belongs in Bedlam. Such a want of breeding, of proper behavior. I would not have believed it of my own aunt. I have a good mind to leave her to endure the consequences of her foolish behavior."

Leaping to her feet, Lydia boldly protested, "You cannot, sir. You must save her from this rash action. She has a truly good heart. She simply does not think situations through very well."

Straightening, the earl coldly retorted, "I am well aware of my responsibilities to my family, Miss Whitney. I shall do my duty and pursue her."

The earl observed two warning flags of color rise on the lady's pale cheeks and her mouth thinned while an angry gleam sparked in her tawny eyes. Why the devil was she annoyed with him?

Hadley, whose gaze rested on the irate young woman, appeared to deem it a good time to intervene. In a matter-of-fact tone he inquired, "Then you shall return Mrs. Trevor to us, sir?"

Miss Whitney lowered her burning gaze from the earl's to the Oriental rug, pressing her lips together tightly. She was clearly resisting the urge to give him a stinging retort.

Puzzled by the young lady's reaction, the earl nodded. "Aye, I am off to Gretna Green."

"Hah, then are you eloping, too, sir?" she said.

"Of course not. Don't be impertinent, Miss Whitney. I intend to reach Gretna Green ahead of Carolyn and Digby."

"Then I should think you will have a great deal of difficulty in doing so, my lord, since they are on their way to the Continent."

Standford straightened his coat and eyed the young woman glaring at him. He cleared his throat. "Perhaps, Miss Whitney, you should tell me what you know."

The young woman pulled a letter from her pocket and held it out to him. He took the missive and scanned the contents.

"The Continent? This is a very strange elopement. I must surmise then that they will go to Digby's yacht. I have seen his craft harbored at Southhampton where I keep my own."

Hadley cleared his throat. "And just what might you be plannin' once you catch the pair, my lord? 'Tis not like Mrs. Trevor is some schoolroom miss to be ordered about."

"Why, I shall convince her of the folly of this scheme. If nothing else, I must warn her of her future mother-in-law." Standford watched as his valet and Miss Whitney exchanged looks of doubt.

Hadley drew his hands behind his back and gave the earl a disbelieving stare. "You and your aunt have rubbed against one another like two hedgehogs in a poacher's sack for a month. Now you think you can convince the lady to give up this mad scheme?"

Placing his hands on his hips in aggravation, Standford stiffly asked, "What do you suggest, Hadley? I cannot allow her to marry that gluttonous fool, Digby. The man is obsessed with his palate, not my aunt. I daresay his mother is behind this ill-planned marriage. 'Tis said it is the only matter about which he has ever defied the old harridan. Obviously she won the point at last."

"I wouldn't be knowin' what's behind any of this, my lord. I do know that in your present mood you couldn't convince Mrs. Trevor to take a pail of water if her skirts were on fire."

The earl shook his head, allowing his hands to drop to his side in frustration. "What am I to do? I cannot shoot Digby, no matter the provocation, and whisk my aunt away as in one of Mrs. Radcliffe's absurd novels."

Stepping forward, Miss Whitney interjected, "Then take me with you, my lord. I have a great fondness for your aunt and can assist you."

"Miss Whitney! 'Twould not be proper." Despite his protest, the earl knew he was not adverse to the lady's company.

Then a thought struck him. Did the young woman know more about this elopement than she'd let on? She had been less than forthcoming about her father.

"Why ever not, sir?" the valet asked, interrupting the earl's thoughts. "You should be able to overtake them in a matter of hours, what with your lordship handlin' the ribbons. Nothin' unseemly about that. Why, I shall come for propriety."

"On the tiger's perch? Hadley, you are too old. You will be rattled to bits at the spanking pace I must travel."

"Old!" the grey-haired man barked. "I am not ready to stick my spoon in the wall just yet, sir."

Eyeing his much offended valet, the earl stiffly said, "Very well, Miss Whitney, Hadley. Be out front in ten minutes or I shall leave without the pair of you."

The young lady uttered a clipped thank you, then exited the room leaving the door ajar. The large black and white cat trailed nonchalantly behind her.

The earl turned to Hadley. "I am not sure of the wisdom of taking the pair of you. You will only slow me down."

"Never fear, my lord," the old man said, ignoring the earl's argument. "The young lady has a quick mind. Between us, we shall think of somethin' to convince Mrs. Trevor to return home unwed."

"How much farther, Mama?"

Carolyn opened her eyes, and forced a smile for Georgette. The child sat on the floor in the aisle of the carriage, her doll in her lap. The widow's head was beginning to ache and she was having second thoughts about this runaway marriage. "We are going all the way to the south coast, Muffin. I think it will be several hours before we reach Lord Digby's yacht."

"I am tired of riding. I wanna go back and play with Boots." The child, discovering a wicker basket under the seat, pulled it toward her, opening and closing the top as if it were some new game.

"Boots will be waiting for you when we return, my dear. For now just play quietly." Carolyn looked to her side where Lord Digby sat, a bored expression on his face while he stared out the window. He'd been in a chipper mood when the trip began, but the monotony of the rocking vehicle had dampened his spirits along with the others'. Georgette's third question about how much farther they must travel had placed a frown on his round face.

Glancing down at the child, the baron winced each time the lid of the basket banged shut. "Must you do that, my . . . dear child."

Across the aisle, a dour-faced Nurse immediately rushed to Muffin's defense. "Miss Georgette is simply amusin' herself. Ain't doin' no 'arm to nuthin'." The servant clearly disliked Lord Digby.

Carolyn closed her eyes again. The continuous sound of the baron's hamper snapping shut echoed in the coach. She fell to wondering what her life would be like with Chester. He was kind, when it did not inconvenience him, and wealthy, but she could not imagine herself in love with the gentleman. Not as she loved Hammond.

Should she tell Lord Digby to turn around and return to London? She would have to face Andrew and suffer his endless lectures on his notion of proper behavior. That she could endure, but she knew he wanted her back in Leeds, living what he thought was the correct life of a widow. Muffin would have no chance for a Season. They would be treated like impoverished gentry who were largely ignored by Society. The thought was intolerable.

Lost in her sad thoughts, Carolyn drifted into a light sleep. She was unsure how long she'd slept when she felt a tapping on her knee and Georgette's faint voice.

"Mama . . . Mama . . . Mama?" The child's voice grew more urgent with each call.

Carolyn instantly awoke to find Georgette looking ghostly pale and rocking limply with the motion of the carriage, a scattering of pastry crumbs clinging around her mouth.

The baron, who was gently snoring, gave a sudden loud snort and awakened. "Are we at the Southhampton?"

"No, Chester," Carolyn answered the gentleman, then asked her daughter, "What is wrong, Muffin?"

"I don't feel good, Mama."

Quickly placing her hand over Georgette's forehead, Carolyn was relieved to feel no excessive warmth, but the dull-eyed look on the child's face concerned her. "Nurse, I think Georgette is sickening."

The old servant leaned forward, touching the child's cheek. Her hand brushed at the crumbs. "What've you been eatin', little one?"

"Apricot tarts," Georgette moaned, slumping against her mother's knees.

"Apricot tarts! Those were mine!" Lord Digby whined, pulling the basket up to his knees and opening the lid. "Cook put lemon ones in for the rest of you."

"I don't like lemon," the child emphatically replied.

A look of horror filled the baron's face as he pulled several napkins from the hamper. "Would you look at this!" He extended the wicker container to Carolyn as his expression changed to one of outrage. "Madam, your child has taken a bite out of every tart in here. There are none left undamaged for me."

Nurse immediately unleashed her sharp tongue on the stout baron. "Aye, and 'twould appear that you've taken many a bite from many a tart yourself, my lord." The woman allowed her gaze to fall to Lord Digby's round middle.

"Nurse!" Carolyn exclaimed. "You will apologize to his lordship for your impertinence and you, too, Georgette, for eating his tarts!"

"Mama, I think I am going to be sick." Georgette clutched her stomach.

With a knowing smile, Nurse leaned back against the squabs. "Beggin' your pardon, my lord. Forgot myself in concern over the little one. But unless you want them tarts back right away, I'd be stoppin' this carriage."

Lord Digby's small, dark eyes grew round, and he looked as if he might leap from the moving vehicle. He suddenly yanked the window open. "Hawks, Hawks, you must stop immediately! Do you hear me? At once!"

The coach jostled the occupants when it veered sharply to the right and came to a jarring halt. Carolyn could see a small inn that looked ancient with mullioned windows surrounded by ivy so thick the surface beneath was obscured.

In the doorway stood a plump little man, a tankard in his hand, who stared at the large carriage in astonishment. A cloud of dust from the arriving vehicle rolled in upon him, sending him into a fit of coughing.

Lord Digby shouted, "The stairs, man, lower the stairs. Be quick about it."

Nurse now held the moaning Georgette. With the aisle empty, Lord Digby, in an ill-mannered rush which belied his girth, exited to the ground ahead of the women after his footman hurriedly opened the carriage door and lowered the stairs. Pulling a handkerchief from his pocket, he mopped his sweating face in relief at his narrow escape.

Carolyn was assisted down by the footman, then she waited to help the sagging Georgette. "Come, Muffin. You will feel more the thing when we have a cool cloth on your head."

With Nurse helping from behind and Carolyn in front, they got the child to the ground. Then mother and nurse each took an arm and the trio began to walk slowly toward the inn door which was empty, the plump man having disappeared.

Lord Digby stood by the entrance fanning himself with his lace-trimmed handkerchief. "Devilishly inconvenient place to be sick. Cannot expect a decent meal in these out of the way hostelries."

A pink-cheeked lady wiping her hands on an apron appeared. "Oh, your worship, we be honored. Don't get much Quality stoppin' at the White Boar."

"My good woman, we need a room for Mrs. Trevor's daughter," the baron stated in a condescending tone. "And I shall require some refreshments."

"There's only the one bedchamber, your worship and ye be welcomed to what there is to eat." The lady backed into the inn, bowing as if royalty had arrived.

"Come along, Muffin," Carolyn crooned.

Just as the trio reached the inn, Georgette gave way to her nausea and deposited a vast quantity of the remains of apricot tarts over Lord Digby's shining Hessian boots. But before Carolyn could utter a single word of apology, the baron's small eyes rolled back in his head and he fell backward to the dirt in a dead faint.

Eleven

The yard at the Royal Arms, one of the largest posting inns in East Grinstead, teemed with a variety of carriages. Standford stood impatiently by the doorway watching two burly ostlers change his spent team. Jostled by a saucy brown-haired chit and her youthful companion just leaving the premises, the earl glared with hauteur at the pair who begged his pardon but otherwise ignored him, so intent was their laughing conversation.

Eyeing the rakish tilt of the chit's hat, he was reminded of himself and Carolyn at that age. His aunt had come to visit Crosswell during his thirteenth summer. Married but a year, she'd at first been all dignity and orders, but within a day her natural enthusiasm had resurfaced. The week was one of the more memorable of his childhood, for his father was in London on business. Standford had engaged in picnics and jaunts to local natural wonders and simply rode for sheer pleasure. Carolyn made him laugh as he never had before.

For that brief time, he'd had no thoughts of the property, the tenants, or his duty until his parent arrived and quarreled with his aunt for taking him away from his studies and responsibilities. Her visits had never again been the same, but he'd developed an abiding fondness for his mother's sister. Their meetings came less and less frequently as the earl aged. Over time Standford suppressed his frivolous side in favor of his father's wishes.

Standford found it hard to believe that the willful widow

who'd come to Town was that same carefree, amusing creature of so long ago. Those fond memories had been lost amidst worries of his aunt's finances and lack of propriety. At the moment, he was excessively angry with Carolyn, but he could not allow her to make the mistake of marrying that fool, Digby.

Coming out of his musings, the earl nodded to the ostlers who shouted they were finished changing his team. Quickly scanning the busy yard, his frustration mounted when he realized that Miss Whitney and Hadley were nowhere to be seen. They must set out at once.

Turning to summon the landlord, the earl spied Miss Whitney coming down the stairs of the inn. Even in his agitated mood, he admired the young woman with her silver-blonde hair framing her pink, wind-kissed cheeks. The purple spencer she'd donned over her lilac gown and matching high-crowned bonnet suited her. He liked the way her eyes lit like burnished gold when they came to rest on him.

"Have you discovered any news of Lord Digby's coach, my lord?"

"No," the earl snapped, suddenly angry with his inappropriate thoughts of her. Controlling his irritation, he continued in a milder tone. "The landlord saw no such vehicle stop. We must find Hadley and set forth for Southhampton. We have lost a good deal of time."

"Lord Digby must change teams, as well, sir, but do let us hurry." Miss Whitney made her way to the carriage without a backward glance. She had been surprisingly quiet during the journey, but none of the trio were inclined to chatter, so somber was their mood.

The young lady was already seated in his carriage, scrutinizing the crowded street for the missing valet, when the earl arrived. He tossed a coin to the ostler at the horses' heads, then climbed up beside Miss Whitney to await Hadley's return.

His aunt and her indiscreet actions troubled his thoughts.

"Have you any notion what could have motivated my aunt to set off on this foolish escapade?"

Miss Whitney cast him a guilty look, then dropped her gaze to her tightly clasped hands. "My lord, you read the letter she left. Carolyn told me nothing but what I related to you earlier."

When she continued to avoid his eye, a thought struck him. Could it be possible that he was the reason for Carolyn's flight? He must know. "Miss Whitney, I am your employer. I demand to be told what you know."

An angry spark glistened in her tawny eyes when her gaze snapped to his face. "Sir, Carolyn is my friend as well as my mistress. I have a great affection for her and as such, I shall not discuss her when she is not present."

"I take leave to inform you that I too have an affection for my aunt. Why else do you think I would dash about the countryside in this ridiculous manner, Miss Whitney?"

"I believe you informed me that duty was your reason, sir." She glared back at him, her beautiful eyes scornful.

Standford made a dismissive gesture with his hand. His lips pursed in annoyance then he growled, "I spoke in anger in the library, but I had great cause. Her behavior is scandalous, but regardless, I do care what happens to Aunt Carolyn and her daughter. I wish to know what caused my aunt's elopement."

"Then you must ask Carolyn." Miss Whitney's lips pressed closed. She turned away from the earl, leaving him frustrated and suspicious that she wouldn't tell him what she knew of Carolyn's elopement.

"Have you in some way aided my aunt in defiance of common sense, Miss Whitney?" The earl felt an urge to shake the young woman beside him.

"How dare you, sir? 'Twas not I who tried to bully and control the woman with every breath. She was used to being the mistress of her own household, not required to look to another for permission for the smallest pleasure. Small wonder she fled your autocratic rule, my lord."

Just as the earl was about to defend himself, Hadley arrived and climbed into the tiger's seat behind the carriage. Turning to stare at his valet, Standford was suddenly aware of a tingling feeling as his knees brushed against the young woman in the close space of the curricle. He drew back as if he'd been stung, then felt foolish that so brief an encounter should set his senses afire. Annoyed with himself for such a masculine response, he forced the thoughts from his mind, trying to focus on his aunt's plight.

Thinking he had his emotions under control, Standford glanced at the young lady. He was determined to learn what she knew.

Miss Whitney's back was rigid and she stared over the horses' heads, ignoring him with studied determination. Standford knew he would receive no information about his aunt from this stubborn miss. Disappointment stirred in him at her defiance, or was he dissatisfied with himself for how he'd bungled dealing with Carolyn and Miss Whitney?

Ignoring the heavy feeling in his chest, the earl turned his attention to the old man behind him who stared straight ahead. His lined face was neutral, giving no indication he heard the fight between the pair in the carriage. Standford waited expectantly but the valet remained unexpectedly silent.

In frustration, the earl roared, "What say you, Hadley?"

"Well, sir, I wonder, do we return to London? I think there was one or two bumps in the road you missed."

"Don't be ridiculous! We did not come all this way to go back before we find Aunt Carolyn and Digby. I warned you not to come. Are you all right?"

Hadley looked from the earl's rigid face to Miss Whitney's erect posture, then replied, "I'm fine, and I'm glad you intend to pursue the lady. The landlord at the inn down the street says Lord Digby's carriage stopped there but two hours ago."

"Deuce take it, Hadley! Why didn't you tell me when we first arrived?" The earl gathered his reins.

"Truth to tell, I weren't sure if the pair of you could make it to Southhampton without coming to cuffs. In my opinion, it don't make no never mind why the lady chose Digby as a tenant-for-life. The first business is to give her time to think better of her choice. Mrs. Trevor might be rash, but she usually comes to the right of it given a little time and patience."

"I quite agree, Hadley," Miss Whitney added, a satisfied smile on her face as she turned to smile back at him.

Without further comment, the earl set the carriage in motion, threading his way through the crowded street. When the vehicle reached the open road, the earl glanced briefly at the mute young lady at his side. Her lovely face held a worried frown and her eyes seemed to have a distant look as if she were deep in thought. Miss Lydia Whitney was definitely hiding something about his aunt from him.

The curricle bowled along at a spanking pace with the earl grimly driving the horses to an inch. Lydia sat quietly, uncomfortable with the earl in such close proximity. She should be thinking of ways to convince Carolyn to return, but each time the earl brushed against her as he tooled his carriage a strange sensation swept up her arm.

With an effort, she ignored her reaction and concentrated on what she must do once they found Carolyn. There must be some way to persuade her to return home unwed. Fearing what the earl would say to his aunt in his present mood, Lydia decided she must speak with Carolyn alone, but how? Standford was already suspicious. Carolyn should be the one to tell about the gaming debts as she saw fit.

Stealing a peek at the stern face of Lord Standford, Lydia believed the earl when he said he had affection for his impetuous relative. Duty and propriety was such a part of his life, however, he didn't know how to show Carolyn he cared.

Unexpectedly Hadley leaned forward, then shouted, "Up ahead, sir! See the old hedge tavern. Is that not Lord Digby's coat of arms on the coach in the yard?"

"Yes," the earl tightly bit out.

A large traveling coach with team still attached stood in front of an ancient building whose looks Lydia thought picturesque despite her worries. Except for two young boys at the head of the restive horses, there was no one about.

With great skill, Lord Standford reined in his team, and brought their carriage to a halt beside Digby's coach. "Lad, walk these cattle until they are cooled. We shall need them again soon."

Jumping down, the earl assisted Lydia to the ground while Hadley exited the tiger's seat. Then Lord Standford started for the inn, leaving them beside his vehicle. The valet called to him. "Sir, best take Miss Whitney or you might frighten Mrs. Trevor."

An incensed look appeared on the earl's face when he paused, speaking to the old man in an annoyed manner. "I come to think that you believe me an ogre who shall eat Aunt Carolyn as soon as I open my mouth."

Lydia cut her gaze to Hadley, who showed no trepidation at the earl's tone. The valet said, "My lord, you've a great heart, but you've a mite of trouble showin' your kinder feelin' to others. Remember that Mrs. Trevor's actions speak of desperation. Miss Whitney might do much to calm the lady's fears, whatever they might be. You must handle her gently."

"Very well. Come along Miss Whitney. Let us see what miracle you may perform." The earl turned and walked to the inn while Lydia followed, relieved to be included in the meeting. There would have been little she could have done if the earl had denied her a chance. She heard Hadley shouting at the lad with the horses to move a little faster.

They stepped out of the sunlight into the dark tavern which

smelled of ale and freshly baked bread. The earl halted abruptly inside the open door.

Lydia moved to his side, her eyes adjusting slowly to the dim interior. They had entered a large public room with rough-hewn benches and tables. The small diamond-shaped windows permitted little light to filter through, leaving the room shadowy.

A gathering of locals stood at one end of a high bar. They whispered among themselves while staring at Carolyn who sat alone at a table near the window.

After taking a deep drink, a plump gentleman in a stained leather jerkin wiped the froth from his upper lip then pointed at Lydia and the earl. "Lud! More of the Quality done arrived, Mrs. Johnson. Next thin' you know the Prince Regent his own self is like to arrive, so fashionable you've become with the swells."

Lydia watched the earl stiffen. The sight of Carolyn being gawked at by common yeoman seemed to add to Lord Standford's consternation.

A woman whose pink cheeks grew quite red came from behind the counter, shooing the men from the room. "Be gone with you, Sully, and take your cup shot mates with you. These folks don't want to hob and nob with the likes of you."

Moving aside, Lydia watched the grumbling men leave. Then she followed the earl to where Carolyn sat, round-eyed at the sight of her nephew. For just a brief moment, Lydia thought she'd seen a flash of welcome on the widow's face but it was gone so quickly she decided she must have imagined the look.

The landlady rubbed her hands nervously up and down her apron as she approached the new arrivals. "Your worship, would there be somethin' I can get for you?"

"Only some seclusion, madam. Have you no private parlor to which we might retire?" the earl asked, never taking his eyes from his errant aunt.

"Aye, sir, but the little miss is lying down sleepin' there and his lordship be restin' up in the one room I let."

"Then this must do, Mrs. Johnson. Pray, excuse us."

"Aye, sir. Would you be wantin' supper, too? The gentleman upstairs done ordered up a meal, the little bit of refreshment I made him earlier not bein' enough."

"No, Mrs. Johnson," Lord Standford stated with finality.

The woman bobbed a deep curtsey, making her limp mobcap fall forward. She straightened the voluminous hat while she rushed to close the inn's front door, then scurried behind the counter, disappearing into the kitchen.

Carolyn rose abruptly, making the straight-backed chair scrape the wooden floor. "Andrew, you have wasted your time coming after me. I shall not allow you to browbeat me into returning to Town."

"Are you completely lost to all sense of propriety?" the earl spat in clipped tones. "Or do you merely wish to make yourself the talk of Society, Aunt Carolyn?"

The widow's eyes darkened. Lydia sensed the lady was about to unleash her temper. Stepping forward, she intervened, "Carolyn, Lord Standford and I have been so worried that you are making a mistake. Do you truly love Lord Digby?"

With a brittle laugh, Carolyn turned away, walking to stare out the mullioned windows. "Love? What does that emotion matter, child? Standford, do you think love important for making an alliance?"

"We do not discuss me, madam. Digby is a fool who cares for nothing but his cuisine and his mother, who is a domineering old harridan. She will make your life a misery. Is that what you wish to achieve with marriage?"

Carolyn turned to stare at the earl with reproach. "It might just surprise you how capable I am at running a marriage, sir. You have never held me in high esteem."

There was a moment of quiet before the earl softly replied,

"You are wrong, Aunt. I have a great regard for you. I simply . . . allowed other things to get in the way."

Lydia noted Carolyn's lips trembled slightly before she turned away from Lord Standford. "You cannot change my mind at this late date, nephew. Too much has passed. I shall not be swayed from this course."

A look of defeat passed over the earl's face, then he squared his shoulders. "Very well, Aunt Carolyn. I shall respect your decision, but I must first speak with Digby and then we can be on our way back to Town."

The earl quietly gestured with his hand as if he were urging Lydia to succeed where he failed. He turned and left the room, his mouth tipped downward in defeat. The sound of his boots on the stairs echoed in the public room. As the footsteps faded, Carolyn collapsed on a bench by the window, dropping her face into her hands.

Lydia went immediately to the distressed woman. "Carolyn, I had a visit from Lord Washburn this morning. I know about the gaming debt."

Carolyn gasped, then raised her tear-stained face to Lydia. "You must think the worst of me. But I did not break my promise, you know, for I only pledged to be good, not to cease gaming. Does Standford know of the loss?"

Taking the widow's hands in hers, Lydia thought back to the morning when Carolyn had given the oath. The widow was correct in the strictest sense, but the point was of no importance now. Bringing herself back to the matter at hand, Lydia replied, "No, I told you before that I would not carry tales to the earl about you."

Carolyn hugged Lydia. "You are a true friend, my dear. Much better than I deserve, considering my foolish behavior."

"Never say that. You have had a difficult time. I do not blame you."

"Andrew will blame me and continue to do so, I assure you."

"I think you both are apt to misunderstand one another. He tried to keep you from harm in his proud, unbending way."

"Perhaps, but 'tis all moot now." The widow pulled out a handkerchief and dabbed her eyes.

Lydia rose and gave the anguished lady a moment to gather herself, then said, "Carolyn, there is one thing about which the earl is correct. You must not marry Lord Digby. The earl would pay the debt for you."

Turning to stare out the window, the widow replied, "No, I have given Chester my word. I cannot pull back now. He promised to pay the debt. Besides, I cannot marry Lord Hammond, so Digby shall do just as well as any other."

Lydia's heart ached for her friend. "You need not marry at all. Wait, give yourself time. You might find another love."

"There is the matter of the money I owe, dear Lydia. Lord Washburn will not wait. I am determined that Andrew shall not be held accountable for the funds. In truth, had I listened to him there would be no debt, but I allowed my arrogance and tenacity to run my own life to blind me to his well-meaning efforts." Carolyn gave Lydia a sad smile.

Filled with guilt for having told Carolyn about her father's skills, Lydia desperately wanted to change the widow's mind. She blurted out, "I shall help you pay Lord Washburn."

"*You?* How kind you are, my dear, but I fear I must pay for my blunder," Carolyn dismissed the offer out of hand.

"No, I am quite serious." Lydia sat on the bench, again taking the widow's hands. "I can use my father's memory trick to recover the lost funds."

Shaking her head, Carolyn smiled sadly. "My dear, I made the mistake of thinking I could use the trick and you see where it got me. We would both end up under the hatches."

"But I have done it before!"

Carolyn became suddenly still, a gleam of hope in her blue eyes. "You have used the gaming trick before?"

Lydia felt her face warm as the old memory flooded back.

She had been but seventeen. Her father had held an entertainment for four gentlemen in their small apartments. Lydia had been determined to do her father proud. Bertie, her usual voice of sanity, was away visiting her cousin.

The gentlemen were quite foxed by the time they arrived, or Lord Frederick's conscience would never have permitted him to allow his daughter to join the game. Lydia had begged to play and with the encouragement of his friends, the gentleman had given his permission.

She easily bested the gentlemen at whist. Her victory had turned to ashes, however, when she'd overheard one of the departing gamesters say he wouldn't be surprised to see Faro Freddie's daughter running a genteel gaming hell by the time she was twenty.

"Yes, I bested several hardened gamesters before realizing I, as a notorious gamester's daughter, would always be tainted in the eyes of Society at any games of chance." Lydia looked down at her hands in embarrassment.

"Then you must not consider doing such a thing to help me. I believe Lord Devere quite madly in love with you. He will be brought up to scratch if you but bide your time."

"Devere!" Lydia scornfully replied. "He is but a callow boy."

"Surely some young man has taken your fancy, my dear. You must not ruin your chances," Carolyn urged half-heartedly.

Lydia knew the only man who interested her would never consider an alliance with someone of her background. She must push thoughts of Lord Standford from her mind. "Don't worry about me. Like you once told me, I would marry only for love, and that seems destined never to happen. We shall win what you need within a day's play. The event should be unremarkable in every way. There will be no scandal."

"What shall I do about Chester?" Carolyn looked up the stairs as she spoke of the baron.

Lydia knew the widow's weakness. "Do you think Lord Digby will make a good father for Georgette?"

A look of disgust settled on Carolyn's pale face. "No! The carriage ride out was horrible. Between Nurse's rudeness and Digby's annoyance at Muffin for eating all his tarts, not to mention her ruining his boots when she fell ill, I felt like the only adult in a horrid nightmare."

Lydia suppressed a smile. Fate and circumstances seemed to be giving her a helping hand in dissuading Carolyn. "There, you have your answer. Simply tell Lord Digby you will not suit. It sounds as if he will be relieved, and as a gentleman he could not be the one to cry off."

For the first time since she'd entered the room, Lydia saw a genuine smile on Carolyn's face. "Yes, that will answer. I shall tell Andrew the same. Lydia, I shall never be able to repay you for this kindness."

"You only owe yourself and Georgette the best life has to offer."

A door closed upstairs, then the earl's boots again echoed on the steps. His eyes were coldly distant as he entered the public room. "Are you ready to leave, Miss Whitney?"

"Your aunt has changed her mind, my lord," Lydia announced. She knew she should feel elated at having persuaded Carolyn, but the thought of going behind the earl's back to game left her feeling sick.

His blue eyes were suddenly sharp and assessing as he glanced from his aunt to Lydia and back. "Is this true, Aunt Carolyn?"

The widow's face became a mask of formality, causing Lydia to long to shake her. "Yes, Andrew. Lydia made me realize that Chester has not the patience to be a father to Georgette. He is truly a fine gentleman, but not one suited to the trials of fatherhood."

The earl's brows rose, but he didn't argue the point with his aunt. "An excellent decision, madam. Do you wish me to tell your intended, or shall you?"

"Really, Andrew, I would not be so cruel as to send such a message through another. You must excuse me." Carolyn sailed past Lydia and the earl going up the stairs with quiet dignity.

Lord Standford looked back at Lydia, a smile lighting his face. "Miss Whitney, I shall not question how you influenced my aunt to give up her plans. Only know that you have my heartfelt gratitude."

Lydia's heart's turned over at the smile on the earl's countenance, which gave his face a boyish charm. She longed to rush to him and tell him all, but her loyalty to Carolyn stayed her. She now had another secret to keep and it tore at her heart.

Turning away, Lydia quietly said, "I did it for Carolyn, my lord. Should you not see to the arrangements for returning?"

"Yes, do you think Digby will allow me to take his carriage and send it back for him later?" The earl frowned as he looked up the stairs.

"I should say that depends on how good a cook Mrs. Johnson is, sir." Lydia brought her chin up, determined not to dwell on the future task she'd set her course on.

The earl laughed. "Judging from the number of empty dishes on the table upstairs and Digby's praise of the woman's talent with pastries, I would say we shall be lucky to see that gentleman in Town within the next fortnight."

A door closed softly, then Carolyn appeared at the top of the stairs. The hint of a smile played about her mouth. She airily stated, "Andrew, have you made the arrangements to leave? Chester put his carriage at my disposal, he being too weak to travel yet."

"I shall see to the matter at once, Aunt." The earl smiled at Lydia as he passed her on the way out, leaving her feeling depressed.

Carolyn came down the stairs, pausing to look at Lydia with a frown. "My dear, if you are having second thoughts about gaming, we can abandon this plan. 'Tis not too late."

Schooling her features to a smile, Lydia glanced at the doorway through which the earl had just exited. With a sigh, she replied, "No, I shall not abandon you in your time of need."

"You are the best of friends," Carolyn said with apparent relief while she gave Lydia a hug. "I shall rouse Georgette and Nurse, then we can return to Town." She walked down a small hallway beside the stairs and disappeared into a room.

Lydia did not feel the best of anything. How had she gotten herself into such a coil? Lord Standford would never forgive her. Lydia knew that the deceit was what bothered her the most. She felt like she was betraying him.

Deep in thought, Lydia started when Hadley appeared at her side.

"Ah, Miss Whitney. You're awfully blue-deviled considerin' the good news his lordship just announced." He peered kindly at her.

"I have promised something I know Lord Standford will not like, Hadley." Lydia's cheeks warmed. Somehow she trusted the valet not to report their conversation, despite his closeness to the earl.

"Well, don't be worryin' about that overmuch. The earl sets mighty high standards for hisself as well as others. At one time or another most of Society has done somethin' his lordship don't like." Hadley smiled gently.

"I fear this concerns his aunt." Lydia glanced over her shoulder to see if Carolyn had returned. The hallway remained empty.

The old man looked up at the ceiling a moment, then scratched the side of his head as if he were thinking about what she'd told him. "Would Mrs. Trevor be returnin' with us now if you hadn't promised this thin'?"

"I—I don't think so."

"Then whatever 'tis, his lordship will understand. Don't

fret yourself about it overmuch. I'm a firm believer in what's meant to be will be."

With a sigh, Lydia thought that was just what she feared. She was destined never to elude the shadow of her father's notorious reputation.

Twelve

The following morning a soft scratching at her bedroom door brought Lydia fully awake. "Come in," she called, rubbing her tired eyes after sitting up in the large fourposter bed. Dawn had been breaking when she'd finally fallen into a restless sleep. She felt groggy from what little rest she'd gotten due to her distress over her promise to Carolyn.

"Mornin', miss." Millie curtsied, a tray balanced in one hand while she entered the chamber. "Mrs. Trevor ordered you a cup of 'ot chocolate this mornin'."

"Thank you, Millie. Have I slept the morning away?" Lydia moved her pillows up behind her, intent on enjoying the unexpected luxury of being served breakfast in bed. She'd made up her mind in the wee hours of the morning not to dwell on her foolhardy offer to game for her mistress.

The maid placed the tray on Lydia's lap, removing the cover to reveal the chocolate as well as toast and preserves. "No, miss, 'tis but eleven of the clock."

"This is a treat. I must thank Carolyn for her kindness." Lydia took the napkin then poured out the rich, brown liquid. After spreading strawberry preserves on her bread, she took a bite.

Millie pulled the blue curtains back, flooding the room with sunlight. "Mrs. Trevor and the little miss 'ave gone to the park as usual. She wanted me to tell you, she's sent a message round to her friend, Sir Jasper. He awaits word of the time and place, she says."

The toast suddenly tasted like chalk in Lydia's mouth. She gulped down a sip of her chocolate to keep from choking on the tasteless fare. Somehow, the plan seemed more real now that Carolyn had set it in motion.

Putting the tray to one side, Lydia said, "I am not very hungry, Millie."

"Shall I 'elp you dress, miss?"

Lydia longed to stay in bed, away from her troubles, but the problem of the funds Carolyn owed would not go away. Lord Washburn would return in five days and demand payment of the vowels.

"Yes, thank you. I shall wear the peach muslin this morning." Feeling little enthusiasm, Lydia rose and allowed the maid to dress her. Then she sat at the small walnut dressing table while Millie brushed out Lydia's braid.

" 'Twas a lovely bouquet of flowers delivered for you this mornin', miss. Seems you've stolen Lord Devere's 'eart."

Lydia smiled wanly into the glass at the maid. Somehow, Devere seemed so youthful to her. She did not want that young man's heart.

The maid seemed to sense Lydia's lack of enthusiasm for the floral tribute and changed to another subject. " 'Tis beautiful silvery 'air you've got, miss. Did you inherit the color from your papa or you mum?"

"Inherit!" Lydia practically shouted, suddenly remembering the legacy from her late uncle. Could there be enough to cover the debt for her mistress?

The maid, who'd jumped at the sudden cry from Lydia, stared at her in the mirror. Lydia smiled reassuringly at the startled servant. "I am sorry, Millie, but you just reminded me of something I had quite forgotten."

"A good thing, I 'ope, miss." The maid resumed arranging Lydia's hair.

"So do I. Millie, is there someone who could take a message to my solicitor?" Lydia felt excitement stir, for she might be able to avoid gaming if her man of business brought her good news.

"Aye, miss. One of the footmen can take it at once." Millie put the final pin into Lydia's hair, then threaded a small peach ribbon around the bundle of curls and tied a neat bow. "There you be, miss, pretty as a picture."

Lydia thanked the maid, then requested the girl wait for the note for Mr. Karling. She went to a Sheraton mahogany highboy against the wall. Opening a secretaire drawer in the middle, she drew out paper and pen, then wrote the message.

"I would like the footman to remain for an answer," Lydia said, handing the folded vellum to the abigail with the man's direction.

"Yes, miss. I'll send it right away." Millie curtsied and left.

Lydia began to pace her room nervously. This might be the answer to her prayers. But what would she do if the amount of the legacy was less than the four thousand six hundred pounds needed? And what about Bertie? She was expecting to share in Lydia's good fortune with a comfortable house in the country. Where should her loyalties be?

Temptation to go downstairs and tell all to his lordship welled up in Lydia. Was she being foolish to acquiesce to Carolyn's wish to handle her own affairs? Lydia was torn with indecision, but in the end decided she was in large part responsible for her mistress's attempt to emulate the infamous Faro Freddie's skill. Therefore, she should be the one to repair Carolyn's mistake, not the earl.

Or was it only reluctance to see a frigid look of displeasure directed at her on Lord Standford's handsome face?

There seemed to be more questions than answers until she met with Mr. Karling, Lydia decided. She did no good pacing about in her room, making herself ill from worry. Perhaps a book of poetry might calm her.

Downstairs, after finding the library empty, Lydia selected a book, then went up to the Rose Drawing Room to await anxiously the reply to her note. She settled herself comfortably on the rose damask window seat overlooking Cavendish Square.

Lydia found herself more intent on watching the people moving about below her than on the poems in Sir Walter Scott's *Marmion*. Closing the book, she gave up all pretenses of reading and watched the south end of the square for the earl's grey and silver livery.

The sound of the drawing room door opening drew Lydia's attention away from the window. The Earl of Standford stood on the threshold. He smiled gently and her heart turned over.

Starting up from her seat, she sent the book tumbling to the carpet. Lydia felt her pulse flutter at the earl's presence. Carolyn had kept her so busy, Lydia had not spoken with him since they'd arrived back at the town house last evening.

Stiffening her back, she determined not to give in to the urge to confess. The gaming scheme might come to naught if her legacy was adequate.

Standford came and retrieved Lydia's book. Handing her the tome, he smiled down at her. "Your book, Miss Whitney."

Lydia was amazed that the earl seemed totally unaware of the torrent of emotions swirling inside her. "Thank you, my lord."

"I learned from Chandler that Carolyn and Georgette are at the park. Would you relay a message to her for me?"

"Yes, my lord."

"I want my aunt to select an entertainment for this evening to which I can accompany you both. Tell her to choose whatever she would most prefer. We don't want any rumors about Carolyn's escapade to be given any credence. I shall ask the Duke and Duchess of Atherton to join us." His gaze never moved from her face.

The news of an evening with Their Graces jarred her. Did that mean Carolyn would be subjected to their eldest nephew's presence? "Shall Viscount Hammond be joining us, sir?"

"The duke told me James's eldest son is ill and they remain

in Portsmouth another day. Do you think you will be able to convince Carolyn she must make a public appearance this evening?"

"Yes, sir," Lydia replied with relief, smiling up at the earl. She was glad she wouldn't have to encourage her mistress to spend an evening with the one man who'd cruelly stolen her heart. Going out this evening with the earl would also mean a delay in Lydia's having to game.

Silence fell between them while they stood looking at one another. Lydia found the earl disturbing to her in every way. She knew it was foolish to think of him other than as an employer, but somehow her emotions could not be coaxed to obey.

"I wanted to—" the earl started to speak, but was interrupted by the door opening.

"My lord, there is a Mr. Karling to see Miss Whitney," Chandler intoned with disapproval at a servant receiving a caller.

"Are you expecting a visitor?" Standford asked, curiously.

"I am, sir. There is a matter which I must discuss with my father's former man of business."

"Send the gentleman up, Chandler."

The earl frowned. He took her hand in his. Lydia's heart jolted and her pulse pounded at the physical contact. She was barely able to concentrate on what he said.

"If you are having some difficulty with your late father's debts, please feel free to confide in me, Miss Whitney. I feel that I owe you a great deal for convincing my aunt to return yesterday."

Reluctantly drawing her hand away, Lydia moved to the center of the room to distance herself from the earl's distracting influence. "Your offer is most kind, sir, but all my father's debts were cleared. This is a personal matter I must speak to Mr. Karling about."

At that moment, the door opened and a small, thin man in a dark grey morning coat entered the room. Bowing deeply, he spoke with a booming voice for one of his size. "Good day, Miss Whitney. You are looking in excellent health." He eyed the earl sharply.

"Good morning, sir. My lord, may I present Mr. Karling, my late father's solicitor. This is the Earl of Standford."

The solicitor bowed so low Lydia thought he might topple on his head. Straightening, the man pulled a card from his pocket, handing it to the earl. "My direction, Lord Standford, should you be needing services."

The earl politely took the card, but placed it in his pocket unread. In a dampening tone, he replied, "I am quite satisfied with my own man of business."

"To be sure, my lord, but you never know when circumstances might change, sudden-like," Mr. Karling replied.

Ignoring the pushing little man, the earl turned back to Lydia. "I shall leave you, but please remember my offer should the need arise." With a nod of his head, Lord Standford left Lydia and the solicitor.

After the door closed, Lydia offered Mr. Karling a seat, then joined him on the opposite settee. "Sir, I was given to understand from my friend, Miss Bertha Armstrong, that I am the recipient of a legacy from my mother's uncle."

"My dear Miss Whitney," Karling said, his loud voice full of condescension. "There is much to be settled before you can consider the inheritance your own. You must first provide me with a copy of your mother's marriage lines. Once confirmed, I shall send word to Mr. Mackay's solicitors in Liverpool. After he agrees that you are the sole daughter of Agatha Mackay Whitney, then said funds will be transferred to an account I shall arrange for you in the city. But I believe the legacy to be quite large."

A feeling of resignation swept through Lydia. All that must take place for her to claim the funds would take weeks and Carolyn had only five days. Her inheritance, no matter the size, was useless in paying the debt.

Mr. Karling droned on about other matters related to her

new income, but Lydia was too lost in her own misery to pay much heed. She would have to game for Carolyn as soon as it could be arranged. There appeared to be no other way out.

"I believe this is my dance, Miss Whitney," Standford said, bowing to the lovely woman when Lord Wellman delivered her to him after the cotillion. The earl thought her exceptionally lovely this evening in a willow-green silk gown with a white sarsenet overdress. Her blonde hair had small white flowers with green leaves set on each side of a cluster of long curls.

"So it is," she replied, a gentle smile curving her lips.

Leading her out onto the dance floor of the Blarewoods' large ballroom, Standford paused to study her while they waited for the music to begin. "I am delighted to have this opportunity to speak with you privately."

Glancing around at the other dancers, Lydia smiled. "Somehow, my lord, I never think of 'being private' in the middle of a crowded room."

"Ah, Miss Whitney, when *you* are in a room, one has eyes for no other." The earl felt strangely lighthearted tonight. He was happy to have his aunt home and in a surprisingly docile mood. She refused to speak to him of her elopement, but promised not to accept any future proposal without discussing the gentleman with him first.

Lydia's eyes widened at the flattery. "I think Her Grace has greatly underestimated your gift for flirting, my lord."

"Flirting?" The earl was startled. Was that what he was doing? Somehow he simply felt at ease with this beautiful lady. "I suppose you are correct. You seem to have a positive effect on both Aunt Carolyn and myself. But I wander from the point of which I wish to speak. I must thank you for your help and good sense, Miss Whitney."

Lydia felt her cheeks warm as she stood beside the earl

who looked handsome in a dark green superfine coat, white
waistcoat, and white pantaloons. His gratitude fanned the
flames of her guilt. Looking across the dance floor to where
Carolyn stood, Lydia again reminded herself she was helping
her friend. "I did what I thought was best for your aunt.
There is no need to thank me, sir."

Lord Standford followed her gaze. "She is rather subdued
since this latest escapade, but I shall not question you about
what you know of her reasons for such a folly. I would only
ask that you continue to guide her."

"I shall do what I think is best for her, my lord."

As the strains of the waltz began, Standford took the lady
in his arms. The sweet intoxicating scent of flowers wafted
up from her as he drew her close. They twirled about the
dance floor in perfect unison. A surge of warmth rushed
through his veins when he gazed down at her sweet face.
Why did this young woman attract him as no lady of the *ton*
ever had?

With determination, he pushed his worries about his fascination for Miss Whitney aside. Just for this evening, he
would savor the feel of her in his arms and drink in her
beauty. Surely such a simple pleasure was harmless.

Lydia stared at the single diamond nestled in Lord Standford's cravat. She knew if she gazed up at his handsome face,
she would lose her resolve to follow through with her promise. Instead, she closed her eyes and gave herself over to the
rhythm of the waltz, relishing the enjoyment of dancing with
the earl.

In her mind, Lydia envisioned only herself and Lord Standford dancing all alone. His arms held her close and she was
smiling up at him. Continuing to dream, she imagined the
music stopping and the earl leaning down to softly caress
her lips with his own.

Shocked at her wanton thoughts, Lydia's eyes flew open
to discover the earl smiling at her. "You dance divinely, Miss

Whitney. I don't think I have ever seen someone derive so much entertainment from the waltz."

Feeling her cheeks warm, Lydia stammered, "I-I have never had such an excellent partner, either, my lord."

When the dance ended, the earl observed, "You appear overheated, Miss Whitney. Perhaps you would like to walk on the terrace, if you are not engaged for the next dance."

Needing to distance herself from the earl and her disturbing thoughts, Lydia started to refuse. "Thank you, my lord, but I am fine. I do not—"

"Good God!" Lord Standford interrupted, his face suddenly a rigid mask when he glanced past Lydia. "We must leave, at once."

Lydia found herself swept out into the darkness before she could utter a protest. The cool night air enveloped her. Taking in deep soothing breaths, she was surprised to discover the earl had drawn her, not to the Blarewoods' terrace, but deep into their garden.

"My lord, I don't think we should stray quite so far from the party," Lydia protested. Her heart hammered as she felt the strength of his hand guiding her forward.

"Forgive me, Miss Whitney, but I fear we are in rather a bad spot."

Mesmerized by his chestnut hair, gleaming in the soft moonlight, Lydia seemed unable to think. "I don't understand, my lord."

Lord Standford cleared his throat. "Lady Pemberton just arrived at the ball. I wanted to protect you from her insinuations and misconceptions about our meeting at Pemberton Hall."

Turning to stare at the four sets of glass doors which opened onto the terrace, Lydia's heart froze. The lady was a notorious gossip. She had it in her power to falsely tarnish the earl's reputation. Worse, Lady Pemberton could add to Mrs. Brisby's lies and besmirch Lydia's own name.

Standford heard Miss Whitney's breathless gasp in the darkness. He felt her trembling hand on his arm.

"My lord, she must not see us together. She is convinced that our meeting at Pemberton Hall was . . . a tryst."

"Did she rake you over the coals terribly after I left?" The earl spoke softly. He watched her head bow, silvery hair glistening in the moonlight.

" 'Tis never pleasant to be wrongly accused of indiscretions and not be allowed the opportunity to defend one's self." Miss Whitney's voice sounded choked with emotion.

Wishing only to comfort her, the earl pulled her gently into the circle of his arms.

The feel of her set his senses reeling.

When her head tilted up at him, Standford could see her beautiful features bathed in the moonlight. With no conscious thought, he surrendered to an impulse. His mouth captured hers, savoring its softness. A torrent of emotions surged through him.

As the kiss lengthened, Standford felt Lydia's hands at the nape of his neck and was jarred back to reality. He quickly pulled away from her, unable to see her lovely eyes clearly in the moonlight. What madness had overtaken him that he should be here kissing a young woman who was in his employ? To be forcing his attentions on her was unforgivable. Never had he behaved in such a despicable manner.

Overcome with his unpardonable behavior, Standford found it difficult to explain. "Miss Whitney . . . I must apologize for this indiscretion. 'Tis unthinkable for a man in my position to even consider . . ." The earl stopped speaking as Miss Whitney took a step back from him, her hands coming up to her face.

The disjointed apology hit Lydia like a dousing of cold water. She'd allowed herself to surrender to the embrace, sending warmth surging through her and causing her knees to grow weak. Now the Earl of Standford regretted his impulse to kiss her. He considered her, a mere companion beneath his touch. She'd been a fool to surrender so completely to the magic of the moment.

Wrapping the shreds of her dignity around her, Lydia tilted her chin upward. "The moonlight must have bewitching powers, my lord. I am sure there will be no such impropriety in the future. Perhaps you would be so good as to find your aunt and arrange for our carriage home. I shall wait on the terrace until you send word, for it would do neither of our reputations any good to be seen together by Lady Pemberton."

Lydia sensed rather than saw that he wanted to say something further as he stood before her in the darkness. Uncertain she could speak calmly, she turned and drew a rose to her, breathing the delicate scent.

"I shall go at once," Standford said, wanting to explain his actions, but uncertain himself what had made him kiss her. Perhaps it was best not to offend her further. Turning, he walked back up the terrace steps in search of his aunt.

He'd fooled himself into believing no harm would come from enjoying the girl's company for one evening. How wrong that had proven. The only solution for his fascination with Miss Whitney was to avoid her. Yes, he would spend his days at the House of Lords and his evenings at his club. Once Hammond offered for his aunt, Miss Whitney's presence would no longer be required. Why did his heart ache at the thought?

A gamut of emotions in her breast, Lydia watched the earl disappear through one of the sets of doors that opened onto the Blarewoods' garden. She then turned her back on the gaily lit house. How could she bear to watch the smiling couples swirling about the room when her heart felt shattered?

One thing was now perfectly clear. The earl would never surrender his love to her. His duty to his title far outweighed any yearnings of his heart and he didn't even know the worst of her yet. The secret of her parentage would only confirm his belief that she was unsuitable.

And what of her own heart? She realized she'd fallen hopelessly in love with Lord Standford. She'd ignored all common sense and now she would learn a hard lesson about love.

The sound of gravel crunching underfoot caused Lydia to turn hopefully. Had the earl realized what was in her heart?

"Miss Whitney?" Lord Devere whispered loudly.

With a sinking feeling, Lydia realized she could not avoid the foolish young man in the bright moonlight. She stepped away from the shadows. "Good evening, sir. What brings you out to the garden?"

"Why you, Miss Whitney. I saw Lord Standford dancing with you earlier and I must say I was shocked to see how he forced you off the floor after the set. Came to make certain you were unharmed."

"As you can see, sir, I am perfectly safe. You should return to the ball and enjoy yourself." Lydia hoped the young man would go away and leave her to order her thoughts.

Grasping her hand, Devere suddenly went down on one knee. "I would ask for your hand in marriage now, before the earl steals you away from me."

"Don't be absurd, Lord Devere." Stunned by the sudden proposal, Lydia pulled her hand from his. "The earl has no intention of offering for me."

"Then he can only have brought you out here to force his attention upon you. I shall call him out for such conduct." The besotted young man rose as if to return to the ballroom and challenge the earl.

"Enough of this foolishness! Lord Standford was merely assisting me when . . . I felt faint. He has now gone to find Mrs. Trevor and we shall leave, for I am not feeling well." In truth, Lydia was sure she was getting a headache.

"But, I do wish to ask—"

Raising her hand to stay his speech, Lydia replied, "You do me a great honor in offering for me, Lord Devere, but I would not want you to be miserable having to give up all your frolics for the staid married life."

"Give up?" The young man sounded shocked.

"Yes. Marriage is about settling down, sir."

"But I have fallen in love with you, dearest Lydia. What are a few lost larks compared to love?" Devere attempted to take her into his arms, but she stepped out of his reach.

"You would miss the fun, and besides, you will fall in love with any number of young ladies before it is time for you to settle down," Lydia replied, kindly. "For myself, I shall only say, I like you too well to spoil your youthful pranks."

Devere spoke with less conviction. "You are the one I wish—"

"Lydia, do I intrude?" Carolyn stood at the bottom of the terrace steps, her face inscrutable in the darkness.

"No, we were finished I believe. I bid you good-night, Lord Devere," Lydia dismissed the young man.

The spurned suitor sighed, then bowed, leaving Lydia and Carolyn in the garden. In time Lydia knew he would thank her for her rejection, but not tonight.

"Come, my dear, Standford has the carriage out front. You should go to bed at once. We don't want you sickening on us." Carolyn put her arm around Lydia and led her back into the ballroom. She was curious about what had happened between her nephew and her companion, for Andrew had been abrupt, even for him, with his request for her to collect Lydia.

Carolyn had seen him take the young woman outside. She worried about what their topic had been.

Entering the brightly lit ballroom, they said their goodbyes to the duchess, then quickly made their way to the carriage. Lord Standford stood stiffly on the pavement. After ushering them into the vehicle, he closed the door and announced, "I am going to my club. Jacobs will see you ladies home safely." Carolyn noted that both Andrew and Lydia avoided looking at one another.

As the carriage jerked forward, Carolyn wondered whatever was going on. Had he learned about her debt?

While the vehicle rolled toward Cavendish Square, Carolyn nervously asked, "Did Standford press you for information about why I eloped? I saw him rush you from the dance floor."

"No. We spoke only briefly of other things."

So, Carolyn thought, their plan was safe. But stay! Could there be a romance between the pair? They behaved as if it were a lovers' quarrel. She'd been aware of his lingering looks at Lydia for some time. A soft smile spread on her mouth, for she could only wish the best for dear Lydia. Besides, it would mean Andrew would be less likely to interfere in her matters.

Relieved about the meeting in the garden, Carolyn put thoughts of Andrew and Lydia from her mind and began to think about her future. "My dear, I did want to tell you that I have decided to return to Leeds with Georgette once my debt has been dispatched."

"I thought you did not wish to return to your home without funds."

"It has occurred to me that Andrew will probably have married by the time Muffin is ready to make her come out. He will be too busy with his own business to intrude on ours, therefore, I shall allow him to assist us at that time. In the meantime, we shall live quietly in the country." Carolyn watched Lydia's reaction closely.

"Oh," Lydia replied flatly. Her hands drew into small fists.

"I have become so fond of you that I wanted you to know that you are welcome to go with us. I shan't be able to pay you . . ."

"Thank you, Carolyn. I appreciate your offer, but I intend to return to my old governess. I have recently learned I have an inheritance coming and we intend to set up house together."

"I am delighted for your good fortune and I shall miss you, my dear, but I know there is nothing like being your own mistress." Smiling in the darkness, Carolyn realized Lydia was enamored with her nephew, as well. Set up housekeeping with her old governess, indeed. Before Carolyn went back to Trevor House, she'd see about smoothing their lovers' tiff.

Lydia felt a sense of relief. Carolyn was returning to the country. She would no longer have to worry about the widow. She was convinced that once the lady returned home all would be well.

"Do you think you will be quite recovered by the morning, my dear?"

"Yes, it is only a trifling headache." Lydia knew that physically she would be fine in the morning. Emotionally, however, she would not recover so easily.

"Excellent, for Standford informed me earlier he is going to be away from home all day tomorrow. I shall send word round to Sir Jasper that we should like him to come for us after nuncheon . . . that is, if you are still willing to help me?" Carolyn sounded hopeful.

"I have given you my word. Send your message to the baronet." Lydia wanted to get the task finished. The sooner she recovered Carolyn's debt, the sooner she could go to Bertie and establish her new life. There would always be that missing part of her heart, but she would have to accept that the proud earl was not destined to be a part of her future.

Thirteen

Sir Jasper's landau came to a halt in front of a sedate house on South Audley Street. Anxiety churning within her, Lydia stared at the dark green door of the residence, surprised to find herself still in Mayfair.

Carolyn sat opposite her beside Masten, nervously tugging at her reticule. Much depended on the outcome of this day's play and well they both knew it.

"Here we are," the baronet said cheerfully. "Lady Halbrook's is quite popular with the ladies and therefore a favorite with me."

"You prefer to game with women, sir?" Lydia questioned, eyeing his purple coat and green striped waistcoat with distaste.

"To be sure, Miss Whitney, the fairer sex gets so delightfully excited or endearingly flustered as the case may be according to their luck. 'Tis a sight to behold."

Lydia was spared making a response, since the footman had lowered the stair and was offering her a hand. Waiting on the sidewalk for the others, she remembered her father had once told her that certain men tended to prey on women gamesters, considering the ladies vulnerable to the superior skills of men. She suspected Sir Jasper was one of those men.

Dismissing his carriage, the baronet rapped sharply on the town house door with his walking stick.

The portal opened at once to reveal a huge butler, but

Lydia suspected that his employment had little to do with serving tea. His beefy hands were scarred, as was his face. A crooked nose and mangled ear were clearly the marks of a former pugilist. He stood mutely gazing at them, neither bowing nor bidding them to enter.

"Ah, Blackwood, I see you are your usual friendly self." Sir Jasper ushered the ladies past the giant of a man.

"Don't get paid to be friendly. Get paid to—"

"Blackwood! How many times must I tell you to simply take the guests' wraps. No chatter," Lady Halbrook reprimanded. She approached the trio in the hall with a smile that did not reach her eyes.

The butler roughly helped them remove their coats and bonnets, then disappeared into a room off the hall. When he returned seconds later, Lydia wondered in what condition they would find their garments when they were ready to leave.

Curious, she eyed the baroness. What kind of a woman ran a gaming house, albeit a genteel one? The woman was lovely, but Lydia nearly blushed as she gazed at the lady's ruby-colored gown which was cut daringly low over an ample bosom.

Lady Halbrook greeted her guests. "Sir Jasper, 'tis good to see you again, and you as well, Mrs. Trevor. I hope your luck proves better today, my dear. I see you have brought a friend."

Carolyn, looking lovely in yellow, tensely licked her lips. "This is my goddaughter, Miss Whitney. She wishes to play whist today."

Lydia saw the measuring look in the baroness's eyes. She'd remembered her father's wisdom about always distracting and disarming an opponent and had dressed herself with that in mind. Her gown was white muslin, with a blue, square-cut bodice and tiny puffed white sleeves. Blue flowers were stitched into a border on the hem and Millie had tied back her pale blonde curls with a matching blue ribbon. She hoped she looked the part of the novice gamester.

"I am sure we can find a game for her. Should it be for chicken stakes, Mrs. Trevor?" Lady Halbrook addressed the question to Carolyn as if Lydia were a child.

"What say you, my dear?" Carolyn asked.

"This chicken game, is that anything like wagering a monkey?" Lydia asked with what she hoped was just the right naivete.

Lady Halbrook laughed and looked at Sir Jasper. "You should not bring such an innocent to play, sir."

The baronet's small eyes glittered. "Both Miss Whitney and Mrs. Trevor were most insistent the gel could play. Why should we spoil her fun? If she wants to game, I am willing to play for such stakes."

Frowning, the baroness drew Masten slightly away from Lydia and Carolyn, but their murmured words reached Lydia's ears clearly. "I do not know this young lady. How do I know she will be able to cover her bets?"

"You know the Earl of Standford. She is living at his residence. Need I say more?"

"Very well, sir." Turning back to the ladies, Mrs. Halbrook asked, "Mrs. Trevor, shall you be joining the game?"

"I fear I am not much in the mood to play this afternoon. I shall amuse myself by watching Lydia."

"We must see if there are two others who are brave enough." The lady turned and started up the wide staircase.

"Come along, my dears. Must make sure we have just the right people," Sir Jasper said, hurrying after Lady Halbrook.

Standing together in the hallway, Carolyn held Lydia back. "How much *is* a monkey?"

"Five hundred pounds," Lydia replied, flashing a sweet smile at Blackwood who stood at his post. The butler watched them as if they were about to make off with the family silver.

"F-five hundred pounds!" Carolyn squeaked. "I think I am going to faint."

Lydia grabbed her mistress's arm, fearing she would make good on her threat. "Blackwood, I need a chair for Mrs. Trevor."

"I don't carry no furniture. I just open this here door and take the coats," he pugnaciously informed her, crossing his arms over his chest.

Carolyn signaled Lydia she did not need to take a seat. In a die-away manner she said, "Oh dear, we shall either be rich as Golden Ball or in debtors' prison by nightfall."

Knowing she was taking a chance by playing for high stakes, Lydia did not respond. She merely wished to get the game over and done. The sooner she was away from this place, the less likely she was to be remembered.

There was also the matter of Lord Standford. He was at the House of Lords today, but should he ask for his aunt at home, Chandler would inform him they had departed in the company of Sir Jasper.

Her sensibilities were still raw from the earl's embrace the former evening in the garden. Lydia's lips tingled in remembrance of the kiss, but the earl's rebuff afterward still made her ache within. With a sigh, she decided she would not dwell on thoughts of Lord Standford.

Drawing the widow forward, Lydia halted as two gentlemen made their way down the stairs, donning their gloves. One recognized Carolyn and bowed before the ladies. "My dear, Mrs. Trevor, we danced at the Washburns' ball last week."

"My yes, 'tis delightful to see you again, sir. Have you met my goddaughter, Miss Whitney?"

Lydia could tell by the vacant look in Carolyn's eyes that she did not remember Lord Rosedale or was too flustered at present to recall his name. He questioned their attendance at the Calloways' ball the next evening and requested dances from each. The ladies agreed and the gentlemen wished them luck before taking their leave.

Following the path up the stairs that Sir Jasper and Lady Halbrook took, they soon found themselves at the doorway of a once elegant drawing room, with cream silk wallpaper and burgundy velvet curtains. The chamber was now filled with green baize tables, each surrounded by card players.

Suddenly, Carolyn turned and said, "My dear, I am too afraid to watch. I shall go to the refreshment room and await you."

Before Lydia could make any comment, the widow dashed back down the staircase. Looking about the crowded room, she took a deep breath for courage. Sir Jasper stood on the opposite side of the chamber near a window, signaling her to come.

Winding her way through the assembled gamesters, Lydia arrived at his table where two ladies were seated. Horror filled her when she gazed at the lady whose back had faced her on entering. Mrs. Eugenie Howell, the woman who'd so callously rejected Lord Standford, was one of the people she must play.

The widow looked stunning in a russet silk gown, her auburn curls glinted with shots of gold. She was engaged in a conversation with Sir Jasper as Lydia approached. Mrs. Howell's blue eyes scanned Lydia with no hint of recognition, clearly dismissing her as no threat in the forthcoming game.

Relieved not to be remembered, Lydia surveyed the lady who sat beside the widow. The woman was older, with grey curls peeking from under a lime-green turban which sported a large emerald. Dark brown eyes examined Lydia from a plump face. A diamond necklace, of gigantic proportions, hung from under her jowled chin, and on the bodice of her lime and yellow striped gown, an emerald-studded turtle was pinned.

"May I present Miss Whitney, ladies? My dear, this is the Marchioness of Seymour and Mrs. Howell who are eager to play."

"Have we met before?" A frown appeared on the widow's lovely face when Lydia's name was mentioned.

A flicker of apprehension coursed through Lydia. Mrs. Howell had been present on several occasions when Lydia had brought Sophia down to an entertainment at Pemberton. Realizing that few people paid attention to servants, she thought herself safe.

Capturing the role she wished to play, she inanely replied, "La, madam, were you at Lady Winfield's 'at home' for all the young ladies who are making their bow this Season?"

The marchioness snorted a laugh. " 'Tis many a year since Eugenie was included in invitation for young ladies coming out."

Mrs. Howell's face flamed red. "Well, my lady, *I* may no longer be considered an ingenue, but at least no one has ever accused me of being overdressed." The widow allowed her scornful gaze to fall to the ornate necklace.

"That, dear Eugenie, is because I hear you spend so much time in undress with a certain Cit," Lady Seymour purred.

Mrs. Howell's fingers curled like talons as they rested on the table. She glared at her plump opponent as if she might swoop down upon her and claw her eyes out. "You—"

"Ladies, ladies, do we play or banter?" Sir Jasper looked gleefully at the verbal combatants.

"I came to play. Miss Whitney, I have heard much of you from my friend the Duchess of Atherton. Would you be my partner for whist?" The marchioness gave Lydia a glowing smile.

Taking her seat at the table, Lydia found herself hoping the older woman's skills were as sharp as her tongue. "With delight, Lady Seymour."

The Earl of Standford sat slumped in a chair at Brook's, a glass of claret sitting untouched before him. He'd gone to the House of Lords earlier, but found he couldn't concentrate on the issues at hand. Only one word in ten penetrated his bewitched brain. Trying to accomplish anything had been useless, so he'd adjourned to his present location.

His mind kept replaying the events in the Blarewoods' garden. Miss Whitney had been utterly irresistible in the soft moonlight. The memory of her lovely lips pressed against his set the blood rushing in his ears even now. Her softness as he'd drawn her close was delicious.

In the clear light of day, it was plain to Standford that he must remove himself from the chit's intoxicating influence. He would go to Crosswell and rusticate for a few days. Surely he could trust Miss Whitney to keep Carolyn out of trouble for a short time.

"Well met, Standford, what say you to a game of casino?" Lord Allister called.

The earl looked up from his musings to see his old acquaintance from Oxford sauntering across the room with two other men. One he recognized as Lord Rosedale, the widower who'd danced with Carolyn at the Washburns'.

"Not today, Allister. I am about to leave. I am off for Suffolk. There are matters at my estate that need my attention."

Lord Rosedale said, "Then I must assume that your aunt, Mrs. Trevor, remains behind, since we met her earlier this afternoon at Lady Halbrook's. She promised me a dance at the Calloways' ball tomorrow night."

Standford's hand clenched the stem of his wineglass. "You just saw my aunt on South Audley Street?"

"Yes, we encountered Mrs. Trevor on the stairs as we left. Sir Jasper was looking for a game for the pretty young lady who accompanied her, a Miss Whitney, I believe. Allister and I were promised to Yardley here or we might have made up the set," Rosedale answered, completely unaware of the torrent of emotions he'd unleashed in the earl.

Standford seethed with mounting rage. He had trusted Lydia Whitney with his aunt. Did that lovely face hide a devious heart? He could not believe that. But Rosedale had no reason to lie about meeting his aunt and Miss Whitney at Lady Halbrook's gaming house.

What treachery was this? Had the girl merely awaited her moment to lure his aunt into a game, matching her talents against the widow's bungling skills? Anyone who knew him would have realized that he would pay any debts of honor to keep his aunt's name from scandal. This simply could not be.

With an outward calm, Standford replied, "My aunt prefers the town pleasures to the country pursuits. I fear I must leave you."

The earl rose and collected his greatcoat. He would go to South Audley at once. If it were true, Miss Lydia Whitney would rue the day she'd decided to get the better of the Earl of Standford.

Willis, the earl's tiger, had never seen the earl in such a state when he came out of Brook's and mounted his curricle. Lord Standford had proven himself to be a credible whip without the reckless disregard some drivers exhibited. The lad was able to brag about his master's skill while tossing down ale with his friends at the local tavern.

Today, however, the gentleman drove the streets of Mayfair as if trying to break some long-standing record. The tiger merely held tightly to the backstrap and hoped his lordship's competence would see them through the wild journey.

Standford hauled on the reins as they reached Lady Halbrook's residence. Jumping down, he ordered the white-faced Willis to walk the horses, he would be only a moment.

A sharp knock on the door brought a quick response and the door swung inward. Standford, about to pass the strange looking butler, found his way blocked by the hulking man. "Yer coat, guvnor."

"I am not staying," the earl barked, haughtily looking up at the scarred face.

"You ain't goin' up with that there coat on. It's my job to take all wraps and take 'em I do." The butler quickly stripped the earl of his greatcoat and disappeared, leaving Standford speechless for a moment.

Deciding he had no time to take impudent servants to task, Standford took the stairs two at a time. The important thing was to find Miss Whitney and unmask her plot.

Pausing at the door to the gaming room, Standford scanned the players. He easily spied the cluster of silver-blonde curls on the opposite side of the room. In the reflected light of the window beyond her seat, she seemed to have an angelic glow about her while she played her card.

Good God! Why did the deceitful chit have to look so devilishly lovely? Grinding his teeth in anger, he straightened his back for the confrontation and started across the crowded chamber.

A scant five steps into the room, the earl found his way again blocked. This time by Lady Halbrook. The lady fluttered her eyes and placed a caressing hand upon his sleeve. "So, you have decided to visit my home, my lord."

"Madam, I have come to remove my aunt and her companion from this establishment." The earl stared over the lady's raven curls in search of his Aunt Carolyn.

"They are both pleasantly amusing themselves at the moment. I could perhaps do the same for you in a chamber upstairs, sir."

Stiffening, Standford brought his gaze to rest on the brazen woman's face. Were the fates working against him, to keep him from rescuing his aunt?

Determined to make no scene, he tersely replied, "I fear I must decline your . . . offer. I am in a great hurry. Would you have a room where I might speak privately with Miss Whitney? I bear bad tidings for the young lady."

"There is a small parlor in the back which you may use." Lady Halbrook moved away from the earl, casting a disappointed look over her shoulder.

What else could detain him? Standford thought. He started forward a second time.

Locking his gaze on Miss Whitney, he ignored the others at the table. He would deal with this scheming chit first, then worry about his aunt, wherever she was.

Lydia saw a shadow fall across the table while she picked up her cards to begin the final game of the rubber. Thinking Carolyn had joined them, her heart leapt into her throat. There, glowering at her, was Lord Standford.

While she sat with a smile frozen on her shocked lips, he suddenly grasped her arm, pulling her to her feet. Nervous fingers released the cards she clutched, causing them to fall to the table in an untidy pile.

"I suppose I could expect little else from Faro Freddie's daughter," the earl growled in Lydia's ear.

She gasped. Lord Standford knew about her father and this foolhardy adventure to save Carolyn from scandal.

Beside her, Lydia heard Mrs. Howell sneer, "Standford, I see you still have no idea how to treat a lady."

The earl's eyebrows rose in surprise when he looked up to discover his former flirt, then his chin came up as the lady's statement registered. "Madam, you would do better to concern yourself with your own affairs."

Raising a jeweled quizzing glass to peer at the new arrival, the marchioness snapped, "Begad, Standford, you interrupt our game."

"I am sure you can find another partner from among this . . . dubious gathering of gamesters," the earl stated contemptuously.

"Sir, I do not like your tone. If I were not so good natured I might take offense," the marchioness quipped.

"Did you not know that Standford excels in giving offense?" Mrs. Howell's eyes glittered maliciously.

"Pray allow me to apologize, ladies, but I intend to remove Miss Whitney from your game." The earl's voice was heavy with sarcasm.

As Lord Standford pulled her away from the table, she

heard the marchioness pronounce, "A very prickly fellow, today. Not his usual repressed manner."

Speechless with guilt, Lydia found herself swept into the upper hallway. The earl drew her down the passageway and opened the door of a small parlor. She was marched forward and unceremoniously deposited into a pale blue wing-back chair.

"My lord, if you——"

Lord Standford raised his hand for silence. "Miss Whitney, there can be no excuse for finding you in this gaming house. I would first ask, where the devil is my aunt?"

"I believe she went to the dining room, sir." Lydia's gaze fell to her lap to stare at her tightly clasped hands. His blue eyes were filled with contempt as they glared at her and it tore at her heart.

"Just how much did you win from her?"

Startled by the question, Lydia's gaze came back to rest on his rigid face. "I did not play your aunt. She has been in the refreshment room the entire time. You do not understand the reason——"

"I understand very clearly, Miss Whitney, that I was duped into believing I could trust you to watch out for my aunt. Even when I learned the truth about who your father was, I gave you the benefit of the doubt and did not dismiss you. For this kindness, my reward was betrayal." The earl turned his back on her and walked to the window.

Lydia cringed at his words. She had said all of these things to herself, but Carolyn had won her over. She deserved his disdain and outrage. "You have every right to be angry. I allowed my sympathy for your aunt's difficulties to override my better judgment."

"Judgment! The daughter of a hardened gamester can surely have no such attribute. A man of your father's stamp——"

"How dare you, sir!" Lydia said angrily, jumping to her feet. "You may rail at me as you like, but I shall not allow you to speak disparagingly of my father. You did not know him and can have no idea the good qualities he possessed."

"I am sure a man whose life was consumed with gaming was a model of respectability," the earl snapped. He felt a twinge of guilt at the mixture of anger and hurt in Miss Whitney's golden eyes, but tried to convince himself he was in the right.

Straightening, she replied, "You measure all of Society by a standard of good conduct that few men can attain, my lord. Perhaps, sir, you should look to your own faults before you judge others, for I have never met a man who has less understanding for the frailties of others than yourself."

Miss Whitney suddenly turned and left the small room, slamming the door with a loud bang. Standford was left speechless. How had his chastisement of the chit been turned around to make him the object of scorn?

Fuming at the accusations she hurled at him, the earl turned to stare out the window. He'd always tried to do what was right and proper. Why did his dealings with those close to him generally end in discord? Both his godparents often warned him he judged his peers too harshly. Were they all correct?

Perhaps, but in this matter of Aunt Carolyn's gaming, he knew himself to be in the right, and so he would tell the pert miss who'd just left him. But first he would extricate his aunt from this gaming house.

As he started toward the door, the portal suddenly opened and his aunt hurried into the room. "What did you do to Lydia? Sir Jasper came to the refreshment room and said you had forcibly removed her from the game. Lady Halbrook says the child dashed out into the street still donning her bonnet."

"After I informed her of my feelings about her despicable behavior in bringing you here, she left in a huff," the earl replied haughtily, failing to mention her criticism of him.

His hand distractedly fingered his single fob as outrage filled his aunt's face.

"And well she might, you poor deluded boy. The girl came here to help me out of a muddle of my own making." Carolyn blushed deeply but continued her tale. "The night you went to the opera, I learned . . . some devastating news. In a fit of distress I foolishly determined to win a fortune and return to Leeds."

"Whatever made you dream you could suddenly win a large sum?"

Carolyn walked to the small marble fireplace before she turned back to gaze at him sheepishly. "I discovered Lydia's father was Faro Freddie and . . . well . . . she told me he used a memory trick to play whist. When she realized why you had hired her, she wanted to inform you of her background, but I promised to be good if she would not tell you she was Lord Frederick's daughter. She trusted me and I failed her."

Standford felt a sick feeling in his stomach. He had it all wrong. He'd falsely accused Miss Whitney of trickery and worse, slandered her beloved father. He'd been too ready to rush to judge her.

When the earl made no comment, Carolyn continued. "The problem was, I couldn't keep the cards straight and lost a great deal of money to Lord Washburn."

"How much?"

"Nearly five thousand pounds."

Looking down at his signet ring, the earl finally understood the elopement. "So, did Digby offer marriage in return for payment of the debt?"

Carolyn nodded her head. "I was determined you would never know, then you arrived at the inn and were . . . well, I felt even more determined to stand by my promise to Chester."

"But Miss Whitney convinced you to return?" The earl

was beginning to see how his own actions had helped bring about this fiasco.

"I still refused to allow you to pay for my foolishness, so the brave child offered to try and recover the money using her father's memory trick if only I would return to London."

The earl knew they each must take a share of the blame for this disaster. But he also knew his own intractable handling of his aunt had been the crux of the problem. "And so here we are. But what was this devastating news which triggered this event?"

With tears pooling in her blue eyes, Carolyn whispered, "I discovered Lord Hammond's wife Felicity and his boys were arriving from the West Indies. I . . . thought the viscount a bachelor and have fallen hopelessly in love with him."

"Deuce take it! All of this occurred because of a simple misunderstanding!" Standford said, his voice full of irony.

"Misunderstanding?"

"Yes, dear aunt, Felicity is Hammond's daughter. His wife died over two years ago. I believe he is even now hurrying his children back to Town so that he might make you an offer."

"Truly?" Carolyn's eyes now sparkled.

"So the Duke of Atherton informed me." Standford fell silent, unable to join in his aunt's elation. He had rashly accused Miss Whitney of trying to fleece his aunt and she'd only been a victim of the widow's impetuous nature. She'd tried to keep Carolyn from the tables and when that had failed, she'd done the only thing she knew how without betraying his aunt's trust.

He felt such a dunderheaded fool. The memory of the wounded look in Miss Whitney's eyes before she left haunted him. She'd been right, he had no understanding of people at all.

Had she gone back to pack her belongings? Yes, the earl

reasoned, she had too much pride to stay where she thought she was not wanted.

With the alarming thought that Lydia might even now be gone, he suddenly felt as if there was not enough air in the small room. She was the one woman he could not live without. What did it matter that her father was a gamester or that she was penniless? Lydia Whitney made him feel alive.

The earl's only hope was that she would forgive him his terrible accusations about her and his insinuations about her father. With some urgency the earl stated, "Aunt Carolyn, we must go home, at once."

His aunt's euphoria about Hammond did not dull her wits. "Were you terribly cruel to dear Lydia?"

"Unforgivably so," the earl spoke softly, walking to open the door.

The fates that day had been with Lydia in all things but love. She'd won most of the money Carolyn needed, but it mattered not now that Lord Standford knew of his aunt gaming. She pushed the painful memory of their meeting from her mind.

After leaving his lordship, Lydia retrieved her hat and pelisse and found a hackney cab who'd taken her straight to Cavendish Square. The young man now awaited in his carriage to take her to the nearest coaching inn.

Donning her old traveling dress, Lydia was determined to take nothing with her. Clearly, Lord Standford thought her some opportunist who took advantage of his aunt's vulnerability. The thought renewed her humiliation at his allegations. She knew she could only blame herself. Things would never have come to this if she'd listened to her own heart and told him about her past. Now she would always be suspect in his eyes, even if he could forgive her this day's folly.

Finally, she stuffed only her three old gowns into her portmanteau. Lydia took a last look around, then hurried down the stairs. Chandler asked no questions, merely opened the door for her with one raised eyebrow.

"Apologize to Mrs. Trevor for my sudden departure. I shall write to her after I am settled."

"Very good, Miss Whitney," the butler replied uncertainly, then closed the door.

"Where to, miss?" the hackney driver asked while she descended the stairs.

"To the nearest coaching inn. I am going to Hertfordshire." Back to dear Bertie, she thought with a dull ache in her heart, and a life of regrets about what might have been.

Fourteen

"Andrew, look out! You almost ran over that poor man and his wife." Carolyn held tightly to the side of the curricle.

The gentleman in question stood in his carriage and shouted abuse at them as the earl's curricle breezed between his vehicle and a large town coach pulled up by the curb.

"What the devil are all these people doing, cluttering up the streets?" Standford snapped, impatient to return home and see Lydia. He would beg her forgiveness. Perhaps, if he was lucky, he might discover she cherished some deeper feelings for him.

"They are most likely going to Hyde Park, just like you do on many occasions at this hour." Carolyn was amazed at her nephew's distracted state, Andrew must truly be in love. "Don't worry, Lydia has a kind and understanding heart. She will not hold your words against you. Slow down, my dear. You are frightening me. Besides, what good will it do you to break your neck trying to get to her?"

"I would not be so worried, but Lady Seymour detained us overlong, making sure we would give Miss Whitney her winnings. What if she has decided not to remain in London? She is most likely without funds." Andrew slowed his team a bit to round a sharp turn.

"No, I believe she recently received an inheritance."

Remembering the visit from the solicitor, Standford suddenly realized the irony of the situation. He had fallen in love with a woman with both pedigree and portion and she was likely to spurn him for his foolish behavior.

Carolyn interrupted his bitter musings. "Besides, where would the child go? That despicable grandfather and cousin of hers do not acknowledge her. How awful to be completely without family."

"I have thought you were wishing for such a circumstance for this past month," the earl said wryly, urging his team again to pick up its speed.

Carolyn gave a light laugh. "Only when you were vexing me." Sobering, she gripped Andrew's sleeve to keep from toppling off the seat when he hit a pothole in the road. "In truth, I would find it rather frightening to have no one who gave me a second thought. The Duke of Graymoor is a fool. Lydia would truly be considered a delightful asset to anyone's family."

"I am glad you think that, for I intend to make her part of ours . . . if she will have me."

"Andrew!" Carolyn threw her arms around her nephew's neck, causing him to veer toward the curb. "I knew it. I think I realized the pair of you were in love with one another even before you both did."

"Do you think Miss Whitney . . . Lydia returns my regard?" The earl held his breath and gripped the reins overly tight waiting for his aunt's answer.

"I think the child has been half in love with you since the morning you brought her to London."

The day seemed suddenly brighter to the earl. He made the turn onto Henriette Place which would bring him to his town house. With a final burst of speed, he tooled the carriage around the fenced green of Cavendish Square to his door. When Willis took the reins, the earl sprang lightly to the ground and assisted his aunt.

The butler opened the door even before the pair reached the stairs. His white eyebrows rose slightly when he discovered his lordship, not only with his aunt, but the couple appeared to be in charity with one another. A surprising circumstance considering that the lady had left with Masten.

"Chandler, did Miss Whitney make it safely home?" the earl asked anxiously, while the servants removed his aunt's pelisse and his greatcoat.

"Yes, my lord. She arrived over half an hour ago. The young lady was here but ten minutes then left."

A wave of despair suddenly filled Standford. She was gone. Would he be able to find her? He knew he must. His voice sounded urgent when he softly asked, "Did she leave a message?"

"Yes, sir, she told me to apologize to Mrs. Trevor for her sudden departure. Said she'd write once she was settled."

The earl was not surprised that there had been no message for him. He'd wounded her terribly by accusing her of preying on his aunt. His slander about her father could only have fueled her pain.

"Andrew, I have just remembered the governess that visited her a few days ago. Did you meet the woman?" Carolyn placed a comforting hand on her nephew's arm, seeing the hurt and disappointment evident on his face.

"I did. Miss Armstrong was her name. Did she make use of my carriage to go home that afternoon, Chandler?" The earl's mood was suddenly hopeful.

"Yes, sir. I notified Jacobs of your wishes and he handled the matter, my lord."

"Bring Jacobs to the library at once, Chandler."

"Yes, my lord," the butler replied. Signaling the footman, he gave the man the orders. "Madam, you have a visitor in the Rose Drawing Room. He insisted on waiting for you."

"Who is it, Chandler? I am anxious to hear if the coachman will know the location of Miss Armstrong." Carolyn didn't want to leave Andrew until she knew he would be able to find Lydia. He was clearly distressed over his misunderstanding.

"Lord Hammond, madam. Shall I tell him you are not at home to visitors?"

"No!" Carolyn practically shouted, her face lit with elation. Then she looked at Andrew and was clearly torn over what to do.

Standford went to his aunt, kissing her forehead. "Go, my dear. I thank you for your concern, but I think the gentleman has something important he wishes to discuss with you."

"Don't worry. You will discover where dear Lydia has gone and she will forgive you." Standing on tiptoes, Carolyn brushed a kiss on his cheek before hurrying up the stairs.

Watching his aunt until she disappeared, Standford felt pleased she would get a new chance at happiness. He also felt a sense of relief to be relinquishing the care of her funds to Hammond.

Remembering his own dilemma, Standford went to his library to anxiously await Jacobs. Restless, he walked to the window and stared out at the garden. The shadows were growing long and he began to worry that Lydia would be out by herself after darkness fell.

A knock sounded on the door. The earl eagerly called, "Enter."

Jacobs, a tall, gaunt man in his forties, came into the library. His hat was crumpled in his hand, and greying black hair poked up at varying angles. "My lord, you wished to see me."

"Jacobs, did you arrange for Miss Armstrong to leave after her visit with Miss Whitney?"

"Aye, sir. Going to 'ertfordshire, she was."

Standford felt an overwhelming sense of relief. Lydia would be at her destination well before dark since the county was only eleven miles from London—if that was where she went. "Where exactly in Hertfordshire?"

The coachman scratched his head, before he said, "Well, sir, I don't rightly know. You see, Brigman was 'ere that day. 'E was goin' to return Mrs. Trevor's carriage, what was used to brin' down the little one's pet. Offered to take the lady in that coach. Said it weren't that far out of 'is way."

The earl's fist clenched with frustration. Brigman was at Crosswell. He wouldn't be able to go to Lydia until he spoke with the servant who acted as his messenger. "Then I shall leave for my estate at once. I must speak with the fellow."

"No need for that, my lord. Brigman's due in the mornin'. Mr. Farlow 'ad 'im doin' somethin' for 'im. You're like to miss 'im on the road if you go tonight."

With a disappointed sigh, the earl realized he would have no choice but to wait until morning. "Thank you, Jacobs. Make certain he comes to me immediately upon arrival. I don't care if it's dawn."

"Aye, sir," the coachman replied, then tugged his hat back on as he left.

After the door closed, Standford slumped into the chair behind his desk. He would have to wait through the long night, but in the morning he would know where Lydia had gone. His mind went over all the things he would say. He loved her. He needed her—but what if his aunt was wrong and Lydia didn't return his feelings? He pushed that thought from his mind. The notion was too painful to even contemplate.

He sat a long time in the fading light, pondering the sudden realizations that had come to him that day. From the hallway, the sound of Georgette giggling and someone trying to quiet her penetrated the library door. Curious and hoping to distract himself, Standford rose and went to look in the hall. Somehow the child's laughter soothed his disturbed emotions.

Opening the door, the earl spied Nurse standing at the foot of the stairs, hands on her hips. "There'll be no special tea if you break one of his lordship's lovely things."

The child was laughing and dancing around a mahogany table with a Chinese porcelain vase filled with flowers. Looking up, she spotted her cousin standing in the library door.

She suddenly stood stock still and stared at the earl, a hint of apprehension on her face.

An easy smile came to the earl's lips as he watched Georgette shuffle her feet. She looked like a small angel with her cheeks flushed with excitement and her white ruffled dress. He went down on one knee, heedless of his pantaloons, wanting to be less intimidating to her. "You are in a very good mood."

"Oh, Cousin Andrew," Georgette cooed, replacing the vase and bounding forward with blonde ringlets bouncing. She placed her hands on his shoulders. "I am to have a sister and brothers. Mama just told me she is to marry Lord James."

"So, you are to have a new father at last. I am very pleased for you, my dear." Impulsively, Standford kissed the child's cheek.

"Where is Miss Lydia? I must tell her, as well."

Standing, the earl replied with more confidence than he felt, "She has gone to Hertfordshire. She should . . . will be home by tomorrow. Then we might all celebrate your mother's betrothal."

"Come, child," Nurse said. " 'Tis getting late and you have not had your tea. Pray, excuse us, my lord."

After the pair left, Standford returned to the library. He would give his aunt and Hammond time alone to savor their engagement, he thought. Restlessly pacing before the stacks, he chose a book of poetry, then settled into a wing-backed chair. However, after scanning several verses, he discovered that his thoughts were too agitated for him to read.

Why had it taken him so long to admit his love for Lydia? Because he'd foolishly dismissed love as of no importance. Only someone who'd never been in love could make such a mistake. Now he had the monumental task of convincing Lydia that he'd changed.

As her beautiful face came to his mind, the earl knew he

would not accept defeat. He was determined she would forgive him no matter what it took.

Sitting alone in the bedroom she shared with Bertie, Lydia diligently plied her needle, ignoring the hollow ache in her chest. This simple diversion helped to occupy her mind, keeping the painful thoughts of Lord Standford at bay. Her old green dress, damaged in the fall at Pemberton, must now be part of her wardrobe, at least until Mr. Karling secured her inheritance.

The playful shouts of four of the Reddingers' six children floated up from the rear garden where they'd escaped after breakfast. Bertie's cousin, Matilda Reddinger, had proven more able to produce children than to manage them. Much of that task had fallen to Lydia's former governess.

The Reddingers had welcomed Lydia the night before with surprising complacency, considering the struggle Mr. Reddinger had to provide for his large family. The solicitor merely hinted that Lydia, if she wished, might lend a hand to his dear Tillie while she visited Bertie.

That lady had taken one look at her dejected friend and agreed with her cousin's husband. Nothing like work to take your mind off your worries, Bertie had kindly offered.

Knowing she could ease the workload, Lydia had risen early and helped the village girl who acted as nurse to the youngest four, all boys. The pair had made certain that the clamoring brood was fed and properly attired before their excursion outdoors.

Bertie had remained behind with the two eldest, both girls, to do lessons in the schoolroom as the boisterous males hurried down the stairs. She'd encouraged Lydia to take a break while Polly took the older boys to the curate for lessons.

The bedroom door opened and Bertie looked into the room. "There you are. I thought you might be resting after the enormous task of helping Polly with the boys this morning."

"No, they are quite a handful, but . . . I enjoyed doing what I could to help." Lydia dropped her sewing into her lap.

Bertie watched her young friend sag listlessly back in the chair. She'd not questioned Lydia when she arrived just before dark the previous evening. The girl had merely announced that she had quit her post and asked if the Reddingers would object to her remaining there until she received her inheritance.

The exhausted Lydia had been put to bed and Bertie assured her they would talk in the morning. She'd harbored hopes the Earl of Standford might develop a tendre for dear Lydia, but the girl's unexpected arrival in Hertfordshire had put a period to those thoughts.

Taking a chair beside Lydia, Bertie asked, "Do you want to tell me about it, my dear?"

In a low voice, Lydia poured out her tale. Her throat felt tight, as tears threatened, but she'd promised herself not to cry. She spared herself not at all, telling her friend every foolish choice she'd made. The story was swiftly told, leaving out only a few details. One being the unforgettable kiss in the garden, along with her love for the man whom she'd failed.

Seeing the pain in the depths of Lydia's golden eyes as she spoke of the events which led her to her present situation, Bertie's heart ached. It was plain as day the girl had fallen in love with the earl and now her hopes were dashed, Bertie thought.

Never one to encourage people to fall into a decline over disappointments, Bertie simply said, "Well, my dear, I would say that you made your mistakes, but your heart was in the right place. 'Twill do no good to think of what might have been different if you'd chosen another course with Mrs. Trevor. Am I mistaken, or have you fallen in love with the earl?"

Lydia gave a defeated shrug with her shoulders. "Does it

matter now? A man like Lord Standford is too duty-bound to think about such a tender emotion."

"Perhaps, but remember you saw something in the gentleman at your first meeting that others did not. A goodness of heart that hides beneath that hauteur. Mrs. Trevor will disabuse the earl of his misunderstanding of your reason for being at the gaming house. The question is, can you forgive the things he said, my dear?" Bertie took Lydia's hand and patted it gently.

Turning to gaze out the window at the Hertfordshire countryside, Lydia pondered the question. She knew she loved the earl and that he'd been excessively angry when he spoke. One often regretted what was said in anger. "Yes, but I sincerely doubt I shall have the chance."

Rising, Bertie said, "Well, there is no point in sitting here wondering about what might happen. Why don't you take a walk in the garden? The older boys go to the curate for lessons at ten and the younger ones will likely not disturb you. The fresh air will bring the color back to your cheeks. I worry when you are looking so wan. I would join you, but I cannot leave the schoolroom just yet."

"Dear Bertie, do not give me a thought. I shall do as you wish and be much better by this afternoon." Lydia rose and hugged her friend. While her heart ached, she was determined not to have Bertie fussing over her like a little girl. The woman had too many responsibilities already, without adding Lydia's disappointed hopes.

The women parted at the top of the stairs and Lydia made her way down to the large garden behind the old cottage. The air was warm and sweet with the smell of wildflowers that grew in great clumps along the stone fencing.

Lydia wandered aimlessly down the path to a wooden bench set under a large elm tree. About to take a seat, she halted at the soft sounds of a child's crying. Following the gentle sobs, she ventured farther down the path until she spied young Edward Reddinger sitting alone in a large tree.

At some earlier time, the children had pulled an old wooden door up the tree and wedged it onto two limbs, forming a large, flat platform. The four-year-old now sat in the middle of that plank, weeping.

"Edward, what is wrong?" Lydia called.

Rubbing his eyes, the dark-haired lad ceased crying, but continued to gulp great quantities of air as he tried to speak. "I-I got up here . . . b-but now . . . now . . . I'm 'fraid to . . . to come down."

Heavens, thought Lydia as she looked around and saw they were quite alone, am I destined to be climbing trees 'til my dotage? Knowing there were few servants about, she asked, "Do you wish me to come up and help you?"

Edward nodded his head as tears continued to roll quietly down his chubby cheeks.

With resignation, Lydia climbed the tree and settled gently on the plank, making sure not to rock the door too much so as not to frighten the child more. "There, now you are not alone."

The boy's lower lip protruded as he edged closer to his rescuer. "I-I didn't think ladies c-could climb trees."

Remembering her meeting with Lord Standford in just such a tree, Lydia spoke in a tremulous whisper, "Yes, on occasion some of us do."

Giving herself a mental shake, she concentrated on getting Edward safely down. That meant calming the lad first. "How did this door get into the tree?"

"My brothers, Robert and Howard, got the man that does the garden to help 'em put it here. We come up and watch the carriages on the road, but . . . it's scary up here by myself." His tears now gone, only the wet-streaked traces of dirt remained on the child's face.

"Where is Polly?"

"She took Howard and Paul to the curate for lessons and I told her I would stay in the garden while she walked 'em over there." Edward pointed to the small house across the meadow which was next to the old village church.

Lydia knew she must warn the young girl not to leave this little one unattended again. It only took a moment for a child to get into trouble, even in the confines of a garden.

Looking at the lad, she saw he was growing calmer. A little more conversation, and she would attempt to help him down.

"What kind of carriages can you see from up here?" Lydia gazed out at the sunlit field through which the road from London cut a swath.

"Phaetons," Edward replied, then pointed to such a vehicle coming along the road at such a pace that dust rolled up behind it in great clouds. "I shall be a famous whip when I grow up."

Lydia paid little attention to the final part of Edward's speech. Her heart was dancing with sudden excitement. Was that Lord Standford tooling the phaeton or was her wish to have him there making her eyes play tricks on her? The distance was great, but there was something about the proud posture of the man as he handled the ribbons that evoked his lordship.

Clutching the edge of the door on which she sat, Lydia closed her eyes for a moment. Dare she hope that he had forgiven her? Perhaps, but she could not return to work in his house knowing that she loved him and that he saw her only as his aunt's companion. If the earl had come to apologize and ask her to return, she would accept his apology, offer one of her own, then refuse to go back with him.

Lydia could hear Edward continuing to tell her of the exploits he intended upon reaching adulthood, but her ears were really listening for the sounds of a carriage. To her disappointment, only the sounds of a lone sparrow chirping nearby penetrated her darkness.

Opening her eyes, she could no longer see the phaeton. It had disappeared in the village and not come toward the Reddinger cottage. A new anguish seared her heart. Why had she allowed herself to hope?

Turning to Edward, she forced herself to concentrate on the problem of getting the lad from the tree. "How do you get down when you are with your brothers?"

A tense look came to the child's face and he backed away from the edge of the plank. "Howard always carried me."

With a sinking feeling, Lydia realized she could not carry the child and manage her skirts, as well. She would have to remain here in the tree with the child until Polly returned.

Standford pulled the carriage into a small lane that ran beside the large cottage which the local vicar said belonged to the Reddingers. He didn't know how long he would be, and the road was narrow there in front of the cottage.

"My lord, ain't that the lady we seek?" the tiger asked, pointing to a large tree in the rear garden of the cottage.

The earl smiled. There, sitting on some kind of wooden plank, sat his dearest love, a small child at her side. He felt a foolish urge to laugh. She looked much as she had the first time he'd ever seen her, only more beautiful.

"Yes, Willis. Wait here a moment, then walk the horse down this lane. I might be some time." The earl entered the garden through a gate he found in the low stone wall.

Walking toward the tree, he could hear the murmur of her sweet voice speaking to the child. Hearing her words, it was clear the child had climbed up and then become too frightened to come down.

"May I be of some assistance?" the earl asked, relishing the way she looked with wisps of flaxen hair curling about her lovely face.

Lydia's heart leapt at the sound of the familiar voice. Gazing down, she could see Lord Standford, dressed in a brown coat and buckskins, smiling up at her. He seemed different. Perhaps it was his cordial manner.

"My lord, what are you doing here?" She could barely lift her voice above a choked whisper.

"Did you think I would not come after I learned the truth from Aunt Carolyn? I behaved unforgivably, my dear, and I have spent a sleepless night because of my actions. Can you ever forgive me?"

Disappointment flooded through Lydia. He'd only come to apologize. "Of course, my lord, you had great provocation, and it would have been very easy to misunderstand what you saw. But I handled your aunt badly. I realize now I should have come to you when I discovered the debt to Lord Washburn. I must apologize that I took Carolyn to Lady Halbrook's."

"Then, when you come down, we shall cry friends," the earl said, wanting to be rid of the small urchin who sat beside Lydia before he poured out his emotions, but knowing he might not be able to contain his feelings of love.

Lydia looked back at the child who'd been listening intently to the conversation. "I fear Edward is afraid to come down by himself."

The earl tossed caution to the wind. "Very well, I shall come up to you, dear Lydia, for I have something else I wish to say and I have been forced to wait all night and will not be put off any longer."

Had he called her dear Lydia? Her heart hammered in her chest as she watched the earl heedlessly toss his beaver hat to the ground and come up the back side of the tree. Was this the staid and proper Lord Standford she knew? She thought not.

The wooden door rocked gently as Standford sat on the opposite side of the child, who eyed him as if he'd just escaped from Bedlam. The earl didn't care, he drank in the enticing floral scent of Lydia's perfume on the breeze.

Lydia sat speechless.

"Are you a real lord?" Edward asked.

"Yes," Standford replied. "And who might you be?"

"Edward Reddinger and I am going to drive a phaeton just like you do someday."

"Better, I would think." The earl smiled back at the child.

"I want a high-perch phaeton to race with, but Robert says he will be able to beat me cause he's older."

Lydia at last gathered her scattered wits. She broke into Edward's future plans and asked, "What did you wish to speak of, my lord?"

Reaching past the child, he took her hand and suddenly felt inspiration. " 'There is a lady sweet and kind, Was never face so pleased my mind; I did but see her passing by, and yet I love her till I die.' " He raised her hand to his lips and kissed it.

Lydia could see the heartrending tenderness in his gaze as he spoke the lines of poetry. Her pulse pounded in her ears when she felt his warm lips touch her hand. He'd remembered her love of verse. Could this be true? Did he love her as she loved him?

"Do-does this mean you have a fondness for me, my lord?"

Standford laughed. "Ah, my love, I think fondness does not describe what I feel for you." Reaching up, his hand caressed her flushed cheek, then he cupped her chin and drew her face to him. He claimed her lips and felt his passion rise as she responded.

The feel of his mouth on hers sent strange and wonderful sensations rushing through Lydia. She wanted that moment to last forever. Her arms came up and encircled his neck.

"Hey, milord, you two are squashing me," Edward grumbled between the pair of lovers.

Standford reluctantly released Lydia. "I am sorry lad, but love makes one forget the conventions. Perhaps I should take you down from here."

"Would you be so kind, my lord," Lydia asked, still in a daze at the turn of events.

"Only if you promise to call me Andrew and to remain here until I return."

At that moment Lydia knew she would agree to anything. With a soft blush warming her face, she said, "Whatever you wish, Andrew."

It took but moments for the earl to get Edward to the ground. Andrew spoke softly to the child, who then ran for the gate and soon fell into step with the earl's tiger who led the horses up the lane.

The earl quickly climbed back up the tree and settled beside Lydia. Encircling her waist, he again kissed her. "Now that we are alone, dear one, will you do me the honor of consenting to be my wife?"

Lydia's eyes grew large. "Andrew, you have no idea what you are saying. You would be aligning yourself with a gamester's daughter. What of your duty to the—"

The earl covered her lips with his in a soul-searing kiss. When at last they parted, Lydia felt deliciously weak and shaken. How could she say no to this man?

"We shall say no more of your father's habits or my father's stern notions of duty. There is only you and I. I love you Lydia, and that is all that matters to me."

"I love you," Lydia whispered, as her feelings of love overwhelmed her.

The sound of children returning to the garden stopped the earl from kissing Lydia again. Thinking he might not wish to be seen in a tree, she offered, "Shall we climb down?"

"Not just yet, my love. I have just remembered a message from Georgette," the earl said, eyes brimming with mirth.

Lydia looked a question at the earl.

"She wants you back tonight for the celebration."

"A party?"

"Not just a party, a betrothal party."

Smiling, Lydia teased, "Well, you were very confident you would succeed."

Kissing the tip of her nose, the earl replied, "No, my dear,

I could scarcely breathe all the way from Town for fear you did not love me. This party is for Aunt Carolyn and Hammond. When I left the house this morning, Georgette begged me to tell you she is to have two new brothers and a sister."

"But I thought—"

"That he was already married. No, dear love, he is a widower. He and Carolyn appear blissfully happy and now I understand the feeling myself." He drew Lydia into his arms again, capturing her soft lips with his own.

Drawing back, his finger traced the line of her delicate jaw. "Shall we stay here all day and forget about the rest of the world, my love?"

Hearing Edward and his brother Robert, just returned from the vicarage and coming toward their favorite tree, she laughed, gently pushing the earl to a more decorous distance. "A delightful thought, but I think you are about to receive a visit from some lads who are very interested in your phaeton."

The earl groaned. "I warn you, my dear, that I shall end up shocking all of Society this evening if you leave me too long with these aspiring whipsters while you pack."

Raising an eyebrow, Lydia asked, "How is that, my love?"

"I, Stiff-necked Standford, shall have to kiss you in front of the entire *ton* to recover the affection I am missing while entertaining these puppies."

"I promise," Lydia laughed, "that before this evening's party there will be time enough to recover your missed kisses."

"You are mistaken, my love, for I shall never be able to get enough of your kisses," Andrew said, moving his mouth over Lydia's.

Encircling his neck, Lydia quite agreed as she surrendered to the sweet bliss of the earl's kisses.